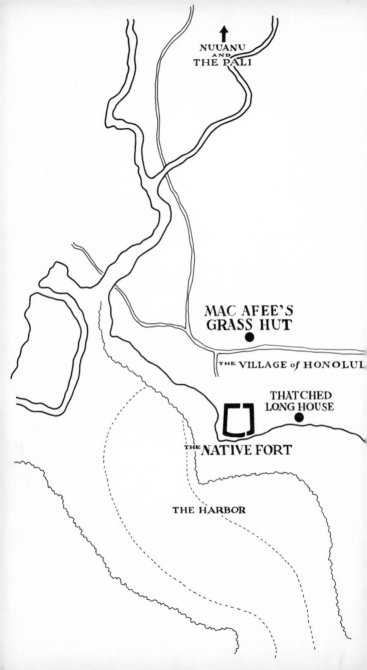

PUNCHBOWL

MANOA →

DIAMOND HILL →

SWAMPS & SPRINGS

ROW of GRASS HOUSES
● (MISSIONARIES)

CONUT
GROVE

HONOLULU
in
1820

TO RAISE A NATION

Historical Novel of HAWAII

MARY COOKE

For Alexandra and Montie

FOREWORD

In historic fact, and in most of its incidents, this is the true story of a band of young Americans who raised the pillars of a free nation in nineteenth-century Hawaii.

With certain exceptions, the principal characters are historical figures. Traders MacAfee and Marley, Captain Silas Gulledge, Maka-lolo and Pualani are fictitious characters. Any resemblance which they or other fictitious characters may bear to real persons is purely coincidental.

Grateful acknowledgment is made to the Hawaiian Mission Children's Society for permission to quote from unpublished missionary letters and journals in its possession; to the American Board of Commissioners for Foreign Missions and the Harvard College Library for permission to quote from ABCFM letters and reports and letters from Sandwich Islands missionaries to the ABCFM; to the Hawaii Conference Foundation for permission to quote from early Sandwich Islands Mission manuscript material in its archives, and to the Kamehameha Schools Press for permission to quote from *Ruling Chiefs of Hawaii* by Samuel M. Kamakau.

I wish to thank the following individuals and institutions for research assistance:

Bernice Judd, Sophie Cluff, Elizabeth Larsen, Lela Goodell, Lee Wild and David Forbes of the

Hawaiian Mission Children's Society; Kay Boyum of the Hawaiian Historical Society; Agnes Conrad and Sarah Nakoa of the Hawaii State Archives; Janet Bell of the Gregg Sinclair Library, University of Hawaii; Captain James Kleinschmidt, Judy Reed, Kenneth Emory and Margaret Titcomb of the Bernice P. Bishop Museum; Joseph Feher of the Honolulu Academy of Arts; Kent Nakamura and Marion Vaught of the Hawaii State Library; D. Goddard of the National Maritime Museum, Greenwich, England; Captain Dale Mayberry of the United States Naval Academy Museum, Annapolis, Md.; Ernest S. Dodge and Francis Bacon Lothrop of the Peabody Museum, Salem, Mass.; Phyllis Mander-Jones of the National Library of Australia; Donald Angus of Tangier; Alfred M. Bingham of Colchester, Conn.; Tucker Thompson, Barbara Lyons and Betty DuBois of Maui; Mabel Wilcox of Kauai and Mrs. Orlando Lyman of Hilo.

For their help and encouragement, I am grateful to Thurston Twigg-Smith, John Plews, Margaret Schleif, William P. Alexander, Dorothy Kahananui, Clare Murdoch, Catherine Summers, Harriet and George Moody, Dr. Oswald Bushnell, Brenda and Scott Pratt, Thomas Kay, Martha McDaniel, Harlo Dillingham, Samuel Cooke, Barbara Dole, Albertine Loomis, Stephen Cooke, George Bacon, Raymond Sato, Alexandra Webster, Montie Cooke, Elizabeth Cluff and to my mother, Mary B. Salisbury, who listened.

M.C.

PRINCIPAL HISTORICAL CHARACTERS

MISSIONARIES	*HAWAIIANS*
Hiram and Sybil Bingham	Liholiho (Kamehameha II)
Elisha and Maria Loomis	Obookiah, Hawaiian student at Foreign Mission School in Connecticut
Asa and Lucy Thurston	Kaahumanu, first regent of the Hawaiian kingdom
Daniel and Jerusha Chamberlain	Kauikeaouli (Kamehameha III)
Levi Chamberlain	Timothy Haalilio, envoy to foreign nations
Gerrit and Laura Judd	Kinau, successor of Kaahumanu
William Richards	Alexander (Kamehameha IV)
Amos and Juliette Cooke	Matthew Kekuanaoa, governor of Oahu

AGENTS AND OFFICERS

Lieutenant John Percival, American naval officer
Richard Charlton, British Consul
James Marshall, American merchant
Lord George Paulet, British naval officer
Rear Admiral Richard Thomas, British naval
  officer

FICTITIOUS CHARACTERS

MacAfee, Sandwich Islands trader
Maka-lolo, sail mender
Captain Silas Gulledge, trader-sea captain
Marley, agent in the sandalwood trade
Pualani, mission scholar

PROLOGUE

Early in the nineteenth century, if a sailor deserted ship at the Sandwich Islands his name could be forgotten. No islander asked him how he was called in other lands, but day and night the *haole* was watched by a horde of amiable pagans who would name him anew.

As he roamed over beach and valley, dark eyes peered at him from behind plaited leaves or through the interstices of thatched huts. Fishermen stared from distant rocks and reef. Brown imps peeped down at him from the tops of coconut trees.

In their hours of palavering by moonlight, ribald kanakas harped on the oddities of the man and they called him by some native word that would identify him forever after.

Anonymity fell like a cloak over pirate and scapegallow, castoff sailor and mutineer—the devils and dregs of white-skinned humanity who wandered barefoot through the south sea islands.

So it was with the old derelict who sat each morning in the shade of his hut near the harbor at Honolulu. Because he sometimes plied a needle and palm disk, he was pampered beyond his worth. The natives gave him food and shelter but he did no work except to mend the sails of ships which occasionally called at the islands for sandalwood. He had one good eye that glittered like a diamond. The other was hidden by a drooping eyelid. In token of the afflicted orb, the natives called him Maka-lolo.

Some distance from the harbor there lived a red-headed foreigner who permitted no tampering with his name. To the Polynesian ear it had a comical sound, but MacAfee remained MacAfee.

In the winter of 1806 natives in a fishing canoe had found the Scot clinging to a spar in the surf off the south shore of Oahu; it was the end of a perilous odyssey after the ship on which he served went down in a blaze at sea.

The fishermen brought him ashore and carried him into a straw hut where he lay insensible for two days and nights. On the third day he cried out. A soft finger was laid on his lips and he understood that by sucking from it he would be fed. The digit was coated with sour paste which the natives called poi.

MacAfee could not recollect how long he lay in the hut and licked nourishment from some unknown hand, but one afternoon he dragged himself across the dirt floor to the doorway and peered out.

He scanned a dry plain on which clusters of dusty grass shacks formed a village. Bronze-skinned natives walked about or huddled in the shade of the hovels which they shared with pigs and dogs. It appeared to MacAfee that whatever labor these people performed must be done at some distance from their dwellings. He saw no farms, nor any herds.

A scant meal was brought to him each day by the brown lass who made her bed in his shack. It was always the same: a young coconut to quench his thirst, a handful of raw fish, half a coconut shell filled with poi. MacAfee wondered if the land had been stricken by drought or famine.

Yet behind the village stood a range of mountains that was corrugated with fertile valleys. One, which the natives called Nuuanu, lay but a little distance from where MacAfee sat. Beneath its cliffs a tangle of green groves and thickets spread like a carpet across the vale.

"An' if the Lord be willin', I'll hie me to yon gorge an' grow a plot o' victuals," the hungry sailor vowed.

MacAfee walked up in the valley at morning and evening when the mountain palisades were capped by soft mist. About a mile above the village he discovered the native farmers working in bogs. Clad only in strips of bark cloth wound between their legs and around their hips, they were digging out the black mire and laying it up to form dikes and trenches.

On other days when he walked that way, the Scot found gangs of kanakas beating the mud embankments with stems of dried coconut leaves while women trampled the sticky bottom earth. The natives pierced the sludge with sticks and laid in portions of taro root topped by heart-shaped leaves. Then they diverted water from a stream and flooded the plots.

The pretty green plants thrived in their water gardens and MacAfee learned that taro root, baked and pounded into poi, fed these natives as rye and oats nourish a Scotsman. But Maka-lolo told him that not a leaf or a root belonged to the men who planted and harvested. Common kanakas were serfs, almost slaves to their chiefs. Every chief was a vassal of the warrior king Ka-mehameha.

"Scratch about in the earth if you like," said Maka-lolo. "You'll be no more than bondman to his heathen majesty. Nay, but show him a bit of canvas or an axe or a musket and turn it to his service. Then, lad, you'll have your plot of ground and the king's men to work it! I tell you the old heathen do love a canny sailor."

MacAfee had not even a cap or a kerchief or a scrap of metal to offer Kamehameha. If the Scot survived he must live by the sweat of his brow, or by his wits.

In the highlands some miles above the Nuuanu taro patches he found streams of water tumbling through the ravines. He knew that in those wild glens he could grow enough potatoes and onions, squash, beans and cabbage to put new life into all the ships' crews that ventured near the islands.

He thought that a proper captain, this far from other ports, would pay well for fresh food. A scoundrel captain, with nothing but rotten stores left in his hold, would be forced to reprovision "...or the most of his scurvy crew, hied off to yon cliffs an' wildwood, would ne'er return to hoist anchor," the sailor muttered to himself.

He knew whereof he spoke.

MacAfee had been forced into service aboard a British ship, a durance so ghastly that the remembrance of it drove him to shun the sea forever. Set down on these shores by he knew not what predestination, he chose to cast his lot with the Polynesian chief whose name the most ancient of pagans called "Tamehameha." In him MacAfee though he detected canny judgment and a disposition to befriend the stranger—if one proved himself some way useful in the land.

The Scot set about rendering yeoman's service to his dusky liege lord whom he called "auld Tammie." He worked with the natives in the taro patches of Nuuanu, but wherever he found a growth of squash, a melon vine, a plantain, a shriveled onion top or any food-producing plant left ashore by some earlier voyager, he stopped to gather seeds and roots.

For, ever in his mind's eye, he envisioned the hungry sailors and the relentless captains of merchant ships driving on through the Pacific to claim rich cargoes at the other side of the world. On such a voyage, and for such profits to the owners of the ship, MacAfee had sailed and starved.

"Me shipmates, wi' the exception o' those that were bound and carried aboard, took to the fo'-castle only to escape hangin' or debtor's prison," he told Maka-lolo.

"As it happened, they made no better choice save that the air above decks blew fresh, whilst below it was as rotten as the gaols they came out of. But matter not what a mon is, if he's to work he must eat!"

With a sharpened stick MacAfee scored a plot of earth in rows and planted the roots and seeds he had found in his wanderings over the island.

"Now, to earn us a little croft o' land," he said to Maka-lolo, "we'll be aboot growin' some crops for auld Tammie to do a bit o' tradin' wi'."

But the old sail mender feigned himself as afflicted about the ears as he was in his blind eye. Not a hand would he lift to prepare a harvest for the ships which inevitably must come to barter at these islands standing midway between the Americas and the Orient.

By 1810 a trade route between the Sandwich Islands, the northwest coast of America and Canton was established. Yankee merchant ships rounded Cape Horn and sailed northwest to Hawaii where their crews unloaded trappings to fetch the fancy of the pagan ruler. Kamehameha bought, and the price he paid was thousands of dollars' worth of sandalwood logs, pigs and chickens, fruits and vegetables.

An agent was sent out on every voyage. At the islands he was put ashore to sell muskets and cannons, mahogany desks, gold-framed mirrors, candelabra and decanters, wine, brandy, linen and broadcloth, lace caps and shawls. In exchange, he demanded sandalwood. The king and chiefs drove their people into the mountains to fell the trees.

When the bargaining was finished and stores of fresh food had been stashed within its hold and on its deck, the ship made a run to the northwest coast of America where master and mates traded with the Indians for furs.

After several months the vessel called again at Honolulu. The captain took aboard his pay load of sandalwood logs and set a course for China. There he exchanged the scented wood (and pelts of beaver and mink and sea otter) for tea, silks, jade, teakwood and China cups and platters.

Even for hardened sea dogs it was a long haul, but a profitable one, and the pivot port was Honolulu.

With the passing of another decade MacAfee half regretted the trade he had helped create. In principle, he still thought it was good. If "auld Tammie" had lived it might not have brought so much evil in its wake.

In the spring of 1819 the old king died and his son Liholiho became Kamehameha II. The sandalwood trade, which the first Kamehameha was shrewd enough to control, became exorbitant. His reckless heir ordered whole forests cut down for the sake of an improvident commerce. Chiefs on all the principal islands claimed the right to do likewise.

American merchants could not float enough ships to carry all the goods that were coveted by these Oceanic princes; but because Hawaiian sandalwood had become a key to trade in the Orient, the Yankees made a mighty effort.

Sea-going agents were replaced by resident traders who lived in grass huts clustered round the harbor at Honolulu. Their function was to sell to king and chiefs shipload after shipload of costly merchandise, and occasionally they sold the ships as well. With a calculating eye on the stacks of logs drying in sandalwood sheds, they hounded the chiefs to drive greater and greater multitudes of their people into the mountains to strip the forests. The natives were forced into human caravans which moved in bands of hundreds and thousands carrying sandalwood logs down to the ships that waited in the harbor.

MacAfee called them "enslaved mortals." The kanakas called themselves *kua-leho* (callous-back) because of the lumps that formed where the picul loads hardened their flesh in calcified mounds. A picul, Chinese measure for the weight packed on a man's back, was one hundred and thirty-three and a third pounds tied to his stooping frame with cords that formed a harness under the arms and over the shoulders. No other means of moving the logs had been contrived.

Worse than the *leho* marks were the foul ulcers and syphilitic eruptions that afflicted increasing numbers of natives. Acquainted as he was with the forecastle of a sailing vessel, MacAfee knew that devil's den to be the source of the malady.

The Scot held to his determination never to board ship again. He agreed to provision the vessels of certain captains in the sandalwood ventures and in return the masters gave him goods to stock a trading shack at Honolulu. For himself, he asked only that they bring tea and coffee and some bottled spirits on every voyage.

"A north mon could no live in such a place, save he take a little stimulant night an' mornin'," he told the mariners. If they occasionally brought him a flaxen shirt and a new pair of trousers he he had no other needs.

His home and his store was a thatched hut which stood a little distance above the traders' settlement at the harbor. In his shack he built a wooden counter on which he stacked his barter goods: cotton cloth, a cask of salt beef, molasses in a stone crock, a sugar loaf and dried apples packed in a barrel of sand. He kept the "stimulants" out of sight beneath the counter.

Three lengths of calico, hung from the ridgepole, insured the privacy of one end of his hut. Behind the flimsy partition lay a pile of *lauhala* mats which was MacAfee's bed. His floor was the ground, strewn with dry rushes and covered by mats. He had one piece of furniture, a round-backed wooden chair that had been given to him by a shipmaster who viewed life in this mud hole with the same horror that MacAfee felt for life at sea.

"But if a man is so disposed," said the captain, "he ought to have something to keep his backside off the dirt."

CHAPTER 1

MacAfee slept sailor-fashion. Not soundly, but with a flickering awareness of wind and voices and movement. The night noises of the valley did not rouse him but a rustling in the thatched wall of his hut brought him to as abruptly as if he had heard the cracking of a mast.

His fingers closed over the stick he kept beside him on his sleeping mat. He whacked the wall and a rat jumped out of the mildewed straw. It dropped a few inches from his head and ran out into the night.

Not night any longer, MacAfee reckoned. A dark winter's morning it was, nigh to dawning.

The rain that had pelted the shack all night had stopped, but the air was so water-laden and his quarters were so confined that the Scot felt as though he were breathing through sodden wool.

He stood up clothed in the rumpled shirt and trousers which he had worn the day before, and the day before that. His chest felt tight and his bones ached; he craved strong coffee with a dram of whisky to the bowlful.

He moved toward the trade goods counter where he picked up his coffee canister, then made for the low doorway of the shack. Bending his body almost double, he hitched under the lintel and slogged off through the mud toward his cooking pit.

It was as though he walked in a nightmare. Volcanic crags and ramparts rose like black walls at the head of Nuuanu valley. A streak of fire moved fitfully across the bottom land. Pausing here and yon in its flight, it touched off a galaxy of flickering red mounds. The valley appeared to be a place of funeral pyres.

Through the smoke MacAfee spied a band of native marauders in a pre-dawn raid for sandalwood cutters. A king's *luna* carried the torch that swept across the vale. Wherever he could not rout a kanaka out of a hut the firebrand touched under its roof and rushed on.

MacAfee gazed at the savage spectacle and, as lonely men will, he cried aloud:

"Hard masters do ravage like madmen, be they goadin' the heathen or be they floggin' a poor sailor before the mast!"

The Scot kindled a fire in the pit of lava stone which was his stove. He balanced an iron kettle on the rocks and scattered a handful of coffee over the rain water that lay at the bottom of the pot. Crouched on his haunches, he waited until the brew began to simmer and its redolence mingled with the musky smell of the earth.

He watched the valley grow dark again. The rout was finished. As quickly as they had sprung up, the fires, all save his, were dying out. When daylight came nothing but ashes would mark the track of the tyrant.

A pink glow touched the cliff that rose like a monument at the top of the valley. On either side lofty palisades knifed skyward in vertical ridges; their peaks seemed to be floating in space above the shroud of night that hid the lowlands.

MacAfee cherished this strange land, but he had little tolerance for its inhabitants. All of the meddlesome, inhumane dealings to which he was daily witness vexed and wearied him. Yet he could do nothing to alter the condition of his neighbors, native or *haole*. He did not presume to set the world to rights—except his own small corner of it.

He rose and walked back to the hut to fetch his chair, a bowl for his coffee and his bottle of whisky. With these few comforts, on this desolate splinter of the earth, MacAfee was content to sit by his fire and watch the mountains at dawn.

❊ ❊ ❊

While the Scot was drinking his coffee and regarding the *pali*, Captain Silas Gulledge, 162 days out of Salem, brought the *Persis Parker* to anchor a mile off Honolulu harbor. He noted the date in his log: February 6, 1821.

Stepping down from the ship's ladder into a boat manned by four burly seamen at the oars, he shouted "Pull away!" and steered for a point of land near the native fort. In the shadow of that sanctuary, on whose adobe walls thirty cannon glinted in the morning sun, there stood a thatched long house wherein lodged Liholiho, king of the Sandwich Isles.

Captain Gullege landed and gained entrance to the royal enclosure without challenge, but at the doorway of his majesty's pavilion a native *kahu* warned him off.

Too early! Liholiho slept!

"Let him sleep," growled the captain and he stumped off to the harbor village to find Marley, resident agent for the owners of the *Persis Parker.*

At Marley's rum-reeking hut Captain Gulledge would not stoop to enter. Instead, he bellowed for the landlubber to step out in the open air where the captain demanded an accounting of trade goods sold and sandalwood due. Suddenly he turned and walked away, cutting short Marley's rambling tale of profits he had made and rum kegs he had emptied in the past twelvemonth. Gulledge set a course for MacAfee's and Marley, obedient to the master's orders, stumbled along in his wake.

They found the Scot feeding a blaze with rushes he had pulled off the floor of his hut. Soggy mats were spread over a pile of lava boulders and a torn quilt hung on the branches of a *hau* bush. Beneath it lay MacAfee's empty coffee bowl.

Captain Gulledge surveyed the domestic welter, moved upwind and bellowed:

"You'll burn down yer bloomin' hut, MacAfee. Sit down and talk business."

He seized the chair, pulled it around to face seaward and sat down. Marley let his bony frame down on a slab near the cooking pit. They waited in silence until MacAfee fetched two more bowls and started to dip them into the coffee kettle.

"Belay that!" Captain Gulledge ordered. He pulled a square brown bottle from the fold of his jacket and told his host to set the crockery on the ground. The captain leaned forward and filled the bowls with brandy that was the color of mahogany.

"I'll land you a cask of this and you'll turn out a harvest for my galley. Eh, MacAfee?" he said.

"Aye," answered the Scot.

With the toe of his boot Captain Gulledge nudged Marley's shin.

"Marley here has been out earning his salt," he announced. "A little rum down the royal hatch and my last cargo sold for a bully good lot of wood!"

Derisive laughter rumbled in his chest.

"The king of the isles won't be roused from his boozy stupor, eh Marley? Look up!" he commanded and thrust a bowl of liquor under the agent's nose.

"A swig of that'll stiffen yer spine."

He handed up a bowl to MacAfee, drank from his own and began to jab the air with a stubby forefinger.

"Five hundred piculs of sandal logs, MacAfee. Swillbelly Marley got that for the muskets. It'll fetch me tea and silk the worth of five thousand dollars at Canton! For the least of the lading— beads and cocked hats and shawls, and his last pint of rum in the bargain—twenty piculs!

"Marley! You'll get a barrel of rum beached this day. See his heathen majesty pays me full measure of wood for my new cargo. I've got damask and silver plate and a billiard table..."

"'Twas no the way o' his father!" MacAfee interrupted. "Ye'd no use the bottle to sell to auld Tammie! 'Tis shame to see the young king strip his forests to the saplin's, wi' no restraint, to buy the likes o' damask an' plate an' a gamin' table!"

Captain Gulledge stared out to sea. He regarded MacAfee's remark as irrelevant blather not worth answering. Marley, who sat like a wizened turtle with half-closed eyes, gave tongue to a confused thought:

"Scoundrels in harbor...buy rum from honest men."

MacAfee raised a bristly red eyebrow.

"'Tis a rarity to behold one, lad!" the Scot retorted.

Captain Gulledge shifted in his chair. He squinted one eye shut, narrowed the other and hitched himself forward to get a fix on something he saw in the distance.

Three men in black suits and three women in long dresses and bonnets were coming down the path from Kawaiahao toward MacAfee's hut. Two of the men appeared to be carrying infants.

The captain said nothing until he grasped the significance of what he beheld. He remembered now. In the fall of 1819 there had been talk in Boston about a group of new-married, psalm-singing missionaries for whom passage to the Sandwich Islands had been bought aboard the brig *Thaddeus*. Gulledge had sworn then they'd be hauled home from a fool's errand.

Yet here, the first time he had called at Honolulu in almost a year, he counted six of them walking this way—with babies!

To get a better look at them Captain Gulledge heaved his bulk out of the chair. He stood with his feet planted wide, arms akimbo, fists digging into his hips. He continued to stare until the missionaries turned *makai* and walked on toward the native palace.

"Plagued fools!" he thundered. "Brought their women! Now they've spawned some puny brats!"

"Aye," said MacAfee. "'Tis wonder they're not all dead, lodged on yon plain wi' nought but flimsy mats 'twixt their feet an' the wet sod."

He watched them step around chuck holes in the path where a pair of pigs cooled their bellies in the mud.

"They have woeful times. Most particularly the thin one wi' the long neck, the wife o' Bingham. I ken the poor lady's lungs are no too strong."

"Then what's she doing here?" demanded Gulledge. "It's no fit place for women that ain't heathen!"

"Oh, aye," MacAfee agreed, "wi' the bare brown lassies shippin' aboard an' all, the sights ain't fit for a lady. An' should the lady happen to come from a hamlet near to his own, sir, a most disturbin' circumstance..."

"Devil take 'em!" the captain barked. "If they're born without the sense to hold a wagging tongue they'll batten down their hatches soon enough!"

He turned his back on the missionaries and glared at the Scot.

"Have an eye to them, MacAfee," he ordered. "They'll make only trouble. Mark that!"

"Weel, sir," countered the trader, "I think they do no harm. They do a heap o' prayin' an' I can tell ye, 'tis a movin' event to hear again the songs o' Zion an' see a mon unashamed to bend his knee before the Lord!

"Withal, they keep a little school o' thirty or forty pupils, mostly orphans sired by the likes o' yerself, but also includin' certain highborn natives. An' there's another thing. Mr. Bingham— he knows a little medicine—he's aboot tryin' to dry up the sores o' the poor natives. Red precipitate o' mercury they brought, an' he dusts it on the sickly limbs o' them that come askin' for it."

"Doctoring their sores!" the captain bellowed. "Would he like to cure the men in the fo'castle, too? There's a heap more riddled sailors and heathen than Mr. Bingham's got medicine for in this ocean, MacAfee."

He seized the brandy bottle, emptied it with a violent thrust at each of the bowls and hurled it to leeward. It hit an outcropping of lava and shattered as MacAfee spoke again.

"I believe, sir, that Mr. Bingham has it in mind to alter the nature o' this particular place. He has announced their intention. It is to preach the gospel an', says he, the word o' God must command the obedience o' all men."

"What else does Mr. Bingham say?" demanded the captain.

"He says the natives are oppressed an' the women are taken in adultery."

"Arrogant donkey! He should have been driven off before he landed!" Gulledge snorted. "But from the pinch-gut look of them, they won't endure another twelve months. If they do, and if I find them here when I next drop anchor, I'll haul the lot of them off and take nothing for their passage, just to be rid of them!"

The missionaries walked on. Their faces were drawn with weariness that ill befitted their years. If Captain Gulledge had looked into those faces he might have resolved at once to rescue the moon-calves from their folly and bear them home like lost children.

But the captain would command and not befriend; he would harass, not aid his unfortunate countrymen. So they looked only to God and Liholiho to alter circumstances which to them had become unbearable.

They went to ask the king to release them from almost a year's confinement in native hovels. They would beg permission to build their own house of pine lumber and glass and shingles. The materials were at hand; they had been shipped out from Boston and lay warping in the sun at Honolulu. The structure they envisioned was a plain, sturdy New England farmhouse. They needed only the king's sanction; they had asked for it repeatedly.

Liholiho begrudged it.

Should foreigners live in a wooden house while he languished in a bower of grass and poles? Pagan pride said No. But at times curiosity almost set aside the royal conceit. Because he could not decide, Liholiho had deferred the issue.

Hiram Bingham vowed it would not be deferred again. Already, his wife was ailing. After she had borne her baby she was put to bed again with influenza. She had lain, first feverish then soaked with perspiration, while wind and rain blew through the thatched walls of their hut. Her fever rose and broke, then rose again. Sybil Bingham prayed she would not leave her child half-orphaned in an alien land.

She was not without fortitude. Before pain and illness tormented her she had written to her loved ones at home:

> Cares in my new situation have pressed upon me beyond anything I ever before experienced... manual labor has made a great demand upon my time. But...I have been enabled to go through that which would once have sunk my feeble frame....

Next to her Lord and her God, Sybil's sustainer in all earthly trials was Hiram Bingham. As befitted a young woman of religion and refinement, she had been taught modesty. Modesty in dress, in manners and above all, in thought and utterance. She adhered to the precept, but the joy she felt in her marriage with Hiram found expression:

> ...So much have I found of every excellence that deserved my highest approbation, that he has secured my tenderest love....[God] has bestowed the rich gift of a kind, worthy, and justly valued partner upon many, but I can never think but that I stand distinguished.

She could not think otherwise. Her husband was not only distinguished, he was one of the most audacious Yankees ever to come out of New England.

On their diplomatic walk to the native palace, Bingham cradled his baby Sophia in one arm and supported his convalescent wife with the other.

Behind them trooped Elisha Loomis, toting his infant son Levi. Maria Loomis, a round-faced girl who had been a teacher and a folder of books before she dedicated her life to Elisha and the

Sandwich Islands Mission, walked beside her husband.

Loomis was a farm boy from upstate New York. One of eleven children, he had never known an idle moment at home and at the age of sixteen he had been apprenticed to a printer. When he was nineteen the American Board of Commissioners for Foreign Missions accepted his offer to go to the islands as the mission printer.

Behind the Loomises walked Bingham's former classmate at Andover Theological Seminary, Asa Thurston, and his wife Lucy. The Thurstons had no infant but each of them carried a mysterious parcel wrapped in linen sheets.

When they arrived at the straw palace they found the court awake. Liholiho and his wives reclined on finely woven mats and ignored ten mahogany chairs and a pair of crimson benches. Overhead three crystal chandeliers hung from the long ridgepole. Their prisms tinkled in the sea breeze.

A pier glass in a carved frame stood at such an angle that, without rising or making the slightest effort, the grandees could study their splendid images. They craved no greater pleasure than to sit indolently together amid the elegance which sandalwood had brought them.

The king wore yards of green Chinese taffeta wound around his girth and loins. A silk *kihei* was draped over one royal shoulder; the other was bare. His queens, having access to the stores of Oriental fabric, had arranged lengths of brocade in the style of their native *pa'u*, a wrapping that swathed them from waist to knee. *Kiheis* covered their ample bosoms. The court circle was ablaze with billows of red, yellow, purple, magenta and peacock blue silk.

Lucy and Asa Thurston stepped forward to place before Liholiho the parcels they had carried thither. The king's pleasure knew no bounds when he drew forth twelve white linen shirts with ruffled bosoms and matching stocks. They were patterned after those worn by the mission men.

LIHOLIHO
Lithograph by John Hayter, London, 1824
Honolulu Academy of Arts

With the grace of an athlete, Liholiho tossed aside his silken drape and sprang from the mat. He seized a shirt and plunged his arms into the sleeves. Lucy Thurston moved behind him and buttoned the garment while the king gazed into the looking glass. She adjusted the stock and he pivoted to show off his finery.

From the waist up, Liholiho had undergone a startling transformation. The wide collar enhanced his chin and mouth and his enormous eyes with their high-curved brows. His was a lofty countenance. The dress of a gentleman became him.

With graceful phrase and gesture he expressed his aloha. Hiram Bingham replied in Hawaiian that the ladies were sorry for being long in the making of the shirts. They would have finished sooner but for the illness of Mrs. Bingham.

"She has been sick," Hiram repeated. "The other sisters have been unable to sew with much diligence because they do the work of nurses and teachers and cooks and homemakers, all in the most trying circumstances."

He added that they were not accustomed to living in houses that had neither floor nor ceiling. He feared the women would weaken, perhaps die, if they must continue to sit and work and sleep on the damp ground.

He might have told it to the wind. Liholiho stood with his back to Bingham. He looked in the mirror, fingered the ruffles of his shirt and felt the buttons at his back.

Hiram crossed to the other side of the mirror and faced the king. He told him that their houses were soaked through and the poles which held up the webwork of thatch were beginning to rot.

He feared that the whole habitation some day would come tumbling down on their heads.

The king heard. He uttered a rippling cadence that said "We will build new houses for you."

Hiram persisted, straining for elusive Hawaiian words that seemed to be mostly vowels.

"We have, already on the ground, lumber to make a durable home for our families," he said. "It is that which we wish to build."

Liholiho smoothed his shirt front and walked away. When he reached the far end of his palace he stood aloof and pondered:

"White men come in their ships, but they go away again—except those who live in grass houses and sell rum and calico. Even those men go away and others come. A wooden ship will sail away, but not a foreigner's wooden house. *Aole.*"

Across the thirty feet that separated him from his visitors, the king's baritone voice carried with the ease of vis-a-vis conversation. He began by saying that he extended love to the missionary teachers and that he had heard *Binamu*'s request. The answer was *aole*. No.

Hiram saw Sybil sway slightly. She was not yet strong enough to be about and the disappointment of this morning's errand made her ready to faint.

"God rest us in heaven," she whispered as Hiram helped her to a chair.

Kamamalu, the twenty-year-old beauty who stood six feet tall when she rose from her place among the queens, moved with regal grace to the rear of the long house. She had decided that Sybil needed food and she summoned the mission men to choose what they would have from the king's stores in the sheds behind the residence.

Lucy Thurston and Maria Loomis stayed with Sister Bingham. Maria untied the invalid's bonnet and removed it. Sybil's hair lay damp and straight across her temples. She was shaking with ague.

As Liholiho moved back across the room he stopped and stared at *Binamu wahine*. He put out a hand and touched her forehead.

"*Wela*," he exclaimed. For a moment he studied her trembling frame.

Lucy Thurston watched him. From some stored-away memory of her academy days there leapt to mind Shakespeare's counsel "There is a tide in the affairs of men...." and four quick steps brought her to the side of the king.

Her command of the Hawaiian language was faulty. She was still unfamiliar with its idiomatic turns and meanings, but she would make Liholiho see the connection between Sybil's feeble state and the fact of her existence on the all-but-bare ground.

Earnestly she groped for words, pressed on with broken phrases, discarded one, tried another, but she never relinquished the attention of the king. Her inspired if halting plea on behalf of those who had come to serve him was that they be allowed to preserve their lives in a house which they themselves would build.

Lucy finished her peroration just as the brethren returned from the food sheds. She trusted they would not regard her as a woman who had misjudged her calling.

But Hiram and Asa and Elisha were unaware of Mrs. Thurston's attempt at persuasion. They set about performing the parting courtesies while

Lucy and Maria took up the babies from the floor mat.

Sybil tied on her bonnet, took her husband's arm and, bidding aloha to the rulers of the realm, she willed herself to start the half-mile walk back to the sodden shacks at Kawaiahao.

"*Binamu!*" Liholiho commanded.

Hiram turned to answer the summons.

"*Hana hana*" (Build), said the king. "When you go away, take everything with you."

Lucy kept strangely silent on the homeward trek. But that uncanny communication which runs like lightning through any Polynesian village was at work. Before the missionaries had walked as far as MacAfee's the news had been told. Liholiho had given them permission to build a wooden house.

Captain Gulledge heard it and clapped a brawny hand on Marley's shoulder.

"Keep a sharp lookout, Marley," he growled. "If you hear of them talking to the chiefs about the worth of this and the value of that, speak up! They'll ruin the trade in a year's time unless they're given reason to belay their prattle."

His brogues left long gouges in the mud as he strode down an incline to stand in the path of the oncoming missionaries.

They stopped to exchange greetings but Captain Gulledge had only one thing to say to them:

"Let yourselves be warned, here and now, that should you make reckless talk in these parts about what don't concern you—the price of the trade goods, d'you see—you'll ne'er get letter or cargo landed off the *Persis Parker*."

CHAPTER 2

"**H**is gracious word, *Lo, I am with you alway*, was sufficient for the first missionaries of the cross; it will be sufficient for you....

"Abide fixedly on this word, and you will have nothing to want and nothing to fear; and by example as well as by instruction, will teach the wanderers of the isles to observe all things whatsoever he hath commanded you."

With this exhortation the first missionaries to the Sandwich Islands had been publicly charged a week before they sailed from Boston.

At an evening service in October, 1819, Dr. Samuel Worcester, first secretary of the Prudential Committee of the American Board of Commissioners for Foreign Missions, stood to instruct fifteen young men and women and one middle-aged couple who assembled before him in the Park Street Church.

"Dearly beloved..." he began, "You are now on the point, the most of you, of leaving your country and your kindred and your fathers' houses, and committing yourselves, under Providence, to the wind and waves for conveyance to far distant islands of the sea, there to spend the remainder of your days.

"You have given yourselves to Him for this service, you have made your vows and you cannot go back.

"If it be not so—and if this point be not fixed with you immovably—stop where you are, nor venture to set foot on that board which is to bear this holy mission to the scene of its labors and trials, and eventual triumphs."

He leaned forward to see if there was a flinching eye, a cheek that blanched or a trembling lip.

The volunteers from Vermont and Massachusetts, Connecticut and New York returned his gaze. Dr. Worcester fixed his eye on one, then another. He must be certain that no irresolute spirit cowered here, particularly among the young women whose faces were framed by curls and flaring bonnets.

Thomas Hopu, John Honolii and William Kanui, young natives who had shipped to America as waifs, stood like dark statues among the fair-skinned couples. They pledged to return to the islands with this company and serve as evangelists to their race.

"Your views," said Dr. Worcester, "are not to be limited to a low or a narrow scale; but you are to open your hearts wide, and set your mark high.

"You are to aim at nothing short of covering those islands with fruitful fields and pleasant dwellings, and schools and churches; of raising up the whole people to an elevated state of Christian civilization; of bringing, or preparing the means of bringing thousands and millions of the present and succeeding generations to the mansions of eternal blessedness ... to obtain an adequate knowledge of the language of the people; to make them acquainted with letters; to give them the Bible with skill to read it. . . . "

He read thirty-three pages of warning, consolation and requirement before he declared this untried branch of the church ready for service on foreign ground.

Seventeen souls, set apart to carry Christ's banner into the Pacific, turned to face the congregation. As they moved forth, their compatriots— those standing within the pews and those who crowded round the portals of the church—silently exclaimed, "What hath God wrought?"

Square-jawed merchants and mariners leveled their glare of scrutiny at the outward-bound pilgrims. Matrons and spinsters fetched kerchiefs to their streaming eyes. The old wives stood rigid. They were utterly drear in their assessment.

They took note of the printer's apprentice, loosed from his bonds in New York; the college sophomore quitting his seat at Yale; the middle-aged farmer leaving his acres in Brookfield—all in haste to go forth upon an unknown sea of troubles. Nor did it escape their notice that all except the natives and the farmer were newly married to a parcel of females suited well enough to parlor or schoolroom but not to a rude habitation among barbarians.

Upon what vain and foolish venture did they now embark!

Provident folk were wont to bide at home, to bear their share of labor on their native heath among their own kind. Why then this exodus, this relinquishing of kith and kin and property and all the comforts and opportunities of civilized life?

Because less than a dozen Pacific islanders were converted in America, was it reasonable to suppose that whole tribes of idol worshipers might be similarly persuaded on their own ground?

Yet, looking at the three Hawaiian youths who now walked forth as Christian missionaries, who could claim mere happenstance? The skeptic no less than the zealot must acknowledge the parish labor and substance which had been spent to rescue these men when they wandered homeless in America.

The most callous witness could not doubt it: Providence moved here, and the miracle had been wrought in a rude clapboard building known as the Foreign Mission School at Cornwall, Connecticut.

In that frugal workshop was begun the fabric of a Christian Hawaiian nation. There the pattern was laid out. There was woven a warp-and-weft that would hold the skeins which every race of man eventually would cast on it.

It would hold, though no one could foresee the maze of interweaving it must yet support. Its binding cords were conceived in righteousness. The bright strands that crossed them were the floss of human liberty, dearly bought in a Revolutionary War by the sires of this firstborn generation of American freemen.

There were among them still old soldiers who had marched on bleeding feet at Valley Forge. They sat as elder hosts at freedom's table, and at that roughhewn board the last of them had entertained an angel unaware.

He was Obookiah, a native youth fetched home by a Yankee mariner. The captain had claimed him at the Sandwich Islands when, all but naked, the boy leapt from the sea and climbed the anchor chain. He implored the shipmaster to deliver him from heathen priests who had held him captive.

The New England families who fed and sheltered Obookiah were baffled by his speech. But they caught the flash of his eye when, in pantomime, he rehearsed a flight of spears hurled by savage warriors that slew mother and father and pierced through an infant brother. Obookiah had been impounded in a temple of wooden idols. He was made a novitiate in the rites of human sacrifice to appease the gods of Polynesia.

From that eerie lair the youth had fled to the northland of America where, upon stone hearth and oaken pulpit, was forged the nation's double genius of righteousness and enterprise. There in the farmhouses of pious folk he learned the Christian creed and tenets. There, on the steps at Yale, one charitable student looked back and harked to the native's plea. The fellow tutored Obookiah and made a place for him on the scholars' bench.

When six years had passed, there came forth in Christian manhood this aristocrat of earthly beings: proof of what his whole people might become if they were offered the quill and the book in place of the stone club.

Obookiah embarked on a course of study for the ministry. He resolved that he would take the knowledge of God's love and law back across the sea and teach his people. The sons of Yankee rebels, singing Hosanna and Godspeed, tithed

OBOOKIAH
Hawaiian Mission Children's Society

and labored to advance his cause.

They inaugurated the Foreign Mission School, stating as its object "the education in our own country of heathen youths in such manner as, with subsequent professional instruction, will qualify them to become useful missionaries."

In it they enrolled Hopu and Honolii and Kanui—and as many more as sought their aid— and prepared them to assist Obookiah when he should lead them back to their island homeland.

"May the Lord Jesus dwell in my heart and prepare me to go..." Obookiah prayed.

He was not to look again on the black crags of his islands. On a raw winter day in Connecticut Obookiah died of fever. He was twenty-six years old.

His sponsors committed his body to the grave. They counted as lost all labor, all expense, all hope of sending native evangelists to the islands. Among the students weeping for their brother, not one was the equal of Obookiah in discipleship or brilliance of mind and method. Without him to lead them there could be no mission.

So spake Reason.

Conscience challenged, and the stoic villagers answered:

"Reckon up the cost."

"Cease vain expectation."

"God has brought matters to an end."

But that which would have been lost through prudence was rescued by one who argued:

"God bespeaks some irrefutable purpose in having brought Obookiah among us; no less a purpose in having called him to Himself.

"Does not this latter event now place the great

design in our own hands? Are we not called to go in place of Obookiah?"

❈ ❈ ❈

Teachers and farmers, merchants and mechanics, students and brewers and weavers and potters donated the funds. The American Board of Commissioners for Foreign Missions engaged passage aboard the brig *Thaddeus* for the band of volunteers, most of whom were not yet thirty years old. On October 23, 1819, the company embarked.

Daniel Chamberlain, veteran of the war of 1812 and a prosperous Massachusetts farmer, sailed with his wife and five children. This one family with six newly married couples and three native youths formed a "common family" for which Mr. Chamberlain was named agent of secular affairs.

His first duty was to account for the possessions carried aboard the *Thaddeus* by his fellow missionaries. Henceforth, the goods and chattels of each were to be owned in common stock. All would be laid up, divided and dispensed according to individual need. No salaries would be paid. The company would be sustained by charity of the Christian public in America.

They sailed with their plow and their printing press, their knowledge of letters, theology, household arts, agriculture and carpentry—and greatest of all, their conviction. As their Lord had said to the first Christians *Go ye therefore, and teach all nations*, He had said it to them.

Except the Hawaiians, none expected to look upon his native land ever again.

❊ ❊ ❊

In the fall of 1819 the Sandwich Islands missionaries had been charged with a sublime objective: fruitful fields, pleasant dwellings, schools, churches—a nation to be enlightened and renovated.

By the end of 1821 the first mission station which they had established on the island of Hawaii was disbanded; the station on Kauai reported less than thirty-five native "learners"; on Oahu no more than forty children and adults took daily instruction in reading and writing.

For visible evidence of their labors, Bingham and his brethren could point to little except the building of the wooden house at Kawaiahao. It stood in a patch of corn stubble and withering bean vines, sorry remains of their attempt at "fruitful fields."

At either side of the central plain of Honolulu lay the great valleys of Nuuanu and Manoa, watered by mountain streams and subterranean springs. They were *kapu*, set apart for the use of the king and chiefs. At the mission plot, salt-smelling marshlands bordered the flat terrain which was little more than coral stone and shells mixed with cinder dust from the crater that brooded over Kawaiahao. Because the old cauldron had hardened in a fluted mold, foreign seamen gave it the name of Punchbowl.

Some miles to the southeast there stood the greater phenomenon which they called Diamond Hill. Between the two extinct craters, no tree or shrub relieved the desolation except a fringe of palms along the shore and coconut groves near

Honolulu harbor and Waikiki.

Farmer Chamberlain first perceived the hopelessness of his task when he found that what soil there was at Kawaiahao was impregnated with lime and salt. He crumbled the gray stuff in his hand. It was all grit and no substance. He held it up to his nose and recoiled from the acrid smell.

"Brine and brimstone," he concluded and let the rubble drop between his fingers.

He could have wished for a more promising corner of the Lord's vineyard in which to labor. But duty was clear: he must produce victuals for his own family, the Binghams, the Loomises, the Thurstons and John Honolii. Moreover, numerous native orphans had found a home with the mission families and sat for meals at their table. Brother Chamberlain had no choice but to bend his back to a futile task.

In the beginning, water was carried from Nuuanu to Kawaiahao in calabashes slung from poles on the shoulders of native runners. Daniel prayed that circumstance might be altered and went prospecting in the mission yard.

He pried up the surface coral and found an old spring from which he threw out hundreds of pailsful of mud. With the help of his brethren he dug and stoned a well. They wrested a pump off a half-sunk vessel in the harbor and when they had rigged the rusty apparatus in the well, they had water. But the sea, flowing in through subterranean passages, mixed with the spring water and made it more or less brackish according to the ebb and flow of the tide.

Daniel and his children hoed the ground and carried buckets of semi-salt water to his rows of pallid sprouts. The plow lay idle; in this country animals were not harnessed in the service of man. The brethren noted in their mission journal that all burdens were borne on the shoulders of the natives "while the oxen and horses look on and enjoy their ease."

They solicited the king's permission to break a pair of animals to the yoke. Liholiho said they might experiment with wild cattle, if they could catch them. Daniel Chamberlain, Asa Thurston and John Honolii set off for the mountain region "to contrive some method to take some of them."

But after taking the measure of pinnacle and palisade—and the beasts that roared defiance from knife-edged cliffs—the missionaries abandoned their plan and all expectation of a proper farm.

Their plight was compounded by the number of ships which, week after week, stood offshore awaiting fresh water and provisions.

In one year the mission families had seen the Hawaiian sandalwood trade double. Every newly arrived vessel was surrounded by canoes loaded with yams and potatoes, melons and taro, squealing pigs and squawking chickens. Honolulu harbor had become a market place in which the servants of the Lord could not compete.

Brother Chamberlain loaded the plow aboard the first schooner that sailed for Kauai. It could be used by Brother Samuel Whitney and Brother Samuel Ruggles on that island where the king had said some of his land should be tilled according to the *haole* method.

"They will of course need a boy who is acquainted with farming to assist them," Daniel told his wife Jerusha, "and I have concluded to commit Nathan. It appears to be our duty, and I willingly give him up."

Which meant that Jerusha also must willingly give him up. Nathan, her second son, was eleven years old.

To obtain their daily bread with some regularity, the families at Honolulu were instructed to list the supplies they would need for the coming year and their petition was forwarded to the Mission Rooms in Boston.

After a six-months voyage food came to them. It was dried, salted, weevily, often moldy. They ate what was meted out, mindful that they lived on the charity of pious folk at home who supported missionary work as best they could, or would. The "widow's mite" which had been dropped into "the Lord's treasury" was not theirs to spend as they pleased.

❀ ❀ ❀

Kawaiahao grew into an awkward-looking settlement of wood, straw and adobe structures, each a different size and shape. When the frame house was finished, a thatched church—fifty-four feet long and twenty feet wide—was built at the *ewa* side of the dwellings. School kept in the largest of the old grass huts; the orphan scholars lived in two others, and one had been given to Elisha Loomis for a printing house.

The missionaries had one fireproof building: an adobe cook house where the sisters toiled morning and evening. When their food was cooked they carried it across the yard and down a flight of steps to the cellar of the dwelling house. There, around a long pine board table, the families gathered for their scanty repasts.

Four couples and nine children shared the two-story house. For a "place of common resort" they set aside a room on the *mauka ewa* side of the ground floor. In that cubicle callers were received and sermons were composed. There the brethren began their work of committing the Hawaiian language to writing. For too long it was an unfinished task that weighed more heavily on the builders than their lack of material assets.

Hiram Bingham and Asa Thurston knew the mechanics of language and the art of translating. They had studied the scriptures in Hebrew and Greek as well as in English. The Hawaiian Bible must be a faithful rendition. They could not begin work on it until they had stabilized the ever-changing word and sentence forms which confronted them in native speech.

They were baffled by some of the most beautiful linguistic sounds ever uttered. Hawaiian phrases seemed to be all imagery and elusive meaning. Word definitions changed according to the whim of the speaker. Vowels followed one upon the other, sometimes fused, sometimes pronounced separately. Depending on such tricks of articulation, one word might express a variety of unrelated thoughts. Yet two or more consonants might be used interchangeably in hundreds of words without the slightest alteration in meaning.

The mission brothers were not the first to be dazed by those mellifluous sounds that were more poetic than precise. Between 1778, the year Captain James Cook discovered the islands, and 1821–1822, the year the missionaries strove to discover the language, *Kealakekua*, the name of a bay on Hawaii, had been written sixteen different ways.

Sea-going map makers, botanists, artists, surgeons and captains heard and spelled all Hawaiian words differently, then went their ways. No one had stayed long enough, or cared enough, to produce a formula of undeviating written symbols for the language. That was a task for men who had been charged with "raising up the whole people...to make them acquainted with letters...."

The brethren concluded that there was no fixed framework on which to base the written language, so they made one. They listed symbols for all the sounds they had heard, including the interchangeable consonants. They set down seventeen letters to establish a Hawaiian alphabet and on January 7, 1822, Elisha Loomis printed Lesson 1 of the first native spelling book.

In the days that followed, crowds of bare brown children and almost naked men and women pressed around the door of the printing hut. They watched the missionary Loomis and kept up an incessant murmuring among themselves. Elisha caught the poetic turn of their language when they compared his nimble fingers to the flying and pecking of small birds.

He had never thought of his work in that way. He simply employed the printer's method of setting type: the thumb and index finger of one hand plucked each letter from the font case and dropped it into a composing stick which he held in the other hand. His fingers moved swiftly and they produced a clicking rhythm as the bits of type dropped into place on the metal stick.

Each morning when the first pages came off the press Elisha handed them round to the natives. The papers fluttered in the wind as plump brown hands turned them this way and that. The new owners tried to discover the *mana* in the sticky black substance that daubed their fingers.

Within a few days Liholiho and the queen regent Kaahumanu sent a message to the mission house: they would come and see the *mea nui* that could make paper talk.

In forty-three years since foreign ships had first touched their shores, no trader had brought them such a tool. They thought it strange that the missionary *haoles* did not say to them, "Be quick to bring us much sandalwood, and the machine will be yours."

CHAPTER 3

E lisha Loomis halted the lever of his press and turned to face the native runner. He was about to reply to Liholiho's message when he saw little Mary Chamberlain scurrying over the coral dust path to the printing hut.

She stopped on the threshold and whispered that Mr. Bingham had just received the king and regent in the common room. So she would not be found loitering in their path when the native rulers appeared, she hitched up the skirts of her long brown smock and sped home.

If Elisha was unprepared for a royal visitation, so were the families at the frame house. It was almost dusk on a Saturday evening. The women were weary, the toil of the week was not yet finished and preparations had to be made for the Sabbath. Now the sisters were in haste to order the hospitality of their home and table.

Little Mary set about folding diapers and throwing unironed garments into a sea chest, as her mother bade her do. Jerusha Chamberlain had no wish to see the sun set on work undone, but she was called to help Mrs. Bingham in the cook house.

The women increased the contents of their kettles and stirred with long-handled spoons. Jerusha plied her task with mute fortitude; she considered small talk a waste of a body's time. Sybil, engulfed in clouds of smoke and steam, held her tongue for want of breath to speak.

Presently both were forced to seek the open doorway. As they stood wiping their faces with linen kerchiefs, young Dexter Chamberlain jogged over the stubble of the mission yard.

Jerusha noticed the untrimmed hair falling pell-mell over her son's ears; his limbs, tanned to the color of burnt biscuit, stretched out of ragged sleeves and pantaloons. He thumped along on bare feet that had grown tough as ox hide.

"Supper is wanted," Dexter croaked. "Mr. Bingham said I was to say they will come from the printing house within the quarter hour."

He handed his mother two clean kerchiefs which Lucy Thurston had thought to send out. Quickly, the sisters clapped lids on the pots which contained their supper. Dexter lifted them by their hoop handles, hunched his shoulders and toted the heavy things across the yard. Sybil and Jerusha stayed a moment to pin up the damp strands of their hair and tie on the kerchiefs. When they left the cook house both women lugged kettles of hot water for the evening tea.

The families assembled in the cellar. Maria Loomis lit three whale oil lamps and placed them down the center of the long table. Mrs. Thurston laid out spoons and forks and crockery and stationed jugs of molasses betwixt the lamps. When

Dexter arrived with his burdensome pots, both women followed him round the table. To each plate they served a slice of boiled salt beef from one kettle; from the other, cakes of hardtack that had been simmered in water.

The orphan scholars descended the cellar stairs single file. Their duty was to set benches round the table, but at the sound of footsteps overhead they stood stark still. If not for their mission mothers' instruction, they would have run and hidden or, failing that, prostrated themselves on the dirt floor. Their wild little hearts beat hard against their ribs but they did as they were told. They stood with the families and awaited the king and regent.

First down the narrow steps came Brother Bingham. He turned back to assist the dowager who followed him. Kaahumanu emerged from the cavernous stairwell; in her bare feet she stood four inches taller than Bingham and she needed no assistance.

There was not her equal in the islands. She was portly, as were all Hawaiian chiefs, but there was that about her which bespoke more than physical power. A daughter of *alii* and the favored wife of Kamehameha, Kaahumanu had been charged with governing his profligate son Liholiho. It was an office that called for unremitting exertion.

Sister Bingham greeted the regent with a little smile of recognition. Kaahumanu was wearing the black silk gown which Sybil had made from a vastly enlarged pattern of her own dress, but the royal coiffure exceeded any Mrs. Bingham had ever seen. The chiefess had wound her hair in a towering knot and secured it with tortoise shell combs. A coronet of yellow feathers circled the mass.

Liholiho descended next, splendid in broad-cloth coat and pantaloons, white ruffled shirt and a gray silk vest. He strode to the table and covered one end of it with printed pages. In a mood of excitement, he wheeled about and extended both hands toward Elisha Loomis. The king announced that his heart was filled with aloha for *Lumiki*.

The silent hosts stood around the table, waiting. They were pleased to pay deference to the king of the Sandwich Islands but it was their duty at this moment of grace to give thanks to the Lord. Elisha acknowledged the king's remark with a sideways bob of the chin and hurried to his place at table.

Liholiho spoke on. He had a tale to tell about the mechanics of printing, of pulling crank and lever and peeling moist pages from the press. He told it, rather he played it as an actor upon a stage, with flashing eyes and extravagant gestures.

Midway through his peroration—rank, fervor and grandiloquence notwithstanding—his audience received a message more imperative than the king's. A silent summons caused them to shift their gaze, as imperceptibly as the movement of a clock hand, to the opposite end of the room. There at the head of the table stood Hiram Bingham.

Beyond the feeble glow of the lamps, the black-clad figure might have appeared incorporeal except for the dynamic blaze of a pair of perfectly balanced eyes. A white stock underscored Bingham's jaw, his straight nose and mouth, the span between those imperious eyes and his high fore-

HIRAM AND SYBIL BINGHAM
Portrait by Samuel F. B. Morse, 1819
Yale University Art Gallery

head. His features appeared in sharp planes and angles, as though they were hewn from some enduring substance.

At once, Kaahumanu perceived the common cause which united that magnetic figure with the stoic beings who stood at either side of the table.

The voice of Liholiho was heard no more. The flashing eye of Bingham sought out John Honolii who bowed his head. So did all the company except Liholiho and Kaahumanu.

John prayed in Hawaiian. Near to his God and heedless that he was the chosen messenger for the families, he poured out his devotion in a soft, purling murmur broken occasionally by a pause for breath before he came to the final amen.

In the hush that followed the children brought the benches and all sat down at the common board. Asa Thurston and Daniel Chamberlain saw to the comfort of Kaahumanu and Liholiho. The royal pair was seated near the stairwell to enjoy what fresh air might find its way down the narrow passage.

The meal began with the passing of the molasses jugs. While man, woman and child poured bitter syrup over their cakes of hardtack, the orphans recited their verses for the day:

"I cannot see God, but God can see me."

"In the beginning, God created the heavens and the earth."

"Jehovah is in heaven and he is everywhere."

"We must pray to Jehovah and love God."

Liholiho had come to his meal in a mood of jubilation. It vanished when he sat on a hard bench and ate scraps of salt meat and a watered biscuit. Nor did he care to hear urchins chanting words he did not understand.

The capricious king suddenly envisioned himself under full sail, headed for Lahaina. The faces of his mission hosts faded from consciousness. With his faculty for lapsing into reverie, Liholiho already was one with the wind and the waves.

But the regent's eye was on the here and now. Not on orphans, not on printed pages—she cared nothing for either—but on Hiram Bingham. Beneath high-arched lids, Kaahumanu's eyes looked straight ahead and took the measure of this man in whom she saw *mana kia'i*, guardian power. Back across the board, Bingham leveled his gaze at her in an obdurate, penetrating fix.

Doughty men, better versed in the ways of the world than Kaahumanu, were apt to quail under that rigorous eye. Kaahumanu was unperturbed. For as long as it pleased her she made appraisal of the mission leader.

"Strong head!" she concluded, and turned from his compelling stare.

She knew nothing of the ways of his God, nor would she hear of them. Kaahumanu saw evil in the pagan tabus and so she was filled with contempt for all gods. But she marked a new element in the tabus of the missionaries. They made strong *mana*, even for these people who got little food and did the work of servants.

It was this *mana*, this extraordinary drive, which foreigners at the harbor talked about in angry voices. Kaahumanu had heard white traders from America rail against these people of their own country. When they said it was because the missionaries were *paakiki*—hard and stubborn— she threw the word back at them and said they were *paakiki* traders. They hounded her for too much sandalwood.

But she knew that Bingham and his brethren had earned the hostility of most of the traders in the islands. Looking round the supper table, she read the cause.

No pliant adaptability subdued these young faces. They were stark, intent, dominant, and the psychic energy that emanated from them was as real as the pine board off which they dined.

Kaahumanu knew that not one of the native children who sat bolt upright around the table would have dared to speak in the presence of the king unless some inspiriting agent had them in custody. When that sing-song of verses began to pour from their mouths, she had watched every scared waif turn toward the lodestar that guided him through his perilous maneuver. She found that it was the mission wife with the long neck, Sybil Bingham.

Despite the bulky cotton dress which concealed her willowy figure, Sybil created an impression of lightness. Tendrils of fine hair curled over each temple to frame her delicate features and the pale eyes in which each child found his encouragement. From her corner she governed with effortless grace "...like gentle rain that drifts through sunshine and brings forth the fragrance of the flowers," Kaahumanu thought.

The regent turned her lofty eye on Asa Thurston, the better to grasp the meaning of a question which he framed partly in Hawaiian, partly in English: Would her highness take a spoonful of sugar to her tea?

He held an earthenware bowl half filled with white sugar. It was not intended to go round the table and the king already had helped himself, generously.

Kaahumanu, perfectly accustomed to special privilege and not to the pinch of a near-empty larder, said she would take two, nay three spoonsful to her cup. With commendable aplomb Asa dug deep into the sugar, after which he placed a cover over the bowl and took up his fork.

Of all the brethren, Asa Thurston least showed the strain of privation which they all shared. So too, that most durable of mission wives, Lucy Thurston. Her every move was a brisk one and her black eyes flashed like polished beads as they darted to and fro.

Seeing the king stare at unsauced scraps on an almost bare plate, Lucy seized a molasses jug and poured a dollop of the black stuff over his hard-bread to render it more tasty, or at least to look more so. She ran a spoon up the outside of the jug to save the drippings. Kaahumanu noticed Lucy took only that as her own portion, having served the king more lavishly than the mission stores afforded.

Midway down the table the Chamberlains and the Loomises sat hedged about by children, their own and the orphans. Long years of "training up a child in the way he should go" had so attuned Daniel and Jerusha to the task that they instinctively knew whether all went well or ill with the dozens who surrounded them. They uttered scarcely a word or correction, but they admonished by reproving glances.

If a child's finger, instead of his spoon, sought to scrape up a last taste of bittersweet bread from his plate, the tot needed only a long stare from Brother or Sister Chamberlain to alter his intention. And if, as Daniel now discovered, fifteen-year-old Dexter sat bewitched by the maturing beauty of the orphan Pualani, his sire brought the lad to himself by tapping one gnarled finger on the table top.

God had provided Daniel with all the physical attributes needed to reinforce the silent messages he sent round the table. He had a long, lean face, a hooked nose and large ears. His blue eyes pierced the shadowy places like a beacon. Beside him, like a second emphasis, sat Jerusha with exactly the same proclivities. She had grown to look very like her husband.

Opposite were the Loomises who derived considerable energy from the idea that nothing is troublesome if it is done willingly. Maria cradled her infant to her dumpling figure with one hand and took her supper with the other. She was blessed with a hardiness apparent to all, including the Hawaiian regent.

But to Kaahumanu, Elisha Loomis was beyond comprehension. Lean as a rake, with straight wisps of blond hair bleached almost white by the sun, he appeared to the giantess as a mere anatomy whose only tinge of color was in his ink-blacked fingertips.

That Elisha was worn to the bone at barely twenty-two years of age was the result of circumstance combined with an overworked conscience. His childhood of toil, and now his obligation to the mission, had conditioned Elisha to a lifetime of acquitting himself creditably at the beck and call of others.

To take no thought of comfort, to dig the earth, to make adobe bricks, to hammer and saw, to teach, to preach, to write and translate and print, to nurse the sick, to make known the words of his Lord, to fast, to pray, to be made a spectacle for men and angels—this was Elisha's lot in life, short though it was destined to be.

It was the lot of all his fellow workers—those in the field and those yet to come—who would spend and be spent in a labor of compassion for the children of paganism. Their solace was the benediction to which they daily became heirs: *Inasmuch as ye have done it unto one of the least of these my brethren, ye have done it unto me.*

Kaahumanu comprehended nothing of the fountainhead from which their authority sprang. She only knew it existed. If their God was good for her people, she would know it. If not, they would have to go away. She would wait and see. Meanwhile, hers was the power in the land and she did not need theirs.

❀ ❀ ❀

Liholiho finished the morsels on his plate. He had sat as long as he would in this room beneath the ground. He rose and announced that he would sail for Lahaina.

Hiram Bingham started from his place at table and walked toward the king.

"Tomorrow will be the Lord's day..." he began.

Liholiho looked back at Bingham.

"Pray to Jehovah to give me a good wind," he commanded.

Hiram quickened his stride and met the king at the foot of the stairs.

"It will be the Sabbath," he repeated. "Will not your majesty defer one day and join with us in a service to the Lord?"

Liholiho pivoted. With an imperious lift of his brow he answered, "If a head wind blows, I will beat this way and that, and go up quick."

Raising one arm in a graceful sweep overhead and reversing its play with a flourish, he specified, "I do not want the wind to blow from this quarter—but from that."

In no less cavalier manner Kaahumanu took her leave. As she approached the stairwell Hiram offered his hand and was ready to repeat his invitation to worship, but the amazon imposed silence when she extended her little finger and walked past him to mount the stairs.

After the royal guests had gone Elisha Loomis turned back to the table to finish his supper. He spied the printed sheets which had so delighted Liholiho an hour before. They lay on a bench where the king had forgotten them.

In his heart Elisha cherished the knowledge that he had fulfilled the charge of "preparing the means of bringing thousands and millions...to the mansions of eternal blessedness." But tonight he ached in every bone and muscle and silently he permitted himself to wonder with Isaiah, *Lord, how long?*

His body cried for rest but he acknowledged that as temporal weakness. The press must be cleaned and new type must be set for the pages he would print on Monday morning. He swallowed his last hunk of beef and, taking one of the whale oil lamps from the table, he walked up the cellar steps and out to his printing hut.

❄ ❄ ❄

Asa Thurston and John Honolii stepped out to attend the royal departure with Brother Bingham. Afterwards they returned to the common room to take up again the tedious business of the Hawaiian vocabulary. It galled them that they made such slow work of it. Their greatest embarrassment was the poverty of abstract words which they needed in order to translate the Bible.

The New Englanders had found that there was a Hawaiian word for every shift of the wind and all the characteristics of rainfall from mist to deluge. There were endless distinctions pertaining to waves and water. Every drift and current to the very depths of the ocean had a name.

But where, in this isolated vernacular, were the words to express the concepts of Hebrew and Christian theology? Without such words there could be no Hawaiian Bible. If they existed they must be found, and if not found, they must be brought into being. The three men sat down and applied themselves once more to the hewing and shaping of a written Hawaiian language. It was the keystone upon which the whole purpose of their mission depended.

❄ ❄ ❄

Below stairs, the sisters hitched aprons over their calico dresses. The high-bodiced frocks which had been made for them three years earlier hung limp except at the waists where the women bound their apron sashes twice around. The pressure eased the aching of their backs.

With the children to help, they cleared the table and carried crockery and utensils out to a wash tub in the yard. They washed them and left them to dry in the wind.

Now infants must be nursed and swaddled and lulled to sleep and Sabbath garments must be ironed. Jerusha and Maria and Lucy carried up their babies and took Sybil's little daughter with them. Sister Bingham laid out work for the scholars.

The children fetched their copybooks and pencils and Mrs. Bingham carried the lamps to the head of the table. As she turned to take her seat, she encountered a tawny angel in rags who went by the name of William Beals.

He was a child of about eleven she thought. Sybil was no more certain of the ages of these foundlings than she was of their paternity, but she was sure that she had never seen a more endearing little face than the one that now looked up at her.

"I can read Sermon on the Mount," said William. "I can teach."

Sybil stared at the radiant imp. His eyes were like dark pools ringed with white. A line of perfect teeth gleamed in the curve of his smile and black curls tumbled over his brow. He was clad in a faded blue smock that hung almost to his ankles.

"I teach!" he repeated.

Sybil needed a moment to comprehend and another to be sure her voice would be steady when she spoke. Not a year ago this captivating child had come to her as a naked urchin. She had bathed and clothed and fed and schooled him—no more or less than the others. Heeding her weariness now, he came forward to make a gift of the things she had taught him.

Surely, thought Sybil, if William sat in her place with the scholars she would get on with her other labors, the sooner to end this seemingly endless day. It was not a thing she would have contemplated, but the child made his offer with such innate grace that she determined to take it in good part.

"William Beals," she answered, "do you now go to the common room and say first to Mr. Bingham that you beg pardon for the interruption. Ask him please to send down, by your hand, the small Bible."

The overjoyed child hied up the dark stairwell and after a few minutes he scuttled down it again with incredible speed. As he walked across the cellar floor he borrowed the gait and posture of Hiram Bingham. He held the Bible in the crook of one arm and took his place at the head of the table. Eyeing the scholars, he turned the pages slowly. At last he began to read:

"*Blessed are the poor in spirit . . .*"

The children cramped their fingers around their pencils and wrote the words.

"*for theirs is the kingdom of heaven,*" William continued. He scanned the table and determined that each child had written the line before he went on:

"*Blessed are they that mourn for they shall be comforted . . .*"

As the beloved refrain fell from the lips of this resolute little pauper, Sybil stepped away from the table. Duty bade her go, but she lingered a moment and watched from a dim corner.

May not the humblest plowboy gaze on the fruit and flower of his industry? May he not mark and measure and hold dear every branch and tendril, the very sight of which is a benison to the weary worker?

Like a shadow figure, Sybil stood beyond the rim of light and looked on the novel scene, the product of her labor. She had gathered these children from the waterfront and had made with them a school. The abandoned fledglings of lust—wild and disheveled, even dissolute in their tender years—now bent clean heads and hearts to the task of learning. They were the homely vessels in which she had kindled a first glimmer of knowledge among the Sandwich Islanders.

"Neither do men light a candle and put it under a bushel, but on a candlestick; and it giveth light unto all that are in the house."

Sybil listened and looked again at the child who read. In a moment, she slipped away to find work for her hands to do while she pondered on the infant prodigy William Beals.

Daniel Chamberlain began to open a batch of newly arrived supplies that was stored at the far end of the cellar. He rummaged around in the shadows and checked the contents of casks and boxes, noting in his ledger under "Item" and "Amount" slates and pencils, dried codfish, shoes, soap, candles, copybooks, flour, blue dungaree and calico.

He turned to the back pages of his book to record the gifts addressed to individual families. Since all property was owned in common stock, such presents made added bookkeeping for him.

It must be noted that one sister received from her parents a new bonnet and dress; another was supplied with ten yards of diaper and half dozen infant dresses, and one of the brethren was the owner of a second pair of brogues. Daniel made a note that the recipients were ineligible to draw similar items from common stock, at least until the brogues or the dress or bonnet wore out.

He began to portion out supplies for the brethren on Kauai. He had their lists. He would fill their orders as best he could, knowing that when it was done there would still remain amongst them a grinding need for tools and medicines and cloth.

As he moved among the chests and barrels, his eye chanced to light on the scholars' table. He noted some irregularity there. Every head but one was lowered and the children strove to write as fast as William Beals read. Daniel perceived that it was his son who gave but a second or two to the business of copying each passage. Dexter's ragged head bobbed up with startling regularity. For what cause? Why, to catch the sly glance of Pualani!

It pained Daniel that this eldest son, who ought to be taking instruction in Latin and Greek, algebra and geometry and history, must forfeit his right to such schooling. The mission afforded neither time nor teacher to accommodate a solitary advanced learner. Perforce, Dexter sat with the native scholars to practice his reading and writing.

He would do so no longer. Brother Chamberlain reckoned on the Devil finding work for idle hands and Dexter was, of a certainty, idling.

Without moving or uttering a word, Daniel captured the boy's notice and summoned him from the table. Dexter was set to work sorting and packing the mission supplies while William Beals intoned "...*wide is the gate, and broad is the way that leadeth to destruction, and many there be which go in thereat.*"

CHAPTER 4

After he put his son to work, Brother Chamberlain took his ledger and started up the stairs. He wanted a quiet place to tally his accounts. He hoped his colleagues would give him a chair at the translation table.

The common room was not quiet; indeed, the voice of John Honolii could be heard all through the house. When Daniel entered, the men at the desk made a place for him but they did not heed him. They were listening to John.

Honolii's task had been to define native words for the brethren. Now he was making words. His loquaciousness was by way of convincing Asa and Hiram that *manao* which meant "thought" and *io* (true) would, if combined, convey the meaning of "faith."

The brethren dipped their quills and wrote *manaoio* into the language. Next, they joined the Hawaiian word for "thought" with *lana* (buoyant) and introduced *manaolana* (hope) into the vocabulary.

They bent over their English, Greek and Hebrew texts to extract precise Biblical meanings which they hoped John could match by hybridizing or combining native words. They weighed and analyzed and argued until Daniel abandoned all hope of balancing his accounts. He had worked against noise for more than two hours and his nerves were spent.

Besides the confabulation within doors, he was aware of a distant thumping of drums and slapping of bare flesh. Suddenly, drumming, clapping and shouting erupted in a wild cacophony that woke the household.

The brothers abandoned their books and ran for the door. Elisha Loomis darted out of the printing house. From windows, upstairs and down, pale faces of mothers and children peered out. Only the orphans remained quiet in their grass huts.

Kawaiahao echoed with the rhythm of gourds striking the ground a half mile away. Silhouetted in torchlight, rows of hula dancers surged to and fro near the coconut grove at the harbor. A chorus of no less than a thousand natives rent the air with strident chanting.

The mission men turned from the scene. They had watched such revels before and they knew there would be no letup till dawn.

As they plodded back to the house they beheld another sight that both fascinated and repelled them. The moon, about to rise over Punchbowl, cast an eerie glow behind the black crater that loomed over the mission compound like a symbol of pagan defiance. Once it had been a chamber for human sacrifice.

No remnants of the slaughter remained there, or at Diamond Hill where more victims of the gods were clubbed and strangled and laid on altars. The evidence had been destroyed when hordes of natives sacked the *heiaus* while the *Thaddeus* plunged through monstrous seas in its struggle to round Cape Horn. The missionaries were told it was Kaahumanu who had loosed the destruction on the temples.

Bingham watched the moon rise above the rim of Punchbowl. So, he thought, do these islanders begin to rise from their long night of tabu. He gazed up at the walls which had echoed with cries of human anguish. They were silenced, not by educated men, Bingham reflected, but by one untutored native.

The thunder of drums ceased and the brothers turned to scan the grove again. No dancer moved; no sound was heard except the wail of a female voice that rose on a prolonged note. It began a weird monologue that carried over the shore in undulating tones, and a new barrage of drumming rumbled up from the grove and loosed pandemonium along the waterfront.

Daniel Chamberlain could bide no more. Asa would not. They strode back to the house. Printer Loomis, pricked by the knowledge that it was an ill use of his time to squander it on such flagrant revelry as now seemed imminent, quit the scene and went back to work. But Hiram watched and John Honolii waited.

Barbarous cries ricocheted over plain and valley. Bursts of flame flickered in the coconut grove. Dark bodies leaped and swayed; their oiled skin glistened in the erratic light. Through the shadows ran scores of naked children who, at Sabbath dawn, would be found lying senseless where they fell. Neither were the mothers, even the grandmothers, exempt from the debacle.

Intemperance, Bingham had discovered, was an evil more to be dreaded than idolatry in his field of mission labor.

As if to mock him, there burst forth from the palmy thicket a clamor that mounted to utter mania. Hiram knew that its first source was a handful of foreign adventurers who lived near the harbor.

Among the common natives, even the poorest had always called to the stranger: "*E hele mai*" (Come to us). When he left a plague in their houses, still they held the rogue in childlike amity of brotherhood and forgiveness. Hiram reflected that the love of man already dwelt within these affectionate pagans who faltered and fell because they knew nothing of the commandments of Jehovah and the wisdom of the Savior.

He envisaged a new order when law and learning and the application of civilized skills should bring to this ensnared people undreamed-of freedom and resource.

Liholiho was neither ready nor, being wasted in debauchery, would he likely become the convert who would lead his people. No more was Kaahumanu receptive to the teachings of the mission. But Bingham knew that of all the ruling class, she was the light among her people. Whatever draughts quickened that flame would shape the destiny of the islands.

That she did not yet crave instruction cast no hobble on his ambition. Hiram saw that the day was at hand when Kaahumanu must fortify herself against the foreign evils that already beset her land. And if, in her quest for mundane knowledge, she should be brought to the gates of heaven, did it matter by what route she traveled?

CHAPTER 5

The *kahunas* had lied.

The gods did not destroy those who violated tabu. Boatloads of foreigners transgressed the ancient laws with impunity. The chiefs, when their senses were numb from strong drink, broke tabu. Neither were they destroyed.

The people knew. They had known for almost half a century but they dared not act until Kaahumanu cried fraud and seized authority.

With psychological brilliance, she had timed her coup on the twelfth day after the death of Kamehameha. First she proposed to the fledgling king that he abolish tabu. When Liholiho remained silent she arranged for him to witness the deception which held him in thrall.

In violation of the centuries-old edict against males and females eating together, five-year-old Kauikeaouli, Liholiho's brother and heir, was ordered to share a meal with their mother.

Instead of death to the participants, the result was civil war.

Temples were torn asunder and the torch was

applied. The monstrous idols went up in flames. Those that would not burn were hurled down the long cliffs to the sea. So were treated the priests who had sacrificed natives who did no worse than set an unwary foot on tabu ground or touch a morsel of food that had been restricted.

The men of the mission knew that Kaahumanu still commanded a retinue of hundreds who voyaged with her from island to island to ferret out remnants of the priests' craft and destroy them.

The queen regent was no stranger to violence. She was a child when fleets of war canoes, arrayed for combat and filled with masked spearmen, were launched by scores, then by hundreds. By the time she was twenty-three she had seen eighteen thousand of her people felled by warfare, famine and disease in the contest that brought all the Hawaiian islands except Kauai and Niihau under the rule of Kamehameha.

When Kaahumanu was thirteen she joined the coterie of wives kept by the conquering chief. As she matured, and he discovered her heroic nature, he favored her above all other queens. At his death he charged her to watch over his son and take care of his people.

With stunning speed, Kaahumanu loosed the debacle that liquidated the priests. The weapon she used was her knowledge of the outer world, shrewdly garnered by observing foreign voyagers who touched her shores as they searched for Pacific trade routes.

Now, like many another innovator, she began to see danger in her work. Liholiho lacked the will of his mighty sire. Repeatedly he dropped the reins of government, if indeed he ever took hold of them. He spent himself in drink and play and

KAAHUMANU
Watercolor sketch, 1816, by Louis Choris,
artist aboard Russian ship *Rurick*
Honolulu Academy of Arts

incessant roving between the islands. Kaahumanu saw that her holocaust within the temples had created, in the place of tyranny, a void.

The battered *heiaus* stood untenanted. Pagan law was abolished. Foreign rascals needed only to beguile the king with rum in order to work their wiles. A pack of mongers and higglers had usurped the power of native oracles.

Kaahumanu was distracted. Her long sight told her that unless Liholiho changed his ways, a master more despotic than the priests would rule in his stead. At last she came to the missionaries and said, "Pray to your god for Liholiho."

They vowed they would, and they did. But when they offered to lead her to church for her own redemption Kaahumanu answered that she would not go to church; she would play in the surf instead.

Does the good shepherd abandon one who is seeking, but who is too headstrong to come into the fold? Hiram Bingham thought not. He resolved to offer Kaahumanu the means and let her discover the way to her own salvation.

That summer the Binghams sat in the presence of Kaahumanu and witnessed a diversion that was unparalleled by anything they had ever seen before.

Paying a call at the regent's house near the harbor, they found Kaahumanu lying on the floor. She was surrounded by her sister Namahana and two of Liholiho's wives, also couchant. The imperial women, each of whom weighed between three hundred and four hundred pounds, faced one another in opposing pairs. Each held a fan-shaped arrangement of playing cards.

Together, they formed a circle of tapa-draped flesh in the middle of a *lauhala* mat. Their brown legs were thrust outward in diagonal lines like the spokes of a wheel; their chins rested on little pillows of colored satin.

At the approach of the visitors, Kaahumanu turned her head and bade Hiram and Sybil sit on the mat. The amazons resumed their game. It was that favorite of English drawing rooms, whist.

How incongruously, thought Hiram, was the tournament transferred from the leather-topped tables of London to a plaited floor mat. With what quick comprehension had these matriarchs learned the game from some British sea captain while he tarried briefly in their company. They played as experts, nor did the posture of the gaming queens diminish in any wise their habitually lofty manner.

An hour passed. The silence was broken by the rustle of cards and the guttural melody of the queens' voices. A rhythmic thud of carpenters' hammers sounded from the decks of sailing vessels in the harbor.

Uninvolved with the labor of ship repairs or the gossip of the chiefesses, Sybil lapsed into drowsiness. She would have gone to sleep sitting up but conscience forbade it and physical discomfort made it impossible.

Having been invited to sit on the floor, she must sit bolt upright, a position calculated to insure wakefulness. Propriety permitted her neither to lean on her husband's shoulder nor, heaven forbid, to stretch out full length beside her recumbent hostess.

They sat in Kaahumanu's reception room on the upper level of a frame house for which the regent had paid a great price in sandalwood. It pleased her that no other dwelling, be it wood, coral or thatch, could equal her manse. She had placed it near the harbor where she could watch the comings and goings of foreigners.

The room in which she took greatest pride was the upper salon where Hiram and Sybil discovered the queens at play. It was fitted not only with windows but also a doorway through which the owner could walk out on a balcony. Madam gained enormous prestige from the novelty of living aloft.

The house faced the sea and its green shutters were thrown open. The tide was out. A faint breeze from the south carried ashore the smell of exposed reef and seaweed. The reek of hot pitch kettles drifted over from the wharf. At closer quarters, the scent of the queens' *hala* nuts leis and the coconut oil on their skin and hair all but overwhelmed poor Sybil.

She was with child again and the humid air, freighted with such heavy odors, brought her close to swooning. She looked to the open balcony and quickly averted her gaze. Brilliant sunlight glinted on the coconut fronds that brushed against the railing. The sound, as much as the sight of them, made her giddy. So did the restless shuffle of the cards as they were dealt and played across the mat.

Suddenly, Sybil went rigid with shock. A shudder ran through her body at the sound of a bestial howl and the crack of a cat-of-nine-tails across bare flesh. A sailor was being flogged on the deck of a ship in harbor.

The lash whistled and fell in relentless rhythm: lay on, cut, withdraw. The victim was subdued; still the hideous punishment went on.

The familiar accent of MacAfee was heard under Kaahumanu's balcony where the Scot stood with trader Marley.

"They'll be aboot cuttin' down the laddie soon," said MacAfee. "He'll no take past twenty lashes. I'd say now he was insensible to the last dozen."

"I'd say he won't jump ship a second time," Marley retorted. "Granted now, the captain may belay punishment. When the poor devil can stand again, it'll be back to the gratings and all hands mustered up to witness final settlement. He'll get another ten sure as he got the better half this day."

"Aye," said MacAfee. "An' pity is, the lad is known to me to be no trouble maker."

"No trouble maker!" Marley hooted. "No trouble maker! It ain't news to you MacAfee that for every jack that bolts ship, a dozen more would follow except for holy dread of the lash? There ain't better ways to keep a crew on every vessel in earshot. All of 'em high in cargo, mind you."

MacAfee minded. He knew the law of the sea. A ship and its cargo, its captain and crew comprised a venture for which one man, the captain, bore sole responsibility. It was his brain and brawn against the treachery of man and nature. Flogging was fair means to force obedience.

"Aye," said MacAfee, "by the scourgin' o' one mon, masters an' mates may be sure o' sufficient hands aloft in the riggin'. But Marley, as to them that's too vicious to be curbed wi' the lash, what's to be done wi' them sons o' the divil?

"'Strike their shackles and beach the lot o' them,' cries the captain whilst he makes ready to sail away. So what have we got but a nest o' bloody cutthroats left in our midst?"

"Warranted," said Marley.

"One day," MacAfee went on, "ye'll see the captains as could ne'er break 'em, but put 'em ashore instead, those same captains I say, ye'll see 'em standin' off an' on beyond the reef, not darin' to bring their ships to port lest the hellcats climb the chain an' seize ship, cargo, captain an' all."

"Warranted," repeated Marley. "Varmints're in a fair way to killing off the trade—if your prattling missionaries don't do it first."

"Nay, Marley," said the Scot, "when ye've sold yerself out on a limb it ain't altogether reasonable to lay the sum o' the blame to the men o' God. Though I dare say the king gets a smatter o' enlightenment from that quarter.

"But if ye'll drop the scales from yer eyes, ye'll see that ye canna forever pin yer hopes on the injudicious fancy o' the ignorant! The day comes when a mon, even a heathen mon, learns he's been gulled, an' then it's whistle for yer pay. Look there, yonder."

Hiram and Sybil guessed where the trader pointed. They heard the clatter of a weighing machine that stood beside the sandalwood shed. The groan of the spring signaled a payment of logs to some trafficking sea captain.

In a year or more, the chiefs had learned that in America a pier glass might be worth eighty dollars, but not eight hundred. A standing wardrobe, for which they paid fifteen hundred dollars worth of sandalwood, cost the white trader no more than three hundred. Moreover, they viewed in a new light the dearly bought silks that were riddled with worm holes and the rotting schooners which had cost them close to a hundred thousand dollars. They had become vague about paying the balance owed on such obligations.

The Binghams could not tell which of the debts was at stake that day, or which of the five captains in port had called for the loading of sandalwood. Nor could they hear what was said when the master loosed his wrath on the natives. But suddenly it began, and it poured forth in a grinding tirade.

The captain hailed his agent who still lounged against the wall of Kaahumanu's house. In a voice that would surmount gale winds at sea, he bellowed: "Maaarrlee!! Ahoy there, Marley!"

Marley shifted his weight from one foot to the other.

"Do you stand idle there?" yelled the curmudgeon. "Do you watch while thieving savages cheat a white man of his cargo? Find the king and see that I get wood, the full measure of the hold, or I'll see you back in the fo'castle!"

"Find the king!" sneered Marley. "Find the missionaries! Boat 'em and bear away, sir, or you'll need not call here again. I tell you they're *printing books* now. So the heathen won't die ignorant!!"

"Ignorant they was born and ignorant they will die," thundered the captain. "Lead on, Marley, and bring me to that donkey of a Liholiho. He'll give not a crooked stick less than full measure, be he the most ignorant man alive. Lead on, I say!"

Hiram wondered that Kaahumanu did not stir. Indolence still marked her bearing but there was a turbulence in her eyes which had turned strangely brilliant in one who lay so idle. Her distraught glare roved about until she spied the banty book which Bingham held in one hand. Her eyelids lowered and she stared at the pamphlet.

All afternoon Hiram had sat cross-legged on the floor and held the pages that were folded and stitched with gray cotton thread. Only now did Kaahumanu choose to notice the gift and its bearer, and in such a peculiar manner that Hiram had no choice but to continue his vigil.

Kaahumanu studied Bingham's hand and the paper book, and they conveyed to her a more vivid account of the man than any word or deed of his. She noticed the long fingers which held the pages with a certain grace; she was *kanalua* of *haoles* who seized their account books with loutish hands.

The regent prolonged her morose gaze, and there came to her mind a first glimmer of conviction touching her dilemma. She understood that Bingham's shield, and hers if she would take it, was not one of thick-woven mats, but the thin pages which he wished to put in her hand.

She heaved her bulk to a sitting position and smote the mat with the flat of her hand, first at the right of her huge flanks then at the left.

"*Hele mai!*" she commanded, startling Mrs. Bingham.

The hours of inactivity had restored Sybil's equilibrium. With the help of her husband, she was able to obey the summons. Hiram placed a hand under her elbow and brought her to her feet.

THE ALPHABET.

—◆—

VOWELS.		SOUND.	
Names.		*Ex. in Eng.*	*Ex. in Hawaii.*
A a---â	as in *father,*	la—sun.
E e---a	— *tele,*	hemo—cast off.
I i---e	— *marine,*	marie—quiet.
O o---o	— *over,*	ono—sweet.
U u---oo	—*rule,*	nui—large.

CONSONANTS.	*Names.*	CONSONANTS.	*Names.*
B b	be	**N n**	nu
D d	de	**P p**	pi
H h	he	**R r**	ro
K k	ke	**T t**	ti
L l	la	**V v**	vi
M m	mu	**W w**	we

The following are used in spelling foreign words:

F f	fe	S s	se
G g	ge	Y y	yi

1

First page of Hawaiian spelling book
printed by Elisha Loomis in 1822 (actual size).
Hawaiian Mission Children's Society

He steadied her as they stepped over the reclining queens and came to kneel at either side of their hostess.

Kaahumanu's face, still clouded with turbulence, veered from one to the other with the look of a sullen child. She kept a woebegone silence as she allowed Hiram to divert her attention to the printed page.

The little volume was only a trifle taller and wider than the whist cards which she had played so knowingly. She held it as he presented it to her, open at the first page.

"A, E, I, O, U," said Hiram, pointing to the letters printed in a vertical row.

She mimicked him. To see if she related the sounds to their symbols, he pointed to the vowels in jumbled sequence. Kaahumanu grunted her responses and proved her comprehension.

Her quick mind demanded more. Hiram directed her attention to the consonants. She mastered them as quickly as she had learned the vowels. Then, anticipating her teacher, the regent chose a vowel and a consonant, combined them, and understood at once the principle of spelling.

"*Ua loaa iau!*" (I have got it!) she exclaimed as she jabbed at the page with her forefinger.

"Ha, he, hi, ho, hu—la, le, li, lo, lu—ma, me, mi, mo, mu..."

With mounting bravado she beat about for new conquests in the alphabetical ranks. She found letters to form simple words. She was boisterous with delight.

Having started down the long road to knowledge, suddenly the regent halted and, with characteristic hauteur, demanded that her entire household must accompany her.

To supply her *kahus* she would need forty copies of the spelling book, she told Hiram. He promised she would have them. Further, he said that when he called again he would bring slates and pencils so that all within her entourage might learn to write as well as read.

CHAPTER 6

Kaahumanu did not wait for Bingham to call again. Early on the Sabbath morning, Hiram looked from an upper window of the mission house and saw a cloud of dust moving up the road from the harbor. At the center of it was the regent's open wagon.

Over the plain it bumped and rattled, drawn by a team of golden lads at either side of the wagon tongue. They bore their lady's chariot at breakneck pace; nor did the tolling of the church bell, heard from shore to valley, curb their frivolous spirit.

The sight of Kaahumanu bounding over the lowlands not only gladdened the hearts of the mission families; it piqued the curiosity of the natives. Where the regent went, her people must be there too. As quickly as the news spread, the chiefs of Oahu and hundreds of commoners followed her to Kawaiahao.

Hiram Bingham escorted Kaahumanu in to church. Dexter Chamberlain placed a bench for her in front of the pulpit and there she sat in splendid isolation. Behind her, the people stepped and squatted and pressed for vantage places on the dirt floor.

The peal of the church bell ceased. Bingham mounted to the pulpit desk and bowed his head. Among the congregation a muttering and scuffling ensued. Wild-eyed natives craned their necks and saw that not only Bingham, but all the mission *haoles* were talking with their eyes shut.

"*E aha la ka poe haole i moe iho la na maka?*" (What are these foreigners doing with their eyes cast downward?) cried an old warrior.

"*E anaana ana ia kakou!!!*" (They are praying us to death!!!) gibbered a raucous crone and she fled from the church.

Hiram commenced the service again. Throughout prayers, hymns and sermon, the populace of Honolulu gaped at him and discussed the curious behavior of all the missionaries.

Bingham offered his benediction in Hawaiian. He pronounced the words with a sharp emphasis that was alien to them, but the natives were overjoyed.

"*Akamai!*" they cried, and they set up a gleeful hubbub of praise and nods and nudges.

Hiram looked down at the vociferous horde and signaled to Kaahumanu. She rose and strode for the door. Her colossal figure was clothed in fifteen yards of yellow satin wrapped *pa'u*-style around her torso. Another twenty feet of purple silk hung over one shoulder and trailed behind her in the dust. A rope of black hair, plaited to the breadth of a man's fist, encircled her neck. At the front of the distinctive hawser she wore a whale tooth hook, symbol of her nobility.

Behind her walked the chiefs of lesser rank,

clad in all the rags and tags of finery which had come their way in years of trafficking with foreign ships. Bingham recognized the red coat of a British officer lately at war in the American Revolution; yonder went a battered tricorn which must have served in the same conflict. He counted some portion of the uniforms of half a dozen nations, but a more outlandish use of them he could not have anticipated.

A cutaway coat, crusted with tarnished braid, skirted the bare brown buttocks of the giant who wore it. On another not otherwise clad, Hiram discovered the breeches and headgear of an admiral of His Britannic Majesty's navy. A pearl-colored satin vest was the Sabbath garment of a third; for his visit to church, he had added a brown tapa *malo* and the woolen cap of a common sailor.

Most of the women of rank wore loose gowns of silk or calico. Grandly, they had added French chapeaux with drooping ostrich plumes. One chiefess, gowned in muslin, clumped forth in a pair of high-laced woodsman's boots and in her hand she brandished a gold-headed walking stick.

The common natives crowded against the walls of the church. Their ragged tapa garments, matted hair and *leho* scars marked them as some of the legions who had spent a decade or more wresting sandalwood from the mountains. If the stories Hiram had heard were true, those who remained in the forests now seized every opportunity to destroy the young sandalwood trees. It was a mute conspiracy to check the tyranny of these gaily-caparisoned chiefs who forced their people to labor in the service of foreign traders.

Bingham scanned the mob and thought, "Something different is needed here. Something to confront voyagers from Christian lands with that principle of government which permits them to be traders instead of slaves themselves."

At the same time, he knew care must be taken to teach the Hawaiian rulers the precepts of human liberty. It was all too evident that they saw no wrong in taking the life and labor of another. As long as the barter was profitable, traders and shipmasters remained aloof. They did not fancy themselves teachers of heathen nations.

On the day Kaahumanu went to church, Bingham and his brethren discovered how quickly that regal dame could move and how widespread were the repercussions of her every act.

Because her presence at Kawaiahao caused a tide of humanity to follow her there, the mission families tarried after she left the church. They wished to extend the hand of Christian welcome to as many natives as would pause for a greeting. There were several hundreds who lingered.

So the brethren and their wives were unaware of what was happening in their home compound. But the Chamberlain children stood outside the church yard and watched with mounting suspicion. Before they could warn their parents, the marauding regent hurtled past them in a cloud of dust.

Kaahumanu ignored the missionaries as she dashed past them in her runabout. Beside her rode William Beals clinging to the jolting wagon frame with one hand and waving to the mission children with the other.

Mary Chamberlain raced down the path behind the wagon. Dust flew over her head and choked her and she pulled up the hem of her smock to cover her face. She could hear Jerusha calling her to halt.

Mary obeyed and when she looked back she saw that every eye was focused on her. Tears streamed down her cheeks. The child was so humiliated that she sat down at the side of the path and hid her face until the natives had gone away. When she saw her parents leave the church she trudged home behind them.

She paused in the dooryard only long enough to hear the orphans' story of what had happened. They told Mrs. Bingham that they had walked directly home from church. On their way, Kaahumanu had passed them in her wagon and when they trooped into the compound they found her waiting. She demanded to know which one of them had learned the most *palapala*.

They told her it was William Beals. The regent said, "Where is William Beals? He will live with me and be my teacher." William had stepped forward and the regent ordered him to climb into her wagon.

Without a word, Mary took the baby from her mother's arms and carried him into their family room. There she remained, nor was she missed until nightfall.

That day such unusual demands were made on the mission that the mothers had no time to serve a midday meal. Before sundown every native of rank in Honolulu had called on or sent a messenger to Bingham and his colleagues.

The king's servants arrived first. They were ordered to fetch one hundred copies of the spelling book for the use of his majesty's retinue. Since Liholiho had decreed that his five wives must learn to write as well as read, the *kahus* said they also had need of tables and chairs. The supply of furnishings at the mission dwelling was sparse, but tables and chairs were carried off.

Then the thing which Mary dreaded happened. The high chiefs came to select their teachers from among the orphans. With her nose pressed against the window pane, Mary watched Mrs. Bingham's scholars as they were called out to stand in a row. The lords of the isles inspected them and made their choices. One statuesque chief, merry as a child himself, swung his small tutor aloft to stand on his shoulders.

"This is my teacher," he announced, and he strode off with the little fellow riding ten feet high.

Mary grieved in silence. That golden urchin and William Beals and all the orphans were her friends. They were the only playmates she had known since she had left America.

She turned away from the window. Her legs felt weak and her stomach was empty. To ease the pain in her middle she lay face down on her mother's cot. Presently she fell into an uneasy sleep from which she would wake to find her little world severely altered.

CHAPTER 7

"Could such as this be called a school?" Sybil almost cried aloud, and in her exasperation she might have done so. But she would not have been heard.

It was late afternoon, past time to dismiss native class, and she rang her hand bell—loud, long and vigorously—but in vain. The mob of headstrong pupils, crowded into her grass schoolhouse in such numbers that the atmosphere was almost suffocating, suddenly united in a recitation of the Biblical generations from Adam to Noah. Why, she knew not.

They sang the "begats" with a jolly gusto. Though they mimicked the ancient spate quite perfectly, Sybil heard in the chorus a tempo that was rather close to the rhythm of their hula chants. She knew that hardly one among them, or among the scores who stood outside the doors and windows, understood what they were singing. Nevertheless, they had learned to sing it.

Since the day Kaahumanu and the chiefs had begun to study *palapala*, hordes of common natives flocked around the mission schoolhouse from morning till night in all seasons. They needed to hear a lesson only once and they could repeat it verbatim.

When they were confronted with the printed word they displayed the same virtuosity. Because there were not enough books for all the would-be learners in Honolulu, those who sat opposite or at an angle to a page read the words as they appeared. They also had learned to write upside down.

Every day hundreds were learning something, somehow. And since it was the habit of the islanders to spread whatever was new the length and breadth of the archipelago, in the autumn months of 1822 *palapala* scattered like pollen in a high wind.

To Sybil Bingham's way of thinking, it was a poor substitute for schooling. To train the developing mind and put it on the stretch to learn and understand, to curb the rudimental will, to mold character, to instill a sense of duty, sound principle, proper motive—these were the bounden duties of one who would educate. Sister Bingham believed that anything less constituted a poorly directed effort.

Her orphan scholars, elevated to the rank of teachers themselves, already were dispersed island-wide, most of them attached to the retinues of chiefs; but some of the little girls and several of the boys had been tempted by the trinkets and promises of seamen. They had forsaken their adult pupils and run off to the ships. When Sybil thought of the fate of those children a weariness of spirit all but overcame her.

She closed her eyes and waited for the uproar

to subside. Seated before her on the classroom floor were natives of all ages. On the limbs of some, foul sores mingled their odors with the fumes of wine and rum. Little children not ten years old frolicked around their elders and advertised by the words of their mouths and the play of their hands that they were no strangers to "carnal knowledge."

There were young mothers here with sucking babes, and the ancients of the race—old nobles whose eyes had beheld the tall spars and billowing sails of Captain Cook's ships of discovery—they were here, too.

Sybil acknowledged to herself that it was one of God's miracles that they *were* here, and in such numbers.

"God, give me strength," she prayed, and she rose from her bench to restore order in the schoolroom.

"*Aloha oukou*," she sang out. "*Aloha oukou*."

It meant "Goodbye...class is dismissed...we will meet again tomorrow."

Her pupils heaved themselves off the mats and began to move out of the hut. As they filed past Sybil their farewells were like the deep-throated cooing of a flock of pigeons. She nodded goodbye to each in turn and when they had gone she took up her cup and pitcher and hurried from the schoolroom.

Sybil was awkward in her pregnancy and she made a nervous passage across the yard, stepping where she could between the natives who sat in the dirt tracing letters with sticks and stones. Near Elisha Loomis' printing hut she saw a dozen or more Hawaiian men standing all but in a state of nature. One of them held a page which had just been peeled from the press and handed out the door. From it he read:

"*I was glad when they said unto me, let us go into the house of the Lord.*"

A bare-breasted woman who lounged in the dust challenged him with a spate of carping that began in Hawaiian and ended with every oath she had learned of hardened seamen.

Sybil hurried on and tried to put the vile words from her mind. She saw little Sophia standing at a window of the mission house. In a moment she would have the child in her arms. She would sit for a while in her rocking chair and hold her baby close while the Chamberlain children recited for her. O precious hour!

She lifted the latch and entered a den of perfect gloom. Her barefoot toddler skimmed over the floor and Sybil swept her up in her arms. The little Chamberlains—Mary, Daniel and four-year-old Nancy—remained seated at a table with their books and slates and samplers. Every face was a rueful mask.

Sybil gazed over Sophia's curls at the three who neither moved nor spoke.

"Oh children, do come away from your lessons now," Mrs. Bingham urged.

"We may not go out," said Mary.

Poor little prisoners. It was true. They must not go out. At dusk, when the throngs had left the mission yard the children might play outside for an hour. But as matters were now, there was nothing to do but to confine them within doors for most of each day.

Sybil did not question the wisdom of it. She would not expose the tender mind of a child to the sights and sounds and contamination which she herself met from morning till night in the schoolhouse and all over the mission compound. But she pitied these little ones and prayed that a change might be made soon for their sakes and for the sake of her own baby, just rising two.

Perhaps Sybil should have left matters alone and spared herself the task of explaining this new order of confinement. But the children looked so forlorn that she felt compelled to do something to engage their attention.

"Do you know why we cannot keep school as we used to?" she asked.

The listless bairns shook their heads.

"It is because the Lord quite suddenly has opened the way for us to instruct many hundreds of the native people. And since they come to us now asking to learn, the way of duty is clear."

Tears welled up in Mary's eyes and slid down her thin cheeks.

"Come, Mary," said Sybil. "Come to the window, all of you. See Mr. Loomis there at his press striking off lesson sheets for the people who walk here and wait all day, hoping to get even one page.

"And there, Mr. Thurston and Mr. Bingham coming up the path now. Do you know where they go when they leave our house in the morning? They must travel many a weary journey to preach and teach and counsel with the people..."

She was interrupted by the sound of childish laughter. Little Nancy, who claimed barely an inch of window space, nevertheless had made a discovery. She spied her mother with Sister Loomis and Sister Thurston at the well. The little girl jabbed a finger against the window pane and pointed to the mothers who were engaged in what seemed to her to be a playful caper.

Sybil put a hand on the child's head and began to explain how, from the store of water in the cellar, the women had lugged bucketsful out to the well. Mrs. Thurston and Mrs. Loomis now took turns pouring water down the throat of the old pump and Jerusha, with a two-handed grip on the wooden handle, jumped up and down in her tracks to get the pump to suck.

Seeing the children's spirits somewhat restored, Sybil put a gentle challenge to them.

"Can you not do your part by waiting, as well as your parents do theirs by toiling?" she asked.

Young Daniel, whose attention was still on the well and the mechanics which caused water to rise out of the ground, answered:

"I would like to go outside and work the pump."

He tried another avenue of escape.

"Mrs. Bingham, Dexter does not stay indoors. Why may I not help him and Father out there?"

He pointed at his brother and Daniel Chamberlain, who was going about his last work for the mission. With Dexter to help him, Daniel had gathered a pile of driftwood from the beach. Father and son were chopping it into firewood.

Sybil looked from the well to the woodpile, but she never answered. There before their eyes was answer enough.

At first, the intruders appeared to be only a gang of seamen from one of the whaling ships that rode at anchor offshore. It was not unusual for sailors to tramp along the strand beyond the mission house, and occasionally one would walk in and ask for a Bible or some tracts. Or they might only wish to speak a word with Christian folk. Sometimes it happened that a youth who presented himself in tar-daubed trousers and a striped frock was the son or nephew of New Englanders who were acquainted with some member of the mission families.

Sybil knew these were no such lads. They were swaggering ruffians who came shouting jibes at Daniel and Dexter. Romping in the midst of the gang were three native girls, naked except for their tattered *pa'us* and some strands of wilted *maile* over their shoulders.

"Come away, children. Come away from the window," commanded Sybil and she tried to turn them around with her free hand.

Mary grasped the casement and jabbered, "Pualani! There is Pualani!"

Sybil looked again and saw that one of the girls was indeed Pualani, the orphan child who had lived at the mission for almost a year.

"Why does she run with the sailors, Mrs. Bingham?" Mary persisted. "And why does she look so...she seems very ugly...."

She could not name the look of fierce contempt in Pualani's face as the native girl pranced in a circle around Dexter and shouted, "Stay work with old man all time!! No come *holo-holo!!!* No *honi-honi!!!*"

"Mrs. Bingham...why?" Mary pleaded. Sybil seemed not to hear.

Suddenly her expression of sorrow changed to horror as a red-faced sailor broke from the gang, grabbed Pualani by the jaw and forced her head back. He poured something from a bottle down her gullet. His thick fingers slid down her front and grabbed one bare breast. With the other hand he hurled the bottle against the woodpile in the mission yard.

The children, too bewildered to speak, felt cold fear creeping into their hearts. Sybil would not have it so; they must think and pray and exorcise this horrible thing from their minds. She ordered them to take their places at the table at once.

She took her seat, settled Sophia on her lap, and waited until each child looked directly at her as they had been taught to do.

"When people fall into sin," Sybil began, "we know that our Heavenly Father loves them still. And so must we.

"Mary, you have read how Jesus said to His disciples: *If a man have an hundred sheep, and one of them be gone astray, doth he not leave the ninety and nine, and goeth into the mountains and seeketh that which is gone astray?*

"Does that not mean that God will watch over Pualani?" Sybil asked. "The good shepherd will seek after her and each one of us will pray for her."

"That sailor..." Daniel began.

"And for that sailor, too," answered Sybil. "Pray for him, children, that he may turn from wickedness. It may be that your prayers will be the first that anyone has ever said for him. Surely if that is so, he is to be pitied and prayed for diligently, for his very soul is in jeopardy."

So they prayed, and when they had finished, the turbulence that had racked their little minds and hearts was quelled—and the mission yard had been vacated.

Sybil went to the door to scan the premises. Seeing no strangers about, and Mr. Chamberlain and Dexter still at their work, she told the children they might go out to play.

They made no move to go. For a little longer they wanted to stay by Sybil.

"Well then, put away the books and slates quickly," she said. "And when you have done, sit here again."

She remembered that she had something to show them. Mary spied the folded sheet as Sybil drew it from her apron pocket.

"A letter from William Beals!" she exclaimed. "Oh please, please Mrs. Bingham, may we see it?"

"It is indeed a letter from William," said Sybil, "and he writes from Waimea on Kauai."

"But why did he go so far away?" Daniel asked, the little forlorn note creeping back in his voice.

"He went because he must go where Kaahumanu goes," Sybil answered. "She took him there with all her *kahus* and now they tarry with four big vessels, waiting for the people to collect sandalwood. But hear what William tells us:

"'My very dear Mrs. Bingham,' the letter begins. 'I long very much to see you. I am in hopes I shall see you in a couple of months. I hope that you are well and Mr. B. and little Sophia. I long very much to see her. I think about her every day, and how she used to play with me. I wish kiss her for me.'"

Sybil delivered a kiss on the baby's temple.

"Now mind this, children," she continued. "Just hear of the work William is doing. He says:

"'You might be pleased to hear I have a school twice a day. I have thirty-five scholars, boys and girls, and the remainder of the time I take to teach the king and queen, so I have no time to write my journal. Once in a while, when they are out in swimming, I have a little time to write.

"'I would thank you to send down some books,

for there are some scholars who have none.... I am going to Niihau in the *Tartar,* and my scholars are going with me, so I teach them there.

"'...I thank you give my love to Mr. and Mrs. Chamberlain and to all the family children. Give my love to John Honolii and James. King Kaumualii gives his love to Mr. B. and to you, and Queen Kaahumanu too. They say they like the *palapala.*

"'Do not forget to pray for me—I am your child,

WILLIAM BEALS.'"

Sybil brushed a tear from her lashes and handed the letter to Mary.

As children will, the little Chamberlains responded to Sybil's skillful ministering and to the joy of sharing William Beals' adventures and his affectionate messages. Just at dusk they ventured to leave the house. But when they opened the door they had to jump aside quickly, for MacAfee stomped over the threshold. His head was lowered and the children saw the angry glower in his eyes.

Directly into the common room he strode and finding Hiram Bingham there he stated his business. Within this hour, the Scot announced, a highborn native woman, the wife of a chief, had been dragged to the beach by a band of sailors. Now they were rowing her out to the mother ship in a whaleboat.

"It was done on captain's orders, an' it may be laid directly to the teachin's o' yerself!" MacAfee charged.

Sybil heard the scrape of her husband's chair as he rose from his desk.

"Explain what you mean, sir," Bingham demanded.

"Within sight o' yer very door," said MacAfee, "eight ships lie at anchor, an' seven more in the harbor. Ye must know that aboard the lot o' them 'tis the common rule for captain an' crew to have their pick o' females. But when the little savages who once went sweetly forth now cling fast to the shore an' prate aboot sinful livin', e'en the captain himself will take a hand, as now has come to pass."

He paused only long enough to draw breath.

"I dinna have to say, Mr. Bingham, that the great object an' the hope o' many a foreigner here is to o'erturn this house an' send ye packin'.

"Take this event as retribution for yer teachin's. 'Tis a punishment to the natives, an' a threat to yerselves. An' mark well the difference in yer numbers an' those o' yer adversary, sir. It be only prudent to do so."

Having never reckoned on the good will of iniquitous men or the advantage of superior numbers, Hiram was unmoved by MacAfee's reasoning.

"Eight ships or eight hundred," he replied, "we do not imagine that lustful men aboard any of them will love the influence of the gospel here. Of course they do not yield without a struggle.

"But the renovation of a nation does not wait for the downfall of Satan, MacAfee. Meanwhile, God has something yet for us to do among the heathen."

"An' would that ye might be permitted to do it!" exclaimed the Scot. "But sir, ye've come too late. O, rightly ye may take it that the natives love yer teachin'. Aye, how they flock around!

But I'm sorry to say that should ye be persistin' in this now, ye'll be doin' the ignorant things more harm than good."

Before he replied Hiram met the fierce eye of MacAfee with a long stare.

"When lawless men feel a check, when they sense that their craft is in danger..." he began.

"Why mon, such a one would slit off yer ears before ye could say him nay!" said MacAfee. "An' have ye thought, sir, what defense might ye have against the carryin' off o' yer own women, should they take it in their heads to do so?"

"We have none," answered Hiram.

"Aye, ye have none. An' I hope for the sake o' the pious ladies that the common talk now heard aboot the harbor may be true."

"What talk?" demanded Bingham.

"I'm told, sir, that Mr. Chamberlain seeks passage to America for himself an' his family, an' I'm prayerful that the rest will follow soon."

Hiram would not have answered this seeming impudence had he regarded it as such, but Mac-Afee looked him straight in the eye and he spoke from manly concern.

"The decline of Mr. Chamberlain's health and the difficulties of guarding his children from the vice that surges over this land, uncontested and unrestrained, have brought him to that decision," Bingham admitted.

"Those of us who stay need not be reminded that if much of the foreign influence in these islands is not soon opposed we may see our own children at the brink of degradation."

"I trust then ye'd have the wisdom to retreat," said MacAfee.

"I believe, sir, we would have the wisdom then

to relinquish what is commonly regarded as a parent's privilege to others more favorably situated in our native land," Hiram answered. "But we would not retreat."

Sybil waited for the furor in her breast to subside. The pounding of her heart was so violent that for a moment she could breathe only by the most determined effort. She felt as though she had lost her footing, but she stood by the table where the children had left their books.

When MacAfee arrived she had been laying out their study drills for the morrow. Through the thin wall which separated their chamber from the common room, she heard all that passed between the two men.

❂ ❂ ❂

That evening Sybil sat in her rocking chair and held Sophia in her arms. The moon rose and flooded the room with such a brilliant light that she could see every feature of her baby's face, the curling tendrils of hair, the eyebrows, the rounded cheeks and sharp little nose.

She did not know how many hours she had sat with the burden of this child pressing on the one yet unborn. Her legs and back ached from the weight of them, but that precious freight was a solace to her. She wanted only to hold her baby close and speak no word to anyone but Hiram. When he came from his desk in the common room, if she could then make utterance she would seek his counsel.

"O God," she prayed, "in the little time left

to us may we still believe that, of all others, this sacrifice will not be required."

At the close of each day it was the custom of Hiram Bingham to record all progress, obstacles and events bearing on the work of the mission. Under the expiring date of August 9, 1822, he wrote a report of the situation at Honolulu. When it was finished he lifted the lid of his desk, took sheets of tissue-thin stationery from the drawer and selected a new quill. He addressed the secretary at the Mission Rooms in Boston and pondered the order of the letter he would draft.

Repeatedly, for more than a year, he had informed the Board of Commissioners for Foreign Missions of the need for reinforcements at the Sandwich Islands. Help had not come and the frail ship of the Hawaiian mission seemed near to foundering.

The decision of Daniel Chamberlain to lead his family back to America already was known to the members of the Board. Hiram had now to acquaint them with a proposal which staggered those few laborers who chose to remain in the field.

He dipped his quill and put the question to his sponsors:

We ask advice...on the propriety or expediency of sending our children from this land...to our friends in America....

Chapter 8

On an April morning in 1823 dawn stole over the island with a light so feeble that it scarcely limned the harsh planes and angles of the mission dwelling. Presently one window was pricked by candlelight. The sickly glimmer shone through a second aperture which spread in a widening angle. The *mauka* door opened and Hiram Bingham stepped out. He was suited in black and wore a stock and shirt of white linen.

He pulled the door shut behind him and went his way. The sound of his brogues tramping over rubble marked his progress toward the thatched church. He walked with lowered head and his shoulders were hunched against the chill of the morning.

Earth, sea and sky were the color of lead. Along the top of the Koolau range, cliffs and clouds merged in a dense mass. From the floor of Nuuanu valley pale shrouds of mist rose slowly, almost imperceptibly, to veil the land.

The sea broke on the reef and grumbled its way across the coral barrier. To Hiram's musically gifted ear, the tempo was marred by a recurring whack that broke each long crescendo of surf. He knew the cause, and soon he saw it looming up like a giant barnacle not far offshore.

It was the *Ruby,* a two-masted vessel that lay at a crazy angle athwart the reef. The waves rushing shoreward burst against its hull and boiled around the ill-fated thing. Still it hung there like a shackled prisoner, its masts pointing halfway between sky and shore, its bowsprit grazing the edge of the reef.

For almost two months the foundered ship had been the property of the mission. The brethren had paid four hundred and five dollars for it with the intent of salvaging its timber. They needed the damaged wood to feed their washing and cooking fires, and they intended that its spars should be the supports and beams of a new printing house. Its planking would provide frames for the doors and windows.

When?

How?

Hiram did not know.

He walked on. At the side of the grass church he stopped before a tiny mound of earth, the perimeter of which was marked by a fence of sticks. Somewhere south and east of where he stood, a vessel now was bearing homeward a letter which he had written to his parents under the date of January 12, 1823.

"How bountifully the Lord deals with my dear Sybil, and with her husband and children," he had rejoiced. "On the eve of the new year, through the goodness of her Heavenly father, she had a pleasant little son laid quietly in her bosom. . . ." Then, with some restraint, he had written of certain cheerless circumstances following the birth of his son:

"The lovely thing has been sick two or three days; we hope it is some better; the mother is now able to walk from her bed to her chair.... I, too, have been somewhat ill about three days, but was able to spend most of the last night in watching with my little family...."

With no physician to attend the infant, and no soup or custard or milk to strengthen the nursing mother, baby Levi Bingham survived less than four days after his father had written the news of his arrival. His earthly crib was a bed of coral dust, his lullaby the rumble of ocean waves pounding near this desolate plot where, one by one, the mission workers would follow when their labor was done.

Hiram's agony was compounded by an awareness that his mission, for which this first tender sacrifice had been made, might also fail. Yet, while the Lord permitted him the use of his head and his hands, the work must not stop.

Mindful that man's days on earth are few, he turned from the infant grave and set out on the path that led to the coconut grove at Waikiki. Thither the chiefs had gone to sojourn in their airy bowers beside the sea, and thither went Bingham.

For months Hiram had traveled after Liholiho's wandering train, seeking to instruct them, hoping to convert them. Still they deferred and demurred. Languidly, they turned aside when Bingham urged them to heed the Ten Commandments. Liholiho exempted himself by announcing: "In five years, I will turn and forsake sin."

"You are not sure of five years or five months

or five days," Hiram admonished. "You can gain nothing by delay."

Such was his belief. Yet all around him stood remnants of his own delayed or thwarted effort. As he walked past the mission compound he did not spare himself the sight of a jagged shell of coral stone that stood across the path from the frame house. It was the foundation of the new printing office. Weeks of back-breaking labor had been spent to cut and haul and mortar together enough coral rock to make this grotesque thing. The lumber for its interior still hung on the reef.

Bingham clung to his only hope for the survival of the mission. Lately he had received tidings from Boston that a new company of preachers and teachers had volunteered to go to the aid of those who still labored in the field. He was told that the reinforcing band would arrive at the Sandwich Islands aboard the whaleship *Thames* on its next Pacific cruise.

Thankful as he was for the promise of assistance, Hiram knew that if it did not come soon one new company of workers could not hope to turn back all the adverse tides that threatened to oversweep the mission. Yet nothing could alter his conviction that the Lord God Jehovah had sent him and his covenanters forth to bestow upon this island people the means of salvation. He was sure God did not sanction the purpose of His servants only to leave them without the means to labor, even in His most distant vineyards.

He walked several miles along the inland boundaries of man-made ponds which bordered the southeast shore of Oahu. Shoals of fish had been taken from the ocean and loosed in the pens where, fed and protected by the king's servants, the finny tribes swam and jumped and grew prime for the *imu*.

"As other men tend their herds of meat-bearing animals, so do these ingenious natives improve the bounty of the deep," Bingham reflected.

But he deplored the tabu which prohibited those who had built the ponds and those who fished, or any person below the rank of chief, to taste even a fragment of the fish. As far as the eye could reach, the food-producing waterways, several hundred of them, were laid out along the shore. Everything in them belonged to the king.

Bingham turned up his collar and wrapped his coat across his chest. Though it was not raining he seemed to be moving through an atmosphere that was only slightly less wet than the bordering ponds and ocean. The air was so freighted with water that, seemingly out of nowhere, chill little splats of moisture blew against his face and damped his clothes.

On the upland side of the path he trod was the bowl of Manoa valley. It was filled, almost to its mountainous brim, with white vapor. Above the cliffs, dark clouds swirled and billowed as though they had burst from a volcano. The sun, which had not yet struck a beam through the reeling mass, shone full on its nether side. The ragged edges of the clouds were ablaze.

When he reached the coconut grove at Waikiki Hiram saw that daylight scarcely had penetrated the dense foliage; only the tallest palm fronds reflected the morning glow. Roused by a breeze, the lofty fans began to move. A dart of sunlight broke through the gloom and the palm leaves glinted like blades of steel. All at once, heaven's splendor burst upon the scene.

The sky was rent by a golden beam that fired the clouds and ignited the rim of Diamond Hill. The new brilliance streamed slantwise to the sea in shafts, routing night ghosts of mist that hovered along the base of the crater. Over the ocean there was loosed a gossamer glow so delicate that, at the sight of it, even the most downcast heart must declare the glory of God. Bingham, witness to these transcendent miracles, felt a buoyancy of spirit which, for too many months, had been denied him.

Looking across the shimmering bay he watched a line of canoes breasting the waves and coursing toward the open sea off Diamond Hill. His attention leapt from the native paddlers to the now visible object of their maneuver. It was a whaling vessel beating a wide arc around the point of the crater.

On it came, white sails shimmering in the morning light. Hiram felt his heart soar within him when he descried the name on its starboard bow. It was the *Thames*.

For as long as she bore her westward course, he did not take his eyes from the noble sight. He bolted across the beach and stood at the water's edge. With his hands cupped at either side of his eyes to lengthen his vision he scanned the rolling deck and tried to distinguish the silhouetted figures standing at the bulwarks. He could recognize only the tall hats of the men and the flaring bonnets of the women who stood beside them.

The ship sailed on. Seamen sprang to the rigging and ran aloft to furl the sails. When the *Thames* stood offshore at a point midway between the two great valleys its anchor was cast.

❋ ❋ ❋

The travel-weary young couples who watched from the deck of the *Thames* knew that her creaking cabin, which had been their home for one hundred and fifty-eight days, must remain so until they had passed the Lord's day in meditation. Before they went below, they met for prayers with the captain on his quarter-deck.

At the close of the service the master directed his passengers' attention to visible evidence that their errand ashore might be accomplished with greater speed than they had dared hope.

"As many as would clap eyes on what your people have wrought among the heathen, squint through my glass," he said. "Aim it yonder as I point."

Each in turn, the sober young men took the spyglass and trained it on a straw-colored mass that loomed up on the coral flats of Kawaiahao.

"'Tis a Christian house of worship, that, and you can see the pagans swarming round it by the hundreds," the captain rumbled.

The travelers passed the glass again and lingered over the thrilling sight. Gazing on this foreign strand, their thoughts turned to the prophetic charge which had been put to them when they embarked at New Haven.

"If you adorn the doctrine of God your Savior in all things," they were told, "if you are found faithful and laborious and devoted servants of Christ; if each revolving year bears cheering testimony of your perseverance; if your Christian virtues shine with greater and still greater brightness; whatever your immediate success may be, every page of your history will be read with unspeakable interest by the thousands of our Israel."

The day of commencement was at hand. They went below to spend the time in prayer before they would sever their last ties with the land they had left and take up their burden as missionaries to the Sandwich Islands.

❋ ❋ ❋

At mid-afternoon, when the heat had become oppressive and all was quiet aboard the *Thames,* the captain twigged one of his passengers emerging from below. Rather, he heard him issue forth, for the sound of a racking cough preceded the young man as he made his way up to the deck.

The master did not wonder that Levi Chamberlain, a gentleman bachelor, should seek respite from the family quarters below. But he did think it strange that a successful Boston merchant should close his business, give his earnings to support a mission half way round the world, and himself sail thither to labor unrewarded in the cause.

Shrewdly, he eyed Mr. Chamberlain who scrutinized the harbor and village of Honolulu.

"No fool he," thought the captain.

Throughout the voyage he had noted with what quick comprehension young Chamberlain had acquainted himself with the business of whaling. From master, mates and crew the merchant had learned all there was to know about provisioning a ship that must roam the seas for three or four years running.

"Should the canny fellow learn a trick or two to keep his own ship afloat, welcome he is to them," thought the captain. He could not but admire gumption in a man, even a business man turned missionary.

He had it on good authority that the governing Board of these roving evangelists pinned its hopes on such judicious management as Chamberlain might bring to their business affairs.

Seeing the effort Levi made to discover something more of the nature of his destination, the captain once again offered his glass. The young man thanked him kindly and put the instrument to his eye.

Training it on church and mission house, he found both places deserted. The only movement he could see was that of heat currents which rose and wavered across his circumscribed view. He turned the spyglass upward to the valleys, then down along the shore.

What he beheld was the multitude of natives whose earlier presence at church had so delighted the new missionaries. Levi now spied the dusky populace lounging in the shade of hayrick hovels.

In Boston, when he had met with the gentlemen of his governing Board, Levi was given to understand that the pioneer mission company had given these people an alphabet, that the language of the race had been produced in written, nay printed form and that Elisha Loomis had, more than a year since, begun to manufacture lesson sheets, spelling books and scripture in the native tongue.

Moreover, Chamberlain had been told that their ultimate aim was that from the common ranks there should rise educated men—ministers, doctors and schoolmasters—and a population skilled in carpentry, mechanics, sewing, farming and all the other arts of civilization.

From the deck of the *Thames* Levi Chamberlain, probing high and low, could discover no evidence save the church itself that book or gospel had ever reached this shore. Dispiriting as were the calculations he made from afar, he did not expect such an impasse as that which he met, and which defied him at every turn, as soon as he took lodging in the mission house.

CHAPTER 9

The *Thames* lay offshore for two days before she was towed into the harbor and her passengers disembarked.

Their arrival at Kawaiahao gave rise to a domestic upheaval which was, in the eyes of Levi Chamberlain, appalling. Into that compound where exhaustion and discomfort already prevailed, nineteen travelers came with their boxes and barrels and sea chests. Within doors and yon, their hosts' books and bedsteads and benches lay just where they had been set aside in the confoundment of altering the menage to admit the new recruits.

Levi stood apart, incredulous. He thought that only the Lord God on high could tell where all the members of this overwrought fraternity might be billeted.

The householders were not without a plan. Directly they specified where the newly arrived couples would lodge, and Brother Chamberlain set about a stint of fetching and carrying which would not cease till long past nightfall.

As he ran toward the row of old grass houses, bearing an armload of trappings, a sudden downpour spurred his flight. The rain shafts pounded aslant the huts and drove like needles through the thatch of the cabin into which he bolted.

He probed the underside of the roof and found a solid patch beneath which he stowed his load. Hampers and boxes were deposited helter-skelter across the dirt floor and a patchwork quilt hung from the ridgepole. It was sodden with water. More than twenty-four hours earlier the bedcover had been rigged as a screen between two domiciles. During the night rain had beaten in along the ridgepole and torn away the crest of rotting thatch.

Levi reached for a receptacle to put under the quilt where it sagged in the middle. The thing which he seized was a white chamber pot. The drips fell into the crock with a monotonous ping, ping, ping that irked him, but he did not move.

The rain clouds passed and sunlight broke through suffocating blankets of vapor. Still Levi tarried, standing almost inert in the doorway of the old hut. He felt as though his strength were evaporating like the steam that rose off the soggy shacks. For a few minutes he could not bestir himself, even to make some provision for his own lodging.

Where he might lay his head this night, Levi could not imagine. There was no room for him in the shacks, nor could he think of a vacant cranny or closet in which a single man might berth at the frame house.

He need not have troubled himself. The brethren had decided that Mr. Chamberlain, being without a wife, would have for his bed the long wooden settee in the common room. It was the last horizontal surface yet unoccupied. Levi understood, of course, that it was also the principal seat in that well-traveled room which served as parlor, study and chapel for all the mission families.

❀ ❀ ❀

Sleep does not come soon to a shy bachelor in a public bed ringed about by married couples and infants. In his unyielding bunk, situated at the hub of the establishment, Levi fell into a fitful doze only to be roused by the crying of children and the persistent glow of a whale oil lamp.

While he waited for babies to be lulled and lights to be extinguished, he could hear the relentless scratching and dipping of quill pens. The sisters and brethren were recording in their journals certain observations which Levi himself might have made.

Certainly he could substantiate Sister Loomis' note that "the health of my little Amanda is quite delicate. Her complaint is in the bowels. She is quite tiresome...." Or the comment of Sybil Bingham: "...it may well be supposed there could be but little time when it could be said to be still around us...ways and means must be devised and labor done, that so many might be fed each day...."

If he had scanned the diary of his fellow voyager, Sister Louisa Ely, Levi would have voiced a weary amen to her findings.

"Brother Loomis," she wrote, "looked so pale and emaciated I could hardly recognize his countenance."

Nor did Brother Chamberlain have to peer into Loomis' journal to read the little printer's own admission: "...I seem to have lost all energy I ever possessed."

Faced with evidence of the grinding drudgery and privation which would be their lot if they went forward in this struggle, did Levi and the other newly arrived pilgrims feel their courage give way a jot? Perhaps they did, and with cause.

If, in the secret places of their hearts, some conflict had to be resolved, if they did falter or hesitate, the issue was concluded in private. Within a few days of their arrival Sister Ely wrote: "We rejoice to relieve these dear sisters who have borne the burden and the heat of the day, for they appear almost worn out."

From a woman's point of view it bespoke that Christian solidarity which carried them forward united, regardless of the cost. For, with Hiram Bingham, they believed that God had something yet for them to do among the heathen.

Moreover, the rulers of the realm gave them cause to think that their hour of opportunity was at hand. Kaahumanu wrote them a greeting:

"Our hearts are glad you have come, very glad.... Give our aloha to all the new teachers and their *wahines*."

Out across the sunstruck sea, Liholiho dispatched his note to the captain of the *Thames*:

"Love to you. This is my communication to you. You have done well in bringing hither the new teachers. You shall pay nothing on account of the harbor—no, nothing at all.

Grateful affection to you.
LIHOLIHO IOLANI"

❀ ❀ ❀

The king and regent, as was their habit regarding anything that took their fancy, considered that these interesting young immigrants were at their disposal. Before the year was out they had dispersed most of the reinforcing company far and wide. In their ado to billet teachers on Hawaii, Maui and Kauai, they caused Lucy and Asa Thurston to return to Kailua, scene of their first mission station before Liholiho ordered them to Oahu.

Having got missionaries on every large island, the chiefs declared that the whole nation must be taught to read and write.

With that edict the way to a cherished goal opened wide before the champions of the Lord. Opportunity bade them advance; royal sanction waved them forward. On every hand they heard the cry "Give us books. Give us teachers." But their forces were scattered and they could not meet the demands of the people.

For new missionaries at remote stations, the first necessity was to learn the native language, to build schools and churches, to doctor the sick and to brook the opposition of foreign renegades who hated a churchman's presence and challenged his existence.

When these things were well begun the brethren still accomplished little because they had not that with which to teach. After Elisha Loomis printed two thousand copies of the Hawaiian spelling book the press stood idle for more than a year because he had no paper.

Brother Chamberlain no longer wondered why

the natives flocked to church and then sat idle in the sun.

Hiram Bingham, in a letter to the secretary of the governing Board, exclaimed: "Do, Sir, give us stationery as well as bread. We cannot live without it."

Levi took inventory of every article owned by the mission, hoping that by skillful bartering he might relieve the shortage in the printing department. No paper was to be found on any of the Sandwich Islands, or on any ship in port.

One day, perhaps in a year's time, the paper would come to hand. Just as barrels of moldy food always arrived when necessity mounted to urgency. But to Levi's way of thinking, something more than printing supplies and dry biscuit was needed here.

He reckoned that the impairment of the missionaries' health already far outweighed the savings they effected by their spartan mode of living. Because of the appalling lack of food and adequate shelter, he thought they could expect rapid deterioration of their most valuable asset: the families themselves.

Levi concluded that if the mission was to meet this rampant desire for instruction which the founding brothers and sisters had generated among the natives, he, as business agent, must make certain changes of a domestic nature. He began by writing to his directors in Boston:

"We are unable at this time to procure fresh provisions for anything but cash, & we have at this station almost entirely denied ourselves in this respect and subsisted on salt food...."

As he had consulted with the whalers, he sought the advice of Sybil Bingham and the other mission wives.

From the first days of their residence in Honolulu they had, from time to time, received gifts of butter and cheese and preserves from the captains of passing ships. The sisters had observed the means by which that life-giving manna survived ocean voyages of many months duration.

"Cheese," Sybil told Brother Chamberlain, "is best packed down in shavings of sweet wood and headed up air tight.

"Apples, perfectly dry and packed in pure sand, can be put aboard vessels sailing any time between October and January. Cider must be drawn off into bottles, then made air tight with good corks and the whole confined with wire. They will make a safe voyage if they be packed in a box filled with sand."

She told him about a little jar of preserved quince that had been brought to them by a seaman who once shared their supper.

"He was twenty-two months out when he called here," Sybil said. "But this quince, scalded and a little sugar added, was quite as relishable as any I ever ate in America."

Brother Chamberlain put it all down in letters he drafted to those men in Boston who purchased and shipped supplies to the Sandwich Islands Mission.

"Let three or four kegs of butter (each weighing from twenty to thirty pounds and put up in brine) be sealed in a barrel filled with a strong pickle," he directed.

"The butter thus put up will keep perfectly sweet. Most whaling ships have their butter put up in this way."

He recommended "Indian meal in tight barrels...for the convenience of landing and transmitting from the depository to the different stations."

Later, he complained: "...we were disappointed that no soap was sent by the *Dauphin* as our supply was at the time of her arrival nearly exhausted."

He noted that "...shoes for the different members of the mission are much needed, also writing paper, quills, ink powder and lead pencils for the missionaries and natives," and he suggested "A hand cart & wheelbarrow would be a very great convenience at most of the stations, & a great saving of expense...."

He turned to the subject of mission families who still lived in grass houses:

"The most durable of the common thatched houses built by the natives will last but a very few years and none of this kind will ever be regarded by any family as eligible for a residence, and even as a *temporary* one, only so long as circumstances prevent the building of a stone house, or the erection of some convenient and more permanent building than one covered with grass."

Pointedly he added: "If the friends of the missionaries in America knew to the full extent how much the mission needs boards, shingles, window sashes, glass, etc., they would strenuously exert themselves to forward such articles."

On a hot August morning the crying of an infant pierced and thrust and finally it goaded Levi into consciousness. When he opened his eyes daylight was at the window of the common room, as though to rebuke the laggard who slept till dawn. More to be dreaded was the prospect that he might be discovered, clad in nightshirt and stretched full length on the settee, when the families assembled for morning prayer.

He braced to spring from his wooden couch, then checked, rigid with shock. Such pain as he had never imagined smote him from neck to ankle. He seized the edge of his inflexible bed and keeled over, inch by inch, until his frame leveled with the bunk.

What collision of strained nerves and muscles and tendons had felled him, Levi could not tell. For months he had toiled with Elisha Loomis, splitting and cleaving and pulling away the hull of the *Ruby*. With the rising of the tide each day, when the men no longer could hold their footing on the reef, they had come ashore to dig coral boulders out of the ground and haul them to the site of the printing office. Together they had set the braces and raised the walls of the new structure. Now, once again, the work would be delayed.

Levi struggled to get up and was brought low a second time. Sweat soaked his nightshirt and his hair clung to his forehead in damp strings. His eyes darkened with pain and the thought that he might be deprived of his usefulness. To the puritan mind, such a calamity—even of a temporary nature—was second only to deprivation of life itself.

He thought it abominable that one, two, and now three men should have exhausted themselves trying to demolish a ship with little more than their bare hands. They had succeeded in pulling the waterlogged hulk asunder, but now whose back would bear the planks and spars homeward, once they were floated ashore? And who might dig more building stones and drag them through the mud to the place where they were needed?

The rack in which he lay pressed on his bones and joints, and the pain put Levi out of temper. He wished all the footfalls and muffled utterances above stairs and below would cease. The atmosphere was stifling and the air was so still that every noise for miles around magnified and rebounded. Otherwise Levi could not have heard, nor would he have been able to credit his ears when he thought he heard the bawling of farm animals.

He held his breath and tried to identify a faint bellow in the distance. Taking account of direction and the power of brute voices, he reckoned they must come from a ship approaching the harbor. Then, like a distant blare of hope trumpeting over the water, came the prolonged and energetic neighing of a horse.

Levi reminded himself that in the time of his probation before he joined the mission he had taken pains to rid himself of any remnant of the acquisitive instinct. Now he examined his conscience to make certain that the purpose which formed in his mind had nothing to do with trafficking for a profit. He was sure it did not.

He had conjured up the irresistible image of four-footed work animals lodged in captivity aboard a ship off port. No doubt they were carried here to be bartered for sandalwood. Levi prayed that his heavenly father would help him rise from the settee and reach the harbor in time to bid for at least one draft horse—if the craft gliding shoreward proved to be the Noah's ark he envisioned.

Chapter 10

L evi pulled himself up from his rack and hobbled to the quay where he beheld a rawboned
critter—long, lean and high in the hips—verily a
workhorse.

Lord knew there was toil enough on mission
ground for the nag, and Brother Chamberlain
sought out the captain who had brought it from
California.

Within an hour almost four hundred dollars of
"a fund for the support of Sandwich Islands missionaries in the year 1823" had been spent for the
horse; two cows, each with a calf, and a yoke of
slab-sided oxen. With the help of a native boy,
Levi drove the animals home and pastured them
in the marsh lands *makai* of Kawaiahao.

When the pain in his back subsided he hitched
the horse to the mission cart and rumbled off to
the village. Stacks of paraphernalia, sent out from
America in response to pleas from the mission
families, had accumulated at the harbor. Levi
reckoned it would take five or six trips to move
the lot.

Coming and going, he drove past MacAfee's hut. Whenever the Scot heard a clatter on the harbor road he came out to have a look. Watching the rattletrap go by, MacAfee drew up one red eyebrow in a grudging salute to the navvy who trundled down the road with his cargo of rocking chairs, stoves, wheelbarrows and crockery.

"To see once more a mon standin' at the helm o' beast an' wheel!" he exclaimed to Maka-lolo. "Now there's a bully banquet for the soul!"

Maka-lolo did not answer. He sat cross-legged before a mound of canvas on the ground and the edge of a torn sail hung on one shoulder. As he plied his needle and palm he paused occasionally to heave the goods over his back.

The spectacle of a missionary riding in a cart did not interest him. But when MacAfee repeated a story he had heard in the village the old curmudgeon pricked up his ears. The rumor was that the mission men were building a rig to which they would harness their oxen and make them pull the wreck of the *Ruby* off the reef.

Maka-lolo harked back to the days of his youth aboard a whaling vessel. He reckoned that one load of ship lumber would be less than the weight common sailors had to pull every time a harpooner struck his mark. Many a dead whale Maka-lolo had helped tow to the side of the mother ship, and many an oar he had bent when his veins were near bursting and his arms almost pulled out of their sockets. Sitting peacefully in his dotage, he brooded over the idea of brutes, instead of men, harnessed to such encumbrances.

Some days later when Levi Chamberlain drove the oxen down to the beach, Maka-lolo left his pile of canvas and trudged after them. Twenty feet from the shore he halted and stood like a derelict sighting a passing ship.

The bullocks lurched ahead. Their necks were pulled low by the yoke that shackled them, and their long horns served as a kind of ballast as they plodded through the sand.

Levi turned the animals around and pulled up the ends of a pair of hawsers that lay in the water. He hooked them to the ox yoke and looked out toward the reef where Elisha Loomis stood on a raft that was loaded with lumber.

Loomis waved his hat and Levi goaded the oxen. The beasts lunged and the ropes jerked taut, flinging sand and spray into the air. The raft began to move over the water. It made a smooth passage until the leading edge plowed into the beach with a dull thud.

Levi ran ahead and goaded the oxen again. The raft pitched forward. It rode the breadth of the beach and bumped over coral slabs and rubble until it reached the mission yard. A cloud of dust rose in its wake and Maka-lolo lost sight of raft, men, oxen and timber. He did not pursue them. His tattered old mind could imagine nothing to interest him at Kawaiahao.

The winter rains commenced in November and the sisters no longer had to muffle their faces with kerchiefs to shield them from the dust. Through the hot days of September and October Levi's oxen had raised billows of dirt around the mission house and it shook from cellar to roof top whenever the team dragged its burdens of lumber and coral through the yard. But by the help of almighty God and the bullocks, the printing office stood finished at last.

Sybil Bingham sat at the *mauka* window of the common room and looked up from her sewing. She rested her eyes by focusing them on the new building. Like everything else connected with the establishment, she thought, its trial for survival had begun. For three days rain had picked at the edges of the mud mortar that was packed between the coral blocks. Now rivulets of brown water ran down the walls and made ugly stains on them.

The cloud mantle that hung over the island darkened. Another storm was blowing in from the sea and Sybil felt a little shiver run across her back. She pulled up her shawl. The room would seem warmer if she lighted a lamp but Mr. Chamberlain had warned the families that their supply of oil was running low. Until a new shipment arrived, strictest economy had to be observed.

Sybil glanced down at her daughter and the two native boys who lay on the floor. They were practicing penmanship in their copybooks. Sophia mimicked the posture of her new playfellows; she propped herself on her elbows before an old notebook and pretended to read as well as write.

If nothing interfered with Kaahumanu's current ultimatum the boys would continue to share their academic skills with Sophia. The queen regent had ordered nine-year-old Kauikeaouli, brother of Liholiho and heir to the kingdom, to spend his days at the mission house and be taught by Mrs. Bingham. With him, as companion, she had sent the other child of noble lineage, Timothy Haalilio.

Of all her edicts, this one revealed the extent of Kaahumanu's anxiety concerning the fate of the islands. For years the old regent had tried to thwart and even to banish certain foreigners whom Liholiho welcomed without question, usually to his detriment. She now decreed that Kauikeaouli would be schooled in the *haole* way. She told Bingham that the boy must be trained up to a pitch of shrewdness and stability unheard of in his flighty brother.

Looking ahead to the day when she would relinquish the charge of Kamehameha: "Watch over my people," Kaahumanu took the first step toward shifting that mandate into the hands of the mission teachers.

Her decision was the result of justifiable foreboding. Liholiho, prompted by some vague awareness of his own inadequacy, had announced of a sudden that he would sail for England aboard the whaleship *L'Aigle* which lay off Honolulu harbor. As his reason for going, the king spoke of his wish to see that nation which was rich enough to send ships and men and merchandise in a never-ending procession around the world.

Kaahumanu's *manao* was that he went seeking British custody. She had not forgotten a similar intent of the first Kamehameha when, some thirty years earlier, the warrior chief boarded Captain George Vancouver's ship *Discovery* and ceded the island of Hawaii to the king of England. Kamehameha had expected that in return Britain would protect his islands from foreign encroachment. But England, having lately lost her American colonies, was not ready to assume the burden of entanglements in the Pacific. The Hawaiian king, the cession and the obligation were ignored.

What might be the outcome of Liholiho's voyage, Kaahumanu could not tell, nor could she alter his intention. But she regarded it as a dangerous enterprise.

Within ten days of sailing, when the king announced that his favorite queen Kamamalu would go with him, there flew into the minds of the mission wives certain misgivings which had not occurred to Kaahumanu but which were, nevertheless, fair cause for anxiety.

Womanlike, the sisters asked themselves, "How would it be if Kamamalu should present herself in England attired only in the loose wrappings of her native dress?"

It would not do. They could not stand by and watch her go forth to meet with stares and smirks and rude gibes. If she must venture uninvited among the courtiers of London, at least she should appear in costumes appropriate to her rank, according to the protocol of her hosts. Therefore, during the last days before *L'Aigle* sailed, the much-used common room was overrun with all the appurtenances of a dressmaker's salon.

From the royal storehouse, lengths of Oriental silk and brocade of crimson, yellow, pink and black were selected as the fabrics and colors best calculated to enhance Kamamalu's beauty. The sisters pondered her heroic proportions, then put scissors to the goods. Over the billowing yards their needles sped as they fashioned a wardrobe of gowns and bonnets and kerchiefs for her majesty to wear abroad. Among the seams were folded many a sigh and a prayer for the vagabond queen.

On this stormy afternoon Sybil expected she might finish sewing the last row of silken bands around the hem of Kamamalu's black gown. The children kept uncommonly quiet, the light at the window was still sufficient to make the fine stitches required for such an elegant robe and Sister Bingham was well begun when the silence was shattered by the snorting of a bullock in the *makai* yard.

Haalilio and Kauikeaouli deserted their books and ran for the door. Sybil called them back to receive their first lesson in "self control, devotion to duty and yielding not to temptation." They might see the bullocks, she told them, but not until they had finished the tasks begun in their copybooks.

Willful children that they were, it seemed unlikely that they would submit to any thwarting of their desires, even by such gentle means as Sybil employed. But when they reached the door Levi Chamberlain stood on the threshold. His presence threw the little truants into a state of uncertainty that stopped them in their flight, but they would not return to their books in the middle of the floor.

Sophia was left there alone, innocent heiress of their soon-to-be-discovered mischief. She sat with a pencil in each hand and made the most of the freedom which the shadowy chamber afforded.

Levi walked to the settee. He wanted his account book, his quill and his inkstand which, for lack of another place to put them, he kept under the bench. He squatted before it, searching for even a hand's breadth between the silken skirts that billowed over the seat and onto the floor.

Utterly baffled by this obstruction of drapes and folds, yet reluctant to lay a hand on them, he turned to Sybil who came to the aid of her reticent brother. Deftly, she lifted the queen's apparel off the settee. He peered beneath it, to left and right. His account book was gone.

Sybil darted to the center of the room. It was as she feared. Sophia was scribbling over Levi's record of "the expenditures and avails of recent instances of bartering in the village of Honolulu."

"O Brother Chamberlain!" cried Sybil.

At either side of the child lay sheets of correspondence paper which Levi kept stored between the pages of his account book and which he used with the most stringent economy. The stationery was divided in two equal if untidy portions and almost every page bore some kind of writing or drawing.

How should such a thing have happened while Sybil sat within this very room? However had Sophia managed to crawl under the settee, unnoticed by either her mother or the two boys?

Sophia was not the culprit. Kauikeaouli, the juvenile prince, had detected the outline of Levi's notebook under the bench. With the aid of a long ruler, and hidden by the screen of Kamamalu's frocks spread across the front of the settee, he had obtained the fascinating quarry. Generously he had divided it: the letter paper for himself and Haalilio; to Sophia, the notebook.

It was a contrite Sybil who gathered up the damaged remnants and returned them to their owner. Kauikeaouli and Haalilio, sensing a change in the manner of the adults, stood like a pair of bronze twins at the farthest end of the room. Even in duress, the aristocratic children bore themselves proudly in their tapa garments.

To one of Sybil's affectionate nature these children were well nigh irresistible despite their depredations. Nevertheless it was her duty to find

LEVI CHAMBERLAIN
Watercolor sketch, probably by A. T. Agate,
artist with Wilkes Exploring Expedition, 1840
Hawaiian Mission Children's Society

some means to enlighten them concerning individual property, the privacy of one's possessions, the difference between "mine" and "thine." The concept was as foreign to their minds as the idea that they might suddenly take flight to the moon.

Just now, the lesson must wait. Brother Chamberlain appeared to be in some haste and oh, poor man! there he stood waiting to use the desk and not an inch of writing space could he find. It was the queen's black silk dress that hindered him this time; in her consternation Sybil had forgotten where she dropped it. She swept the gown off the desk and put it on the settee.

Levi sat down and separated one clean sheet of paper from the blemished lot. He wrote several lines and sanded them. As he leaned over the desk Sybil observed his high cranium, the aquiline nose and patrician mouth in contrast to his crude garments. Brother Chamberlain bore the profile of a man of intellect but, drawer and hewer and burden bearer that he was, he had no time to tarry at the scholar's seat. He rose quickly and bolted for the door while Sybil tried to express her regret for the children's misbehavior and her own delinquency. Levi held the door ajar and turned around.

"Do not reproach yourself, Mrs. Bingham," he said. "It was for want of a lamp to shed some proper light on the matter. I am pleased to tell you that I go now to make settlement with a whaling captain who has spoken for the keel of the *Ruby.* In return I shall get a supply of oil for our lamps."

Sybil scarcely expected him to pause for conversation, but Levi appeared ready to speak of something else. She held her tongue and waited for him to say on.

"I believe, Sister Bingham," he began again, "in view of the needs centering on the common room, it would be well if I took up my lodging in the cellar for the present. A field bed, with my books and papers convenient to my hand, will be all I shall require."

Having said it, he took his leave.

Sybil watched him walk toward two black silhouettes on the beach. One was the figure of a man dressed in a long coat, narrow trousers and the billed cap of a shipmaster. The larger form, which listed precariously in the sand, was the inverted keel of the *Ruby*.

The bullocks stood where Levi had left them. Their heads drooped and sharp ribs and hipbones protruded under their hides. Veils of vapor rose off their overheated bodies. Beneath them, and all around the compound, the ground was crisscrossed with the tracks of cart wheels and gouges of hooves—scars of the summer's drudgery.

"Like the old ox," thought Sybil, "we begin to lurch out of our slough and move ahead."

They still lacked much, but by sagacious management and bargaining Levi had eased some of the pain of their privation. The draft animals relieved the brethren of their hardest labor; the cows provided pitchers of milk for the family table. In countless ways Levi had bolstered the mission and put its house in order.

But for Brother Chamberlain there was no balm for aching limbs and overtaxed patience unless he might find it in the retreat which he now contemplated: a bed behind boxes and barrels in the cellar.

Before he returned to unyoke the bullocks and

turn them out for the night, Sybil hastened below stairs to see what she might do to add some comfort to the miserable lodging of her brother in Christ.

Chapter 11

In his hut near the foot of Nuuanu valley, Mac-Afee woke to the moan of a conch shell. The distant trumpeting was broadcast by some native who played the mollusk as Gabriel must have played upon his horn. MacAfee sprang off his mats and ran from the hut. In the silence of the pre-dawn hour he stood stark as a post in his dooryard.

Mountain, cliff and cloud seemed melded together in a celestial highway upon which he saw a caravan descending in single file. Its progress was marked by a flow of streaming torches. As the travelers emerged from a ravine and passed over a wind-swept precipice, their flickering lights leapt high. MacAfee reckoned that the oncoming legions numbered more than a thousand souls.

So fantastic was the spectacle on the mountain that, had he not possessed the steady nerve of a stoic, MacAfee might have fancied himself the victim of hallucination—a disorder not unknown among his fellow exiles in the south seas. What he witnessed was not the coinage of his brain;

nevertheless he felt a need for strong coffee and spirits. He set about building a fire in his cooking pit.

MacAfee fetched his chair and a bottle of brandy from the hut and sat down to watch the progress on the mountainside. The forward ranks already had descended into the valley and they moved along a winding course through the taro patches.

Just *mauka* of the trader's hut they turned east.

Trade winds swept the torch fire in a horizontal stream over the heads of the natives and MacAfee saw that on their naked shoulders the men carried poles from which pairs of calabashes were suspended. He could hear their marching song:

> *Praise ye the Lord*
> *Praise ye the Lord from the heavens*
> *Praise him in the heights*
> *Praise ye him, all his angels*
> *Praise ye him, all his hosts*
> *Praise ye him, sun and moon*
> *Praise him, all ye stars of light*
> *Praise ye him, ye heavens of heavens*
> *And ye waters....*

> *Hoike!*

At the shout *Hoike!* MacAfee understood the phenomenon. He guessed correctly that Kaahumanu had ordered the people of Oahu to muster at Kawaiahao for a grand review of the progress they had made in the new *palapala* in this year of our Lord, 1825.

As they had journeyed to pagan festivals in the days of their youth, here now came the new "schools"—platoons of commoners and their chiefs—to meet at daylight on the plain, to vie with one another in English recitation, to add and subtract in full cry and to pour forth the lessons of psalm and scripture in a mighty chorus.

MacAfee had seen the mission-taught scholars at Honolulu perform such exhibitions, and he had heard some talk of the impending conclave. But he could scarcely credit his senses when he saw the inordinate ranks of provincials, carrying their food in swaying calabashes, still coming thick upon the land.

He was all the more flabbergasted when he considered the cause of it: the peaked little printer had got his press working again. Loomis had deluged the land with spelling books and hymnals and lesson pages—enough to generate this human avalanche—and noted the consequence in a single line of his journal: "Much attention is now paid to learning in all the islands."

"So it be." marveled the Scot, "an' 'ere long some new grievance will be, I'm thinkin'."

The sky was beginning to pale. MacAfee dipped up another bowlful of coffee from the iron pot. As he turned toward his brandy bottle he descried another line of torches moving in from Waikiki. A third was advancing out of the hinterlands of Ewa.

"'Tis most like the Jews coming up to Jerusalem!" MacAfee exclaimed aloud.

From the pocket of his flaxen shirt he took out his copy of the Hawaiian hymnal which Loomis had printed. Hiram Bingham had given it to the trader as a token of gratitude for kindness he had shown the mission families.

Bereft of a Bible from the days of his calamity

NA

HIMENI HAWAII;

HE ME

ORI IA IEHOVA,

KE

AKUA MAU.

—◦+◦—

E hoonani ia IEHOVA, *e oukou na aina*
a pau: e hoorea ia Ia e oukou na kanaka
*a pau.—*Davida.

———

OAHU:

PAIIA I KA MEA PAI PALAPALA A KA
POE MISIONARI.

1823.

First Hawaiian hymnal (actual size).
Hawaiian Mission Children's Society

130

at sea, it was his habit now to read, by first morning light, hymns and scripture verses in the native language. MacAfee was not an acquisitive man, but from the day he received his hymnbook it had never been other than in his hand or in his pocket.

It was a coarse little volume, the contents of which were printed on some scraps of cartridge paper that were merely folded and stitched. In it MacAfee found the hymns of Watts and he fancied that he could hear them once again pealed forth in the rich brogue of his kinsmen half a world away.

As he studied the hymnal, he wondered what element in the Christian utterance had possessed Kaahumanu lately. She had taken to ranging about from island to island and declaring with the air of a constable: "This is Kaahumanu who speaks. Make good your hearts and obey the word of our Lord."

"Sure," thought MacAfee, "the law do be with her now, with it pleasin' God to strike down her wanderin' king. The poor, poor laddie..."

He sorrowed anew at the thought of those radiant birds of passage Liholiho and Kamamalu who had made a safe voyage to England only to sicken and die among strangers in the city of London.

Even before the sad news had reached Honolulu Kaahumanu, with the zeal of a new convert, had set about reforming her people "according to the word of God."

Summarily she had outlawed murder, theft and non-observance of the Sabbath. This, coupled with the prodigious output of printer Loomis, had advanced the cause of the missionaries with uncommon speed.

"Aye," MacAfee reflected, "'tis sure that a mon must be a better mon if he have some religion than if he have no piety at all."

But he feared that the stream of events ran too swiftly. The brethren had got on the high road now and MacAfee scented trouble ahead.

While he watched the lines of torches, up from the harbor trudged a distraught and surly being. From the nasal whine of his hootings, it would be Marley, thought the Scot.

Marley it was—rum-smelling, rum-talking Marley who brayed out:

"Be it tribal warfare, or be it they've all gone *crazy*?"

He lurched into the yard like a carouser bellowing through a temple, and as unwelcome. To MacAfee, who did not sit in church with other men, the valley was his chapel and early morning was his time for reverence. It was shattered by this fool who stumbled perilously near the edge of the cooking pit and kicked dust over the coals.

"Belay there!" MacAfee ordered and Marley slumped to the ground.

Another drink of rum, which he demanded, certainly would prolong the visit; coffee might prompt a speedy exit. MacAfee put his hymnal away, fetched a clean bowl and dipped it in the kettle. He handed the steaming brew to the intruder.

Instead of spurring Marley on to his pursuit of sandalwood debtors, the coffee only sharpened the focus of his waspish mind. Unbidden, he poured out its venom where he sprawled.

When he had drained a second bowlful his mood changed. He grasped the significance of those lines of torchbearers which still moved across the island from three points of the compass, and he set up a cantankerous whine of defeat.

"'Tis a fact!" MacAfee agreed. "Ye did lose yer taskmaster when the king o' the isles went scuddin' off. An' him ye'll see no more.

"Think ye that Kaahumanu might drive these clans back into the mountains, for to bring ye more, more an' more o' the scented wood? Tut! She calls 'em forth to heed the word o' God, no the bark o' the trader! I trow, sir, the time has come for ye to think no more o' gettin' wood, but rather to crawl aboard some stinkin' vessel an' float off!"

He pulled his hymnal from the pocket of his blouse and thrust the open book under Marley's nose.

"Ye'll no turn her back, mon! See, here the evidence. This be the helm the auld woman steers by now."

With stubby thumb and forefinger he leafed through the pages and read the scripture headings:

"For as many as are led by the spirit o' God, they are the sons o' God.

"He shall no fail nor be discouraged till he have set judgment i' the earth, an' the isles shall wait for his law."

"*Law!*" Marley yelled as though he'd been stuck by a goad. "Now it's the lord god Bingham a-handing down *law* under kivver of a song book!"

He stared murderously at the pamphlet.

"Trade gone to smash. Tribes won't cut wood for that *law* hounds 'em to church!"

He snatched the hymnal and scrabbled to his feet. Before MacAfee could stop him, he ripped out the center pages, cast them into the fire and stumped off toward the harbor.

Afterwards, as long as the two men dwelt in the Sandwich Islands, Marley never again dared set foot in the Scotsman's bailiwick.

❊ ❊ ❊

Later that morning MacAfee called at the mission house. He had a favor to ask and another to bestow. When he approached the compound he spied the lass Sophia Bingham sitting atop the coral stone wall. He bade her show him in.

The sedate little miss, dressed in gingham frock and pantalets, hopped from her perch where she had been watching the *hoike* throngs. Following behind his barefoot guide, MacAfee was brought to the threshhold of the common room, but no further. Miss Sophia halted and the visitor had to stop behind her until Hiram Bingham rose from his desk and stepped forward to extend a hand of welcome.

MacAfee saw the look of strain in the dark eyes that leveled with his. Bingham's lean body had grown taut and angular and the lines in his face were drawn with a sharpness that magnified the force of that overdriven man. But when the Scot held forth a bundle of flannel and said, "For the babby," Hiram's severe stare altered to a look of gratitude.

At the back of the house a second Bingham son, perilously sustained past his infancy, lay struggling to draw breath. The constrictions of croup threatened to suffocate him and day and night Sybil had to strive with him to ease his pitiful throes.

"Pray excuse Mrs. Bingham," Hiram said as he

took MacAfee's gift. "She must bide with the child, but she will receive your present with a thankful heart. There, Sophia, take it now..."

No sooner had he handed the bundle to the little girl than a rising whoop of strangulation tormented the environment and Hiram bolted for the door.

To divert his mind from the sounds that followed, MacAfee glanced around the room and looked for something on which to fasten his attention. He found it on Bingham's desk.

Had he wandered into the den of a master mechanic, the drawings which caught his notice would have gone unheeded. But how this? Bingham—dominie Bingham—plying the architect's rule?

"An' sure 'tis so," breathed the astonished trespasser, and he lifted the edge of the topmost page to peek at those that lay beneath.

On one sheet after another he discovered parts of the plan of a great stone church that had been drawn by the hand of Bingham. Here was a profile of the stately thing sketched with a pencil. Beneath it, as though set down at a later time, Bingham's pen had figured the height and breadth of arch, turrets, windows and tower. At the bottom of the pile lay a second rendering with new specifications: a structure one hundred and twenty feet long, and forty-eight feet wide—to be built of hewn coral.

Now MacAfee could not but take thought of how, yonder on the plain in full view of the sandalwood traffickers, there lounged hordes of native woodcutters who had been drawn out of the mountains as by a lodestar, which was Bingham.

Bingham would stand to hear their lessons,

their psalms, their declarations of Christian faith, and Bingham would bless them in battalions. Would Bingham dare, as well, to propose that they raise this vast church even before a settlement was made in the dispute over sandalwood debts?

Weighing the phenomenon already at hand, MacAfee concluded that Hiram Bingham could

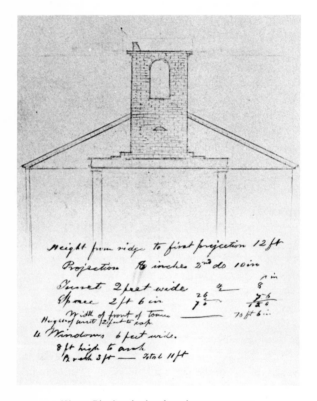

Hiram Bingham's sketch and measurements
for Kawaiahao Church.
Hawaiian Historical Society

not but see his purpose *whole*, nor did he aim to accomplish less than the whole, regardless of hazard, cost or sacrifice.

"Survive or perish, the lad weel ne'er peep through a millstone," he thought, and he sat down on the wooden settee to wait.

Presently the turmoil in the sick room diminished and the sound of Hiram's tread bore down on the common room. Without altering his pace he entered and made straight for the desk. He wiped streams of sweat from his forehead with the blade of his hand and when he spoke his voice betrayed exhaustion.

"Neighbor, your charitable thought and the new flannel already begin to relieve the sufferings of both mother and infant. Did we but know of some necessity of yours, and were it in our power to provide it, believe me we would count it privilege to do so. Failing that, be pleased to sit a moment, MacAfee, and say how you fare."

Deeming the invitation to be genuine, MacAfee kept his seat on the hard bench.

"Ye know, Mr. Bingham," he said, "'twas ne'er habit o' mine to ask ought from any mon. But I did walk this way wi' the hope that the wee printer might spare me a page or two more o' the hymns. I've lost some innards o' the book ye gave me, due to the turbulence o' Marley."

He pulled the mangled shell of the hymnal from his blouse and concluded, "'Twas for vexation o' seein' such hordes o' natives mill aboot, givin' tongue to the psalms."

He stepped to the desk and laid the tattered remnant of his hymnbook on the drawings of the stone church. Since he was a straightforward man— as straightforward as Bingham—he added, "The traders like it little that Kaahumanu claims she need no pay the sandalwood that's wanted."

Hiram looked at the ruined pages of the hymnal.

"I regret that your book was destroyed," he said. "You shall, of course, have another.

"The matter of the sandalwood debt comes not within our counsel. But when a once-pagan ruler begins to act from Christian conviction—and each day grows more benevolent toward her people—it follows then that some curb will be made on the profits of those foreigners who feel no such benevolence."

"Aye, ye may say so," MacAfee agreed. "But still they like it not that the auld woman should scrape up gist for her law makin' from the pages o' yer song book!"

Bingham sat down at the desk.

"We've not sufficient paper to print a variety of books; the hymnal must serve both church and school," he answered. "If Kaahumanu discovers in its pages some basis for civil conduct, that is not without precedent in the work of a countryman of yours who, in even more reduced circumstances than ours, still found the means to establish a Christian colony on Pitcairn Island."

He reached for his letter box and pulled out a stained sheet of paper.

"By a recent vessel this letter has come to me from John Adams, last survivor of the band of mutineers who seized the ship *Bounty* and escaped to Pitcairn. Adams has learned of the establishment of this mission. He writes now to ask that some one of us visit his island to baptize the families there.

"They have one Bible, from the pages of which Adams has drawn their only code of law. For more than thirty years he has used that same Bible as a text to teach the children of the colony to read and write. The old man makes one last request. Before he dies he wants the marriage service read for him and the native woman whom he has called wife during the years of his exile."

"To think on it, sir!" exclaimed MacAfee. "No doot he be a good mon, this Adams, an' glad am I that such a laddie dinna hang for his part i' the mutiny. Time comes when 'tis no more than right to strike down so cruel a mon as Captain Bligh o' the *Bounty*. But, sir, 'tis mutiny at every turn now, an' catchin' as the pox it is!"

Hiram returned Adams' letter to the box and drew out a larger square of paper.

"It is so," he replied. "From America I am informed that one hundred and thirty-seven persons, whose business it is to send whaling vessels into the Pacific, wrote to warn President Monroe of the peril. They have requested a show of naval force in these waters. From Nantucket comes advice that a band of derelicts who make their lair in the Sandwich Islands may seize some oncoming vessel as it touches here for provisioning."

MacAfee squinted at the sheet which Bingham handed him.

"Yer president need only send hither a sloop o' war, wi' orders to seize an' be off wi' the cutthroats," he said. "An' might be King George would claim *his* scapegallows. 'Tween the two, they become most too plentiful 'mongst us here.

"The more so King George, I'm thinkin'!" he added. "Do you know, sir, this Richard Charlton—lately come upon us wi' the high-soundin' name o' Consul for Great Britain—this Charlton declares to one an' all that native rulers may ne'er punish an Englishman! Matter not how villainous the rakehell might be!

"'Nay, ' prates he, like the lord o' creation, 'they'll make no law for any foreign man ashore...'"

Bingham sprang from his seat and walked to the front of the desk.

"It's such as this that keeps the land in turmoil," he said. "All around us now the chiefs strive to put a check on vice, hoping to achieve a civilized state. Yet these people, just rising from their mats, may not survive. They will not, without that right of any free nation to administer civil law."

"Nay but," cautioned the Scot, "should the law be framed too swiftly, 'twill be said that it came no from the rulers, but from oot the wee song book—or be it so, from oot the head o' Hiram Bingham."

He rose and started for the door. At the threshhold he turned and admonished his host:

"'Twill no do, lad, to build so quick, though the buildin' do be good. Still, ye canna keep the auld woman boxed up, now ye've schooled her. She'll no be stopped, an' may God put a hobble on the Divil."

❊ ❊ ❊

The Devil bided his time. Within a few months Kaahumanu and Bingham gave him new provocation. Hiram made a Hawaiian translation of the Ten Commandments and Kaahumanu understood it to be the law of Jehovah. Therefore she declared that it was suitable basis for law in the Sandwich Islands.

Had she proposed a revival of the Inquisition she could not have stirred up greater consternation along the waterfront.

Though *Owhyhee*'s idols were no more, traders and sea captains recalled that, to the native mind, God (no matter what god) *is* law. They had not forgotten the heathen notion of punishment for some slight violation of religious tabu: the gouging of eyes, snapping of bones and smashing of skulls.

The soldiers of fortune from Christian lands were struck with unholy horror at the prospect of Kaahumanu enforcing the Ten Commandments. A tale was circulated that "the old woman" reckoned the death sentence a fit penalty for transgression of any one of the Ten!

In this charged atmosphere, the regent and the chiefs assembled to consider Bingham's list of sanctified aids to governing. The boy king Kauikeaouli was hailed from his lessons at the mission house as, six years earlier, Kaahumanu had summoned him to be the pivot figure in a crisis.

A band of foreign seamen and traders advanced in a rage and invaded the royal conclave. So quickly did matters swerve from peaceable palaver to a shindy of insult, ridicule and bullying, that when Kaahumanu rose and proposed that the Ten Commandments be adopted as the foundation for a new code of island law, Kauikeaouli did nothing.

He turned his back and said, "It would be well to defer the laws."

No sooner had the royal child been silenced than officers and crews aboard the ships at anchor cried riot. Kaahumanu, without consulting man, child or missionary, had decreed that at least the seventh commandment would be kept. She pronounced a thundering Tabu on the custom of native women swimming through the surf like shoals of sea nymphs and boarding the vessels that lay offshore.

When she scuttled what was looked upon as a seaman's inalienable right, hot-blooded sailors (subject to harsh discipline in all matters except this one) suddenly found themselves in bonds of harmony with their captains. Like any other disaster, Kaahumanu's edict had struck forecastle and quarter-deck alike. It generated a ship-wide accord which, in the normal course of events, would have been unimaginable.

The masters and mates liberated their crews. Boatloads of sailors carrying knives and marlinspikes rowed shoreward. To sustain her ultimatum, Kaahumanu called up a guard of several hundred natives. She ordered them to patrol the village and she armed them with the muskets which Liholiho had bought with sandalwood.

For a time, the old queen prevailed. It was tabu for native women to board the foreign ships.

One morning while the ban was in force, Levi Chamberlain hastened to the harbor and sought out the captain of a departing ship. Chamberlain offered a packet of letters to be carried to America. The master ground his teeth and glared. His eyes were like cold blue stones.

"I'll take no letters of missionaries!" he barked.

For as long as Levi stood in his presence the captain remained as immutable as the figurehead on the bow of his ship, nor did he alter his stare by a trace.

At the end of the quay a longboat came to its mooring and Levi watched the crew leap ashore like a pack of invading foxes. A giant of a sailor, who wore nothing but a pair of striped trousers, brandished his oar aloft and sent a long shout across the harbor:

"Are the missionaries' houses burned and all their damned throats cut?"

As Brother Chamberlain walked back to Kawaiahao he recalled that it would be his turn to conduct family prayers that evening. Earlier in the week he had considered taking for his text:

The souls of the righteous are in the hand of God, and there shall no torment touch them.

However, in view of the worsening situation, he decided on:

If thou faint in the day of adversity, thy strength is small.

Chapter 12

Through the village the sounds of fury mounted until, with the onset of a southerly blow, the seamen's rampage gave way to a tropical storm. The surf, which usually played a gentle cadence on the southern strand, turned into a thing of violence. White combers lunged over the reef and rushed shoreward to explode on rocks and beaches. Spume-freighted gales slammed against the island. The tops of coconut trees were set reeling.

The noon sky turned black and a wall of rain moved in from the south. Thunder cracked on the mountains as though it would split the cliffs which, with every flash of lightning, showed their pinnacles in lonely silhouette.

The frail habitations of men toppled and fell in rain that beat down week after week without cease. When the land was inundated, fresh gales pummeled Honolulu and the sodden wreckage of thatch, poles, mats and calabashes took flight in a crazy dance across the plain.

The island was ravaged. The walls of fish ponds burst and the banks of taro patches collapsed.

Nuuanu stream flowed like a torrent, carrying hundreds of muddy taro roots down to the harbor. They surfaced and floated like drowned rats, bumping the hulls of ships that lay in port.

Before the deluge was over the United States Navy schooner *Dolphin* came to anchor in the mud-stained waters off Honolulu. It was a dazed, half-sick population which assembled to greet the American officers and sailors.

Such a torporous welcome did not please Lieutenant John Percival, commander of the *Dolphin*. He bridled when the chiefs sent out a message that they would not return his salute until the day after he chose to fire a barrage. Because he had come to port on the Sabbath, such noisy courtesies would have to be deferred until after the Lord's day, they said.

The lieutenant deferred nothing. He fired away.

Riding north on the gale which devastated Honolulu, Percival had become addicted to the heady stimulant of power. His commission in Pacific waters vested him with no small authority: he had been dispatched to hunt down a gang of escaped mutineers and murderers of the captain of an American whaling vessel.

Having found his quarry on an island southwest of Hawaii, Lieutenant Percival next came to grips with the fury of a Pacific storm. Boldly he drove his ship through tumultous seas. He set a course for Honolulu where the schooner could be repaired, and the crew refreshed.

Seasoned to the idea that intractable men—and women—came under his superintendence, Percival immediately took up the matter of the tabu which prohibited native women aboard his ship. He demanded to know who had framed this intolerable restriction. Forthwith, he was led into the presence of Kaahumanu.

With blood in his eye, he began to instruct the regal chiefess who sat before him. He spoke of harlots. He said they were treated with leniency in nations far greater than hers. He told her that in England and America prostitution was not punished.

From beneath her heavy eyelids Kaahumanu darted a fierce glance at the intruder.

"Then let Americans get their prostitutes there," she answered. "It is the wish of the chiefs here to obey the laws of Jehovah."

"By whom are the women tabued?" Percival demanded.

"It is by *me.*"

"Who is your teacher that has told you the women must be tabu by the law?"

"It is God."

"It was not by *you*; it was by Bingham!"

"It was by *me*. By Bingham the word of God is made known to us. It is for *us* to give directions respecting our women. It is for *us* to establish tabus."

"Declare to me the man that told you the women must be tabu," said Percival, "and my people will pull down his house! My vessel is like fire...."

Within an hour the conversation had been reported verbatim at the mission house. Over and over, the harsh words dinned in Sybil's brain until, by a determined effort of will, she slammed her mind shut against them.

"No more, no more!" her anguished soul cried out. Though vicious threats were heaped up and repeated by every tongue in the village, she knew it served her ill to think on them.

Her scrawny arms worked furiously, as if by physical toil she would exhaust the grief within her. On hands and knees she scrubbed the pine board floor and wrung water from her mop rags into a tub which she dragged behind her. Sophia lay on a cot and watched her mother working in a pool of rain water that stood beneath the window.

When she could step across the room without wetting her slippers through, Sybil took up the bowl of cold supper which she had carried in earlier. She asked Sophia to swallow a spoonful of ship bread soaked in milk.

The child was flushed with fever and the pain in her throat made her cry, but she ate what her mother offered. When the trial was over Sybil permitted herself to remain seated on the edge of the cot.

It was the lowering time of day on a February Sabbath and the other families had walked out to afternoon prayer service. For this brief hour, no beck or call could separate the two who remained at home. The child, despite her pain, knew a sweet contentment.

It was not altogether so with Sybil. Her eyes reflected a torment of anxiety. Beneath them deep circles of gray depressed the pallid cheeks. She watched over her child with a peculiar tenacity.

At last Sophia's breath came deep and slow. Sybil tucked the little arms under the patchwork quilt and got up from the cot.

Would that the mother might find some calm

retreat, but sorrow is a tyrant that does not release its sufferers willingly. Sybil felt compelled to wander over to the window that faced two little burial mounds. Beneath them lay her baby sons; the second had been put down by his grieving parents eight months past.

The graves were sinking in pools of muddy water and their stick fences were broken and cast helter-skelter by the storm. If ever a dolorous scene bespoke the suffering of a human being, it was those half-submerged graves. Whoever looked on them might find in Sybil's heart an equal desolation. She would not give utterance to the thought, but she knew that she herself, no less than her children's coffins, stood on sinking ground.

❀ ❀ ❀

Three years were gone since Daniel Chamberlain had delivered his family from this outpost of lawless renegades.

"Unless much of the foreign influence in these islands is opposed, our own children may be brought to the brink of degradation," the brethren admonished one another.

As long as she labored in the mission cause, Sybil never walked free of that foreboding.

Forfeiting all but the most meager prerogatives due the mother of a rising family, she had gone out day after day to call at the doors of native huts. She had trudged over dusty paths, stopping where dejected women languished in poverty, and she had taught them something of nursing and sewing and swaddling and cleansing.

Nor, except for illness, had she dared to fail her *Poalima*, a gathering of native mothers who met with her every Friday for prayers and talk about the teachings of Holy scripture. Afterwards, if they restrained their daughters and themselves from committing the sin which caused sickness to spread among them, it was because they had learned God's law.

Sybil had made those toilsome rounds with a conflict in her heart. It seemed a necessary thing to loose the grip of vice on the land, and she had resolved to make amends in her neglected nursery when she could muster the strength to do it.

Now she was bereft of all but one lonely child, skimpily taught even in her sixth year. The mother no longer could hope to make amends; nor could she offer any alternative to the plan on which Hiram was determined to act. Within a year, he said—perhaps two—Sophia must be sent away to be schooled in New England.

Into Sybil's trembling heart there came the apprehension that when she was called to give up this last cherished child, she could not do it. Her mind reeled at the thought of Sophia, carried off to America alone and forlorn, a friendless orphan wandering over two oceans...

It was not to be borne! Not ever, while life was in her, would she relinquish her child to such a plan! Though she pay out the last jot of her harrowed being to fulfill a mother's duty in this alien land, mother she was and she could surrender no more.

Nor could she bear to look any longer at the muddy barrow to which her infant sons had been committed. She drew back in the dark room; then, like a prisoner weary of eternal gloom, she veered toward the opposite window and stopped there.

She wondered what, on a Sabbath afternoon, had set off the band of natives who were running toward her door. Why the chiefess Namahana at the vanguard, thundering and plashing through the mud in her black silk dress?

Suddenly, two sailors, clad in ragged canvas trousers and red waist bindings, ran across the path. Brandishing clubs, the bearded demons rushed headlong toward Sybil's door. One made a catlike pounce to the window where she stood.

He crouched under it and squinted up at her. His mouth widened in a leer that showed stubs of broken teeth clenched over a dirk. The crazed eyes lowered, then flicked sideways in their red-rimmed sockets. With every limb convulsed and the blood pounding in her head, Sybil lunged at the door and shot the bolt.

Whirling round, she saw Sophia jerk like a wounded rabbit as the sailors' clubs bashed against the door and set it dancing on its hinges. Sybil tore back the quilt and caught up her child. Carrying her as she would an infant, she fled to a rear chamber. Through the din of shattering wood and glass she tried to hush Sophia's screams.

Unaccountably, the pounding ceased. Sophia left off her shrill cries and whimpered hoarsely. The mother, more wary than relieved, sensed some new peril in the lull.

A roar of angry voices went up:

"You are the man! Let us have women or we will pull down your houses!"

With Sophia clinging to her skirt, Sybil sped back across the clutter that lay in her path. Through the shattered window she saw a band of seamen holding a man captive at the edge of the yard. She was certain it was Hiram.

The sailors crossed their clubs around him in a menacing barricade. The natives, crowding close, did not lift a hand against the *haoles*. But when, through some nervous crotchet or intent to murder, one of the sailors raised his club, the whole company was jostled by the chiefess Namahana.

She flailed her arms and swept aside the cudgels that confined Mr. Bingham. At her sudden approach, whacking and thumping the sailors as though they were tiresome children, madness seized the man who held his club aloft. In the grip of his brute fists the truncheon swung round and up again, then drove with murderous aim at Bingham's skull.

On its downward thrust the weapon collided with Namahana's arm which stopped the blow as effectively as if that colossal limb were in fact related to a tree.

"We are not willing that our teacher should be killed!" she shouted at the fiend whose weapon lay athwart her arm.

He dropped the club and lunged at Hiram. Every native eye caught the flash of a knife blade as, an inch from its mark, it drew the breadth of Bingham's throat.

In a trice, the fellow was laid by the heels. His arms were pinioned, his legs bent double. His shipmates dodged and scattered, beset by angry brown giants who chastised them with a hail of stones.

"Why do you not obey your God?" demanded Namahana of the fleeing sailors. "We will write letters to your *alii* in America. We will speak of the things which you do among our people!!"

She stepped about on enormous brown legs which sported a pair of green kid gaiters. Beneath those stylish frills her bare feet churned up the mud as she went shouting and rapping her hands and commanding her people to punish the sailors.

Bingham's assailant lay groaning in the mire; nor could he reasonably expect to rise again except by Christian intervention. A mighty kanaka, clad in black for the intended prayer meeting, towered over him. He held a rock as big as his head, ready to crush the sailor's skull with a single blow.

Sybil leaned on the window casement and lowered her head.

"Mama!" cried Sophia.

Sybil turned and saw her child standing like a tiny ghost beyond the debris of wood and glass that separated them. The little girl, halted in her flight by the rubble that cut her feet, made no sound until she saw her mother's head sink forward.

In an instant Sybil was at her side, taking her in her arms and holding her close. She shut her eyes to the wreckage underfoot, but she could not erase from her mind the pitiful image of Sophia standing alone in her white nightdress, calling to her across that atrocious barrier.

Always the child had to wait—wait for a reassuring word, wait till the natives were taught, wait till evil was vanquished, wait to claim her birthright.

Yet how many times had Sybil heard repeated in her memory—and shrunk from them—the words of Hiram's far-sighted resolution: "... *we must relinquish what is commonly regarded as a parent's privilege to others more favorably situated in our native land."*

When the heart is ready to fail, duty—that center pillar of the puritan soul—prevails. If it were not so, Sybil could not have made her tortured soul be still and taken her first long look down the path that led to sorrow indescribable.

Chapter 13

The Lord tempered the wind to the shorn lamb. Before Sybil was called to surrender her first-born she was blessed with another little daughter whom she named Lucy, and a new friend whose name was Laura Judd.

By 1828, of the first two companies of missionaries sent to the Sandwich Islands, only nine men and seven women remained in the field. Most of them labored at lonely billets on Kauai and Maui and Hawaii. When a third band of evangelists arrived from Boston that spring, Dr. Gerrit Parmele Judd, sent out as physician to the mission families, was stationed at headquarters in Honolulu.

The Judds began housekeeping upstairs in the *ewa* side of the frame house where, of the four men who had built it, only Hiram Bingham remained. With Sophia and baby Lucy, he and Sybil occupied the Waikiki end of the dwelling.

Sister Bingham welcomed the young Judds. With their warm hearts and inexhaustible energy, they filled a void which had come into her life.

Printer Loomis, worn down at last to a skeleton of 118 pounds, had taken his family and followed the Daniel Chamberlains back to America. Lucy and Asa Thurston were gone to toil on the island of Hawaii. Levi Chamberlain, having claimed a bride from among the single ladies of the new company, moved his bed out of the cellar and set up a domicile in the printing house.

After one month of married life, Brother Chamberlain reported to the Mission Rooms in Boston: "I perceive no reason yet to repent of the step which I have taken."

The old order at the mission house was gone and Mrs. Judd soon initiated the new. She had not been in residence more than twenty-four hours before she took charge of all domestic concerns.

Sybil could not recall such freedom from hard labor as that which she enjoyed under the management of Laura Judd. Certainly the mission distaff ranks never had afforded such a tower of strength as this new sister from upstate New York. A tall, dark-eyed girl of twenty-four, Laura was blessed with infinite capacity and enthusiasm for life. Her emotions ran deep; she was prone to tender sentiment. She longed to bolster the spirits of all those with whom the world had dealt harshly.

As a girl of sixteen Laura had become a country school teacher. In her late teens she began reading the reports of Sandwich Islands missionaries published at Boston in *The Missionary Herald*. She pored over the graceful phrases quoted from Sybil Bingham's journal. In imagination she dwelt on the faraway scene and the heroines who labored there to such high purpose.

What greater calling could enlist her own restless spirit than to go there too and bear a part in the endeavor?

When she came, she saw at once how matters stood and set about lifting the burdens from Sister Bingham's frail shoulders. Nor was she long in learning enough Hawaiian to enable her to teach a new generation of islanders who flocked after their parents to the Kawaiahao schoolhouse.

In time, as bonds of affection drew them closer, Sybil whispered to Laura the secret fear that gnawed at her heart. She confessed that, though it was long in coming, the hour she shrank from with all her soul was the one in which she would hear some God-fearing sea captain declare his willingness to give a child of missionaries free passage to America.

If Sophia were to go, it could only be arranged in this way. Hiram had no salary and although Sybil, before her marriage, had saved close to eight hundred dollars from her earnings as a school teacher, she had given all to the American Board of Commissioners for Foreign Missions.

For twenty-four months the day of her affliction had waited on finding a captain who was willing to take the child. With each sighting of a ship off Diamond Hill, Sybil must divert her steps to some private place and try to calm her agitated soul. She could not. Secretly, she prayed that the master would not consent to take Sophia aboard.

Time and again her prayer had been answered, but it would not always be so. The agony of that expectation had reduced Sybil to near invalidism.

Never, in her girlhood conception of the mission woman's task, could Laura have imagined the multiplication of woes which had crushed Sister Bingham. On the night Sybil confided that her only child, not yet eight years old, was to be sent away, Dr. Judd's bride was plunged into such a mood of desolation that to sleep was impossible.

She could not seek her husband's counsel; Gerrit was gone across the island channels to relieve the suffering among his brethren. Though the clock hands stood at midnight Laura knew that she must be up and doing. Nothing would rout her depression except the undertaking of some work.

Her household paraphernalia wanted sorting. Her clothes needed shaking and folding; Gerrit's books waited to be set on shelves.

She needed no lamp or candle. Moonlight flooded her chamber with such brilliance that she could mend the rents and sew buttons on their travel-worn clothing. Well then, up with the lids of the sea chests, and to those long-delayed tasks—with fervor!

Laura piled her possessions on the bed and reached for a last dark something that lay in a corner of the chest she had emptied. It was her purse. She had not laid eyes on it since before they sailed from Boston. As she drew it forth it weighed a little heavy in her hand. A muffled clink at the bottom of the pouch proved to be that of four shillings.

Laura knew her duty. The money was hers before she made covenant with the other sisters and brethren. Now, since it had traveled here with her, it should be given over to their fund of common possessions.

In the solitude of that early hour, only the silver moon saw the glint of the shillings as they lay in the palm of Laura's hand. Carefully she slipped them back in the purse and, folding it over so the coins would not rattle, she returned it to the dark corner of the chest.

If, in the day of Sybil's grief, there should be wanting some material comfort, the purchase of which might be forbidden by communal rule, it would be well if she did not have to ask.

It was characteristic of Laura, more so of Gerrit, that often they did not ask or wait to be asked. Murmurs soon ran abroad that the Judds were too bold in their self-appointed tasks. Yet Hiram Bingham, upholder and preserver of discipline within the mission ranks, found no fault in them. He perceived that their will to do had lifted the spirits of those exhausted workers who still remained in the field.

Gerrit Judd was a frontiersman born and bred. He was the son and grandson of circuit-riding country doctors in what was, not many years before his birth, a north American wilderness. Pushing westward through the forests of upstate New York, his father had followed trails that were crossed as often by bears and wolves and hostile Indians as by settlers from New England. A dynamic independence and a knowledge of medicine was the patrimony he bequeathed the son who chose to sail eighteen thousand miles into the Pacific to his field of labor.

Mindful of the Biblical admonishment, Gerrit put his hand to the plow and did not look back. But his vision ranged incessantly in every other direction. As a missionary, he was bound by the most stringent rules of human organization, but his nature was such that he could not walk in traces.

It was not enough that he roved between four islands to minister to those sisters and brethren and babies who were committed to his care. He also turned his hand to the printing and binding of books and the training of Hawaiian choirs. Betwixt times, he advised young native men in matters of farming and carpentry and the treating of disease.

Since charity and healing know no boundaries, Dr. Judd also strode the ruffian precincts of Honolulu harbor when he was called to the grog shops. The hosts of those dens offered shelter for wretched offcasts of the sea who were in the last stages of disease or insanity. The village afforded no other ward or asylum and no physician except the mission doctor. For this cause, and this cause alone, bawdy traders and mariners stopped the curses in their mouths when the missionary Judd advanced on their harbor stronghold.

He was a match for any sea captain just stepped from the quarter-deck. His chest was broad and his jaw was square. If he were challenged by a rascal, he would sooner call him one than pray for his salvation. Thick-thewed and stocky, Judd drove a blunt course over hostile ground. The very sight of him threw the inhabitants of the foreign quarter into paroxysms of wrath.

Their gathering place was Kaahumanu's house which she had abandoned in favor of a peaceful retreat under the cliffs of Manoa valley. She went off in high dudgeon, declaring that Honolulu had become too wicked for her. Particularly, she railed at the high chief Boki for his drunkenness and the fact that he could scarcely read or write.

Boki reciprocated by turning her house into a lair of worldly pleasures and, serving as the cat's-paw for hostile foreigners, he opened the way for the near destruction of almost ten years' work by the mission.

He was drunk a good deal of the time. Even when sober, he was so bloated and his legs were so covered with sores that he could hardly move about. Instead of a smile he displayed a barbarous gap where, in a frenzy of mourning at the death of Kamehameha, he had caused four front teeth to be knocked out.

After piling up a debt that was even greater than the king's, Boki became a bizarre entrepreneur. With reckless nonchalance he bought the entire cargo of a British trading ship from Canton and set up a store in one half of Kaahumanu's house. In the other half he spent more thousands of dollars to furnish a hostelry of sorts which he called the Blonde Hotel. He named it for the British ship which had returned the bodies of Liholiho and Kamamalu to Honolulu.

Having voyaged to London in the entourage of his fated king, Boki tried to pattern his den of confusion after the demimonde rendezvous he had visited in that ancient metropolis. Bottled spirits, gaming tables and, it was whispered, dusky daughters of joy all were to be found behind the green blinds of the Blonde Hotel.

Neither Kaahumanu's wrath nor Hiram Bingham's preaching would turn Boki from his path of destruction. But, to their sorrow and alarm, the boy king Kauikeaouli soon was captivated by the enticements within the chief's pleasure pavilion.

Hailed by Boki as the true ruler of the islands,

whose kingship was being usurped by the old queen regent, the fifteen-year-old boy was drawn into this perilous refuge from reality. Abruptly, he abandoned his studies at the mission. He refused to obey Kaahumanu and he fancied no greater joy in life than the camaraderie of indulgent sea captains and traders who were his hosts at the Blonde Hotel. With the tasty punches he imbibed, Kauikeaouli was offered every inducement to cast his lot with the men of commerce.

When he would reign as Kamehameha III, did he wish for his people to return to their carefree pagan ways? Surely, then, a lad of his bright wits could see the folly of listening to teachers who would foment riot by outlawing such a natural pursuit as fornication on the decks of ships—or be so rigid as to presume that everyone ought to obey the Ten Commandments!

Did Kauikeaouli wish for a life of ease and luxury? At his service then were these spellbinding traders who would provide him with a never-ending flow of vessels filled with delightful toys from round the whole wide world.

As they alternated between sweet blandishments and dire threats, they drew the infatuated lad under their influence and congratulated themselves on having taken a long step toward the day when they might drive Bingham and his ilk out of the islands.

The cock-of-the-walk at the Blonde Hotel was the beefy, red-faced Englishman who functioned as south sea trader and British consul to the Sandwich Islands. He had not been long in Honolulu before he conveyed to one and all the impression that he, Richard Charlton, was a man of exceeding consequence.

Dr. Judd, riled by the braggart who, for all he knew, might be an imposter, demanded of Hiram Bingham:

"Charlton? Who's Charlton? Never heard of him!"

He could scarcely credit the evidence, supplied by Bingham and echoed round the village, that this Charlton fancied himself the lord high protector of a British colony. The English trader-consul had become altogether fantastic in the overreaching of his authority and there was no one to dispute him except Kaahumanu. But for her antagonism, the Englishman shortly would have become judge, jury, lawmaker and disciplinarian in the land.

His method was grotesque. Systematically, he complained that the non-British elements of the island population—missionaries, Yankee traders and natives—were guilty of offenses against the Crown or resident or visiting Englishmen. He denounced, demanded punishment and called for reprisals.

MacAfee was exempt from any fealty to the Crown, and he did not feel obliged to hold his tongue concerning Charlton.

"Why sir!" he said to Dr. Judd, "the British bashaw already do have our laddie king in leadin' strings! The auld woman did blow wise to the turnin' an' whirlin' o' this Charlton, but she canna make the lad look straight on him. It harrows up the soul o' me to think what 'twill be when she's gone to the grave."

His fierce blue eyes explored Judd's countenance as he might study a map.

"Ye may find it hard to credit, sir, but the little king an' all the chiefs did suppose that there could be no bindin' law 'mongst us here unless it first be sent off to King George for *him* to say aye or nay to it!"

"Atrocious piece of trumpery..." snorted Dr. Judd.

"Nay but have in mind, sir," MacAfee interrupted, "have in mind that this Charlton declares that the chiefs an' their people are but *subjects* o' Great Britain. For reason that auld Tammie once did offer his kingdom to the Crown, though ne'er was he thanked for it!

"Then, says he, should the royal laddie proclaim any law wi'out the sanction o' Britain, a great army shall come at once an' take possession here. That bein' the case, sir, 'twas weel ye stepped ashore when ye did, for might be ye'd have come to find yerself peerin' into the muzzles o' King George's carronade!"

Judd was outraged to the depths of his Yankee republican soul. Not since the rebels stood fire at Bunker Hill had he heard of such preposterous ultimatums being handed down in lands abroad. Nor could it be expected that these natives would outlaw the swashbuckling redcoat in their midst, so violently did he threaten them.

"Where one arrogant freebooter thrives and prospers," the doctor reflected, "a like host will follow, though they come from the ends of the earth."

In his evaluation of near crisis and real mischief which he found in the Sandwich Islands, Dr. Judd returned again and again to an obstinate question: To what purpose do evangelists labor to enhance the native race if, simultaneously, they do not venture to preserve the nation?

Was his contention premature, or did the

sponsors of the American mission hint at it in the instructions which they had given this third band of Sandwich Islands missionaries?

"Our brethren at the islands," warned the Prudential Committee, "have, for two or three years past, been suffering from the cruel opposition of unreasonable and wicked men. This opposition... must be counteracted and checked, or the condition of the natives is hopeless."

As a means to check such opposition, they proposed "causing all classes of residents to feel that they act in full view of the civilized world."

If they had searched the country over they could not have found a man better suited to the task than Gerrit Judd. Of all his endowments, none was more pronounced than his faculty for contention. Having found a prime contender, he took to the scent with relish. Nor would he withdraw or desist until, after fifteen years, his contest with the agents of the British Crown did at last come into full view of the civilized world.

Chapter 14

As he took his seat at the desk in the common room, Dr. Judd noticed a list of translation assignments which Hiram Bingham had made for the brethren. Those who were most familiar with the native language had begun to work on the Hawaiian Bible.

It appeared that the monumental task would fall mainly to Bingham, Thurston, William Richards and Artemas Bishop. Now Gerrit found the names of three of his shipmates—Lorrin Andrews, Jonathan Green and Ephraim Clark—also enlisted in the work.

Dr. Judd, being insufficiently versed in theology, was not asked to join his brothers at the translation table. He confined his academic efforts to jotting down phrases for a "Treatment Book" which he intended to write in Hawaiian. Only on rare occasions did he spend an hour or two in the study.

It was mid-October when Hiram relinquished the desk to Gerrit and Laura for an evening. The Binghams bade the Judds goodnight and withdrew to upstairs quarters. The time of their affliction was at hand; before the sun set again, the homeward-bound ship *Enterprise* would bear their child Sophia away for America. They scarcely hoped to see her ever again.

Laura Judd sat immured in woe too deep for words. As if to bolster her spirit by some physical means, she braced her feet flat on the pine board floor and her coarse shoes protruded beneath the hem of her brown cotton skirt. Mrs. Judd was not a woman of modish aspect but there was a kind of raw queenliness about her figure.

Her eyes were cast down and the lamp glow caught the sheen of the straight dark hair dressed aslant her high forehead. As she bent to a pile of sewing in her lap the ill-suppressed tears kept falling and damping the garment on which she worked.

She wept for little Sophia who would wear it and for the mother who, having no means to outfit her child, must put together some little frocks out of remnants of woolen dresses she herself had worn as a bride. Now, while Sybil Bingham sought the help of God Almighty, Laura plied her needle against the hour of Sophia's sailing.

Where was solace for the Binghams? What resting place could they find when they had committed their child to wind and waves and the mercies of common seamen?

They had taken some comfort in their discovery that the captain of the *Enterprise* was a God-fearing man. Moreover, Mr. and Mrs. Ely of the mission made haste to sail on the same ship. But like the others who had gone before, the Elys left the islands because their health was broken. If they should not survive the voyage, who then would guard the waif Sophia as she tottered fore and aft about the deck in mournful peril?

Nor was this the parents' only apprehension. Where Sophia would find a home they could not be certain. Among their kinsfolk in New England, several had offered sanctuary for the wandering orphan, but they would not settle the matter until the little girl came among them. April next, when Sophia might be expected to arrive in America, more than a year would have passed since her relatives had written their intent to care for her.

Hiram put the thing before his Lord. Down the stairwell, through the cracks and interstices of imperfectly joined floor timbers, the drone of his intercession carried to the ears of the Judds. His voice rose and fell in a plea for compassion on the helpless little voyager. He prayed, too, that in the hour of their trial neither he nor Sybil would shrink from doing that which was required for the cause of the mission and the benefit of the child. Like a muffled accent, the sound of Sybil's hollow cough accompanied his supplications.

Gerrit pondered the ill-boding symptom. Considering the fevers and wasted flesh of certain other members of the mission band, the doctor suspected that Sybil's decline was not an isolated case among them.

He put aside his papers and glanced again at the list of work which Bingham had laid out to produce the single necessity of a Hawaiian Bible. Taking that together with the overwhelming burden of their other labors, Gerrit wondered how many more young mission couples must join the numbers returning to their homeland, many of them so enfeebled that they were past cure or mending. And how many children, his own perhaps, must be taken from their parents, never to know them again?

Etched in the mind of every missionary to the Hawaiian people were the words of the epic mandate "...to give them the Bible with skill to read it...a nation to be enlightened and renovated and added to the civilized world."

Not one had embarked for the islands without the realization that he must spend and be spent in a labor of love. Where throngs of natives looked to the missionary and his wife for the care of parents and teachers, each came knowing he must sacrifice all selfish desires and worldly comfort.

But having renounced the home and affections that bound him in America, did one suppose that as a lonely exile he must yield up his progeny too, and they of tender years?

Gerrit folded his arms across his chest and clasped his elbows with his broad fingers. A peculiar blaze of energy played in his eyes as he sat thinking. He had the look of a man who did not intend to bow to circumstance.

Appalling as it was to send Sophia Bingham on a six-months voyage half way round the globe, Dr. Judd was convinced that her prospects for a safe passage over life's long track far exceeded those of her royal playmate, Kauikeaouli. The young king ran before the wind like a graceful pleasure craft destined to split on hidden rocks. In Gerrit's eyes, he appeared as pathetic in his cast-off foreign uniform as did Sophia in her mother's made-over dresses.

Kauikeaouli spent his days in gaming, his nights at tilting the inebriate's bowl and he bore himself with the grace of an English lord. Oftimes Gerrit had watched him enter the Blonde Hotel in his blue midshipman's jacket and glazed black hat with its jaunty ribbons. He wore it on the back of his head and his dark curls tumbled over his brow in careless confusion.

The lad seemed destined to play the role of a pawn in the machinations of his elders. When he was a child of five, his was the hand put forth to topple the ancient gods; at eleven, he had stood helpless while foreigners curtailed his regent's right to rule. At fifteen, instead of some promise of the kingly mold, it appeared that Kauikeaouli would remain at best a weak jelly.

In his moods of fitful discontent he seemed tragically fated to oppose the plea of Obookiah for the whole race.

"A tree once cut will fall," mused the doctor. "When a ruler falls, the fatal mischief is loosed upon his people."

Dr. Judd reckoned that the thing which had paralyzed Kauikeaouli's will was fear: fear of abuse, threats, even ridicule. In how many devilish ways, both broad and subtle, had the boy been driven to retreat! How often was he given to understand that to assert himself in kingly ways would be to collide with the heads of nations abroad. How much safer then to appease, to defer...

"Gammon!" exclaimed the doctor.

He reasoned that when a tumor endangers a man's life, the surgeon's duty is to excise it. Why not his duty then to rid this spoiling king of the bloodsuckers which were disabling him? Was it not the missionary's province to lead the future monarch of Hawaii out of a vulnerable state of confusion? Why not develop his will to think and to act so that he might at last take his place among

Christian rulers?

There were those who said it could not be done. There were more who said it should not be done by a missionary. Dr. Judd believed that it must be done. He knew that the time left in which to do it was very short.

❋ ❋ ❋

To the parents of twenty little mission children who, one by one, must sail away in strange vessels for the cold northland of America, the years of bolstering the Hawaiian kingdom would seem an unending agony. Until they could see the thing accomplished, they had no choice but to fix their minds and hearts sternly on their purpose and relinquish their children.

In the weeks and months after Sophia Bingham sailed, Sybil's memory of the ordeal presented the ever-recurring image of her little girl as she had last looked on her. Dreaming and waking, she saw the pale child looking down the side of the *Enterprise* at her parents in the longboat below.

The Binghams were rowed out to the ship which stood a mile offshore and Sophia was taken aboard. Sybil heard the order "Heave anchor up short!" and she watched the sailors run aloft to set the topsail. Like the slow beat of her heart the anchor chain struck against the ship's side with a relentless rhythm. Slowly, mournfully it seemed, out of the sea the huge chain rose before her eyes. The spurtles that drained off it wet her dress as the wind drove the spill toward their open boat.

Numb with grief and half-blinded by tears and spray, she looked up the slope of the wooden hull and strained her head back to catch a glimpse of Sophia. The Hawaiian sailors who manned the longboat dipped their oars and pulled away from the ship. Then Sybil saw the tiny figure of her child, dark hair drawn behind her ears, her face a solemn mask, the dainty fingers gripped around a wooden doll which Hiram had made and Sybil had dressed.

Sophia stood motionless as if, like the doll, she were a little figure carved in wood and set upon the busy deck of the ship. Behind her, to and fro, below and aloft, ran the boisterous sailors to whose brawn and skill the life of the child now was entrusted. She had been given up, utterly and finally, to others.

Ever in her memory as long as she survived that fateful day, Sybil heard the thin, labored voice of Sophia uttering her last words as she stared at her broken-hearted parents:

"It is very odd for you to leave me so."

How odd indeed. How comprehend it at all? Reasons are set down. God's mercy is invoked. Yet the heart rebels.

The westering sun glinted over the sea as it heaved and fell in sickening billows. The open boat started its long pull back to shore. Hiram and Sybil saw the sails of the *Enterprise* spread like great white wings and the ship quickened to the draw of the northeast trade wind. She began to move. She surged and rolled. She was homeward bound.

After that day Sybil never regained the courage which had marked her course, even in failing health, during the first eight years of her service in the islands.

When more than a year had passed, and she and Hiram still had received no letter to tell them of Sophia's safe arrival in America, Sybil took pen in hand. Unburdening her tortured soul, she wrote as she felt:

When shall I cease to labor in vain and spend my strength for naught?

When I look upon the natives . . . see their head, a youth not only, but the dupe of foreign influence; see their laws trampled upon by those whom they feel too weak to control; view their local situation, where the eye of cupidity, self-indulgence, and the love of domination fixes with eagle eye upon them, I have no hope save in what may be the sovereign will of God to make them a nation to his praise.

They may melt away before the overflowing tide of commerce, cupidity and ill-gotten power, and bright hopes in thousands of hearts, with respect to these distant islands of the sea, may be blotted out . . . .

For this staggering cause she had sacrificed three children and her own vitality.

Chapter 15

In the decade of the 1830s a succession of naval officers stepped ashore at Honolulu to demand redress for their countrymen.

The procedure of a newly arrived commander was to call Kamehameha III to account for the restrictions he imposed on foreigners; the officer declared he had the honor to visit these shores because his compatriots claimed grievous treatment at the hands of the Hawaiian government.

Through the clamor of many tongues, Bingham and his brethren recognized the prelude to French, British and American rivalry for possession of the islands.

The French not only claimed entree, they demanded favored treatment. Yankee traders took umbrage because they were not permitted to deal in Hawaiian land. Britons cried abuse because the king arbitrarily deported foreigners when it pleased him to do so.

Kauikeaouli was rebuked and his laws were ridiculed. A British lord, commander of one of His Majesty's fighting ships, flourished a treaty and a threat. He would fire on Honolulu if the king did not sign. Kauikeaouli signed. The man-of-war sailed on; when it was out of sight Kauikeaouli said that *haoles* still must have his permission before they could build houses in his islands.

Infuriated, the foreign residents went back to wrangling with the native rulers.

"Government in the Sandwich Islands?" exclaimed a red-faced trader. "Chaos!"

And it was.

Kaahumanu was dead. Succeeding her as regent in 1832 was the chiefess Kinau. She fared no better than Kaahumanu in her efforts to govern the unpredictable Kauikeaouli.

Kinau was a daughter of Kamehameha the Great and a half sister of both Kauikeaouli and Liholiho. She had been one of the five consorts of the late king. Now she was wife to Matthew Kekuanaoa, the governor of Oahu, and their sons Lot Kamehameha and Alexander were destined to rule.

Soon after the infant Alexander was born, King Kauikeaouli looked in on the mother. He took a fancy to the baby and when he left, he stuck a note in the thatch of his sister's abode.

"This child is mine" read the king's message.

It was enough to addle the wits of foreigners. When they were confronted with such royal ambiguities in realms of business and diplomacy, tempers flared. Quarrels were quick and violent. The harbor community became as inflammable as a tinderbox.

Kinau was aggrieved because of the tongue lashings she received from foreign factotums. She was so baffled by the demands of military men that she was ready to abdicate. In her perplexity, she sought the counsel of Dr. Judd.

"I have come to tell you my thought," said the heavy-hearted regent, and she eased her bulk down on the settee in the common room.

Laura and Gerrit waited for her to speak again but Kinau sat in silence. She looked out over the sea and let her tears flow. After a while, she resumed the telling of her thought.

"I am quite discouraged and can not bear this burden any longer," she said. "I wish to throw away my rank and title and responsibility . . . bring my family here and live with you. Or we will take our families and go to America. I have money."

So little time, thought Gerrit. So little time had God allotted the Polynesians. How much more swiftly than other earthlings must they discover the good and evil of two thousand years!

It waked his sympathy to see poor, bewildered Kinau casting about for some escape. There could be none. He counseled the unhappy chiefess to take up the duties that were her lot and never abandon them voluntarily. Then, as sisters and brother, the Judds knelt down with Kinau and prayed that God would light her path.

Because he believed in works as much as in prayers, Gerrit now took the first step toward shifting his career from that of missionary to statesman for the Hawaiian monarchy. He set up a little government office, the first in the islands. In that rickety shack he taught Kinau and Governor Kekuanaoa the rudiments of administration.

Here, he said, was a ledger in which they should record all disputes between chiefs and foreigners. On the pages of a second book he showed them how to list taxes and harbor fees—those that were owing and those which had been paid to the king.

A third tome should contain the registry and dates of arrival and departure of every vessel that called at Honolulu. Above all else, the doctor insisted, they must keep an account of their transactions with foreign consuls and naval commanders.

Henceforth, those officers would be told to wait upon the regent at her office. No longer would they have carte blanche to invade her chambers and scatter abuse and threats at what o'clock it pleased them. The man to whom they must present themselves was the highborn native John Ii who would serve as Kinau's secretary.

At Kawaiahao the men of the mission reasoned together. They debated their obligations, arguing for and against a deeper involvement in the affairs of the nation. Notwithstanding Dr. Judd's ado to set matters straight for Kinau, government business did not fall within the purview of missionaries. So they were instructed, so they believed, and so the most of them remained scrupulously within bounds of their prescribed tasks. Judd contended that the time had come to examine a wider concept of their duty.

There persisted among the natives a craving for alien tools and knowledge. Aware of this readiness of the people to advance in technical skills, the brethren resolved to produce a corps of native teachers for every island.

They sent Lorrin Andrews, Jonathan Green and Ephraim Clark into the hills of Lahaina on

Maui. There, with little more than axes and ingenuity, was raised up a training school for Hawaiian educators.

Brother Clark surveyed the needs of the builders wrote to Levi Chamberlain:

> With regard to our wants, we want immediately one yoke of your good oxen from Honolulu, if we can get them . . . . We want also a light ox cart like the one at Wailuku. A heavy cart will not answer on this hill . . . .
>
> I have felt today much like giving up. We have . . . no houses to live in and no houses to teach in. My goods are scattered from Lahaina *lalo* to Lahaina *luna,* some in one place and some in another as I could find a spot for them.
>
> But to go on with my wants . . . . Some chains, an iron bar, a stone hammer and two or three stone axes will also be needed . . . . Lumber for my dwelling house will come along, I trust, in good time. I shall build small and with strict regard to economy.

Their first scholars, twenty-five young native men selected by chiefs and station teachers, came from mission settlements island-wide. Together, teachers and students of two races built and furnished Lahainaluna Seminary. It became the fountainhead of continuing gains toward the literacy of 125,000 Hawaiians, most of them in a state of abject need and oppression.

When four new companies of missionaries arrived between 1831 and 1836, some of them were assigned to teach the natives practical skills. They taught the trades by which a man might earn his living, and the duties of a woman to protect her children from wayward influence and instill in them habits of industry.

Bingham believed that unless the common people acted on these principles they could not hope to rise out of their feudal state. He was convinced that a race which remains too long in bondage may hope for nothing but extinction—or new masters.

The brethren conceived the idea of vocational boarding schools for Hawaiian children. Isolating groups of boys and girls from disruptive elements

VIEW OF HONOLULU, 1836
Lithograph by Lauvergne

and from each other, mission couples undertook to rear them in the regimen of Christian home life.

The girls were taught to cook and to sew, to spin and weave. The boys learned to plow, to raise and grind sugar cane and care for dairy herds. When they became adept with saws and hammers they fashioned tables and chairs and beds; they also built wagons and fitted them with wheels.

Honolulu Academy of Arts

As the sun rose and set, the "families" assembled to read the New Testament, not only in Hawaiian but also in the language of Yankees and Britons. Classes were formed to study arithmetic, geography and map making. The mothers gathered their tapa-clad pupils in choirs to sing the stately harmonies that would be their common heritage—the first Hawaiian *himeni.*

In Hilo, Mr. and Mrs. David Belden Lyman established a farm school for twelve native boys; eventually they educated more than eight hundred. In the same hamlet Mrs. Titus Coan taught Hawaiian girls to read and cipher and keep house.

Later, on Maui the Jonathan Greens and the Edward Baileys and Miss Maria Ogden trained classes of boarding students at the Wailuku Female Seminary.

At the remote Waialua station on Oahu, Edwin Locke and his pupils converted a wasteland into "fruitful fields" and produced a community of skilled native farmers.

The initial efforts proved the worth of the plan, but it had to be sustained. With their resources stretched to the last notch, the mission leaders in Honolulu drafted a letter to the governing Board in Boston. Their message was that they had need of forty-six more missionaries in the Sandwich Islands, and they needed them at once.

Through the ages, wherever men have caught a vision of freedom, and for as long as it prevails, there is an epic ring to their language. Their declarations resound like mighty anthems down the corridors of time.

Into the literature of liberty was written a prophetic appeal by the Sandwich Islands missionaries on behalf of the Hawaiian people. Drafted in the summer of 1836, it was directed to the American Board of Commissioners for Foreign Missions.

In it, the mission leaders laid down reasons for advancing beyond their religious mandate:

> ...We...would wish to see *the rights of the people better defined, better understood, better respected by those in power....*
>
> They need competent instruction immediately in the science of government in order to promote industry, to secure ample means of support, and to protect the just rights of all....
>
> Unless something more can be done for the people, they will not provide well either for the rising or future generations.... But foreign speculators may be expected to seize on the advantages which the country affords for agriculture, manufactures and commerce....
>
> An inevitable influx of foreign population, induced only by the love of pleasure and gain, would doubtless hasten the waste of the aborigines; and at no distant period, the mere mouldering remnants of the nation could be pointed out to the voyager....

The brethren termed their deposition a "Memorial" and the bearer of it to Boston was William Richards of the Lahaina mission station. With his wife and six children, he sailed for America in the winter of 1836. His twofold errand was to present the Memorial and to find homes in New England for his sons and daughters.

On the voyages when Richards roamed twice around Cape Horn, the sailors who watched at the mastheads occasionally descried other wing-like sails. Passing at night or in a tempest or at a great distance, the ships sailed on through the great south sea, all hands unmindful that each played some part in the destiny of the Sandwich Islands.

While Richards' ship rounded the Horn and turned north for New England, the barque *Mary Frazier* heaved her bows through mountainous waves and entered the Pacific Ocean. She carried a company of thirty-two missionaries, the largest reinforcement ever sent to Honolulu.

To the northeast, some unknown ship bore on for England. In her captain's cabin was a letter to King William IV from Kamehameha III and his high chiefs. It was a plea to the British monarch to take back his consul Richard Charlton whose tyranny had become unbearable, even to this oppressed but forgiving race of Polynesians.

The native rulers had written:

...A man, a Briton, bearing the title of Consul, is now residing with us in the midst of our nation, who has spoken evil of us in the highest degree, ridiculing us, and bearing down heavily upon us on account of our ignorance....

These are words which are very common from his mouth, "When a British man-of-war arrives then all the chiefs and people of the Sandwich Islands will be slain." He also says the people shall be hung. He is firmly bent on exalting himself over us....

On account of these things we respectfully and humbly implore you to assent to our entreaty which we make, and call said Consul to account.... And should you find him guilty, remove him from amongst us, and return him to the land of his birth, and put an end to his acting as Consul on these Sandwich Islands.

How many times would be heard some echo of that plea from rulers of other Pacific islands, and how often ignored. How easy for courts and ministers half a world away to remain officially uninformed of the methods of certain of their consuls and naval officers.

In time, the politically unschooled, all-but-unclothed natives would subside.

They were duped? Plundered? How unfortunate. The incident would be concluded with the signing of a treaty.

The pattern was beginning to emerge when those ships bearing Sandwich Islands messages and missionaries set sail between 1836 and 1838. Even then, somewhere in the great south sea the French frigate *Venus* was gliding westward toward the Oceanic Islands. France, under Louis Philippe, had begun her hunt for colonies in the Pacific.

Chapter 16

The ship that carried Mr. Richards to America and the one bringing new missionaries to Hawaii reached their destinations almost simultaneously in the spring of 1837. Touching land again, the voyagers on both errands had cause to look heavenward and exclaim:

"The world is too much with us!"

In the Mission Rooms at Boston the solemn-faced secretaries, perceiving Mr. Richards in their midst, gave him to understand that for a missionary to journey home without leave was too much. The occurrence would call for some discipline.

In Honolulu the thirty-two new recruits, released at last from cramped quarters aboard the *Mary Frazier,* learned that they had arrived in time for the annual meeting of the Sandwich Islands Mission. Preachers and teachers and their families were arriving daily from their stations on five islands.

Almost half a hundred children and parents already had taken temporary lodging at Kawaiahao. The young bridal couples, who scarcely could find a place to step among the veteran sisters and brethren and their abundant issue, thought it wise to hold their tongues and await the bidding of their hosts.

At mission headquarters four new dwellings, a schoolhouse, storehouse and book bindery had been built. Still, the numbers who had to be accommodated were too many. Only by discounting any concern for their comfort would a way be found and the thing be done.

Out came the patchwork quilts to partition off a cubby here, a vestibule there, a wee compartment yonder. A man and wife might need six feet this way, six feet that. A babe could sleep on a sea chest, or in it; a little girl or two would lie snug on a pallet beneath their parents' bed.

Come night, the whole tribe of lean-faced boys—never mind to whom related—must climb to the attic of Levi Chamberlain's house and drop their bony frames among ropes and kegs and blocks and pulleys.

So dispatched and uncomfortably clapped together, the host families blessed the Lord and made room for the travel-stained voyagers from America.

With what would they all be fed?

Those mothers who had been long in the field knew that a tin cup of arrowroot pudding with molasses, given each child before supper, did wonders to stretch a meager food supply. Thus they reckoned to feed many mouths with something.

They could even calculate the number of days on which their incoming sisters, and some of the brethren, would care to be fed with nothing at all.

There was scarcely one among them who had

not known the agony of crossing inter-island channels aboard schooners that reeked of bilge and quivered with rats and roaches. Those who refused to enter the infested cabins lay retching and fainting on a sun-scorched deck. If the winds proved fickle the craft might wallow on its sickening way a full week or two or three. At journey's end the emaciated passengers would be carried ashore more dead than alive, the sight and smell of food quite beyond their endurance.

However it might be with the inner man, and however many stragglers still pitched about on the open sea, at the appointed hour on the appointed day, General Meeting convened in the adobe schoolhouse at Kawaiahao.

Those who were staunch and those who were

Mission houses at Kawaiahao, 1837
Drawing by Daniel Wheeler

ready to swoon made uneven work of their hymn of solidarity:

Blest be-e the tie-e that binds
Our hearts in Chri-istian love
The fe-ellowshi-ip of ki-indred mi-inds
Is li-ike to tha-at above.

When they had got through the first stanza, a rustling of calico and alpaca coincided with the turning of heads to see from whence came one clear female voice that soared forth in perfect address:

Before our Father's throne
We pour our ardent prayers
Our fears, our hopes, our aims are one,
Our comforts and our cares.

Hawaiian Mission Children's Society

The singer seemed to steady those about her who halted and quavered. At the same time she inclined the robust to a more precise tempo. The company more nearly harmonized as one, for verily, a gifted musician had taken the lead. It was the new Mrs. Amos Cooke from Sunderland, Massachusetts.

Miss Juliette Montague she had been until three weeks before the *Mary Frazier* sailed. During the voyage her shipmates had remarked that, despite their serious errand, Sister Juliette seemed in no hurry to put on the solemn face of matron. She set forth on her pilgrimage with the buoyancy of a robust country lass.

It was she who had ranged the deck in storm and in calm. With girlish excitement she saluted the first white albatross that wheeled round the masthead and followed the ship. At the captain's nod, she ran to and fro, watching schools of porpoise play under the bows and applauding the dainty prowess of flying fish that skipped the waves on wing-like fins.

As Juliette revered God's handiwork in that wondrous ocean world, so did she admire the ingenious ways of men with a ship. The common sailor, scorned by polite society around the globe, won her respect. She sought to learn something of the mariner's skill from the fellows who worked the *Mary Frazier*.

Right gladly they answered the lady's questions, and great marlingspikes! if one day they did not come upon her practicing to splice rope. Juliette was a teacher by profession, a tailoress by trade. To work with strands of hemp instead of flaxen thread presented a curious challenge. With her skirts spread out around her, she sat flat on the deck and busied herself at the seaman's task.

If her ragtag tutors were flabbergasted by this, they were altogether bowled over by her next intent. In the manner of a schoolmistress laying out a plan for her pupils, Mrs. Cooke proposed to mend the sailors' clothing as they could spare a coat or a blouse or a pair of trousers. They were a threadbare lot, and she thought it the least she might do for neglected deck hands who had suffered not only the presence but the quizzing of a female landlubber.

The ship sailed on. From time to time a sailor approached the mission wife and handed her his tattered raiment. The men in the forecastle swore they never heard the likes of a sea dog going to his grave dressed in rags that were patched by a lady. For some of them, hers was the first act of kindness they had ever known.

Before the *Mary Frazier* reached Honolulu Juliette took note of her twenty-fifth birthday.

"One quarter of a century gone, and all my work yet to do," she chided herself in her journal. "Let me keep this constantly before my mind, and do with my might what my hands find to do...."

As she sat in General Meeting at Kawaiahao, Mrs. Cooke permitted herself the opinion that whatever her hands might find to do here, the risks which attended the doing of it must be considerable.

She listened to the brief reports which told how it was with the families of the mission corps:

"In the twelve months just concluded...fourteen infants born, five deaths...fifteen members embarked for their native land.

"Among those remaining in the field, six wives of missionaries in a feeble state...common causes of debility may be noticed...dyspepsia, bilious attacks, fever, cough, bleeding from the lungs...."

"And," Juliette might have added, "some little spirit of contention amongst the families." For that had been her observation.

Walking about the mission settlement at recess one day, the Cookes had looked in at Levi Chamberlain's house. Amos hoped he might get a post there as assistant to the business agent. Certainly Levi needed help. The community to which he catered now tallied more than a hundred men, women and children living at sixteen stations on five islands.

Every hinge, nail, button and biscuit that came to their use came cheap and in bulk from the A-merican Board of Commissioners for Foreign Missions. The Board dispatched its pinchpenny purchases to Mr. Chamberlain. The families, whose lives depended on receiving some part of them, had to wait until a quota was counted out, recorded and vouchsafed, usually at the time of the annual meeting.

Amos and Juliette climbed the narrow stairs and harked to the sounds of murmuring and discontent.

"Much of this clothing does not appear to be adapted to the human form," they heard Mr. Chamberlain admit.

"Ready-made slops!" thought Juliette as she glanced at the trousers which Levi offered to a missionary from Maui.

On the desk lay a wooden chest filled with tight-sleeved, short-waisted, scant-tailed gentlemen's coats. Seizing up one of the garments, Juliette confirmed her guess.

"A great bargain in Boston, no doubt," she

thought and she dropped the ill-conceived thing back on the pile.

"These shoes, Mr. Chamberlain," began a hoarse female voice at the other side of the room, "all these shoes are made of such stiff leather. They chafe the ankle bones quite raw..."

The poor soul spied a pair of brown prunella slippers among the lot. She bolted for them—but too late.

Or was it?

A long-limbed mission wife who stood opposite her held one shoe. She the other. The tall woman, whom Mr. Chamberlain had just helped to a vial of turpentine, appealed to the business agent.

Levi had seen her touch the slippers first, but he declared in favor of the smaller woman.

"The shoes will fit her better," he told the plaintiff, "and of our small supply of turpentine, you have secured a portion and she has none."

Still the pair of slippers remained divided.

"I appeal to you, sisters," persisted Levi. "Which of you has the greater need for shoes or for turpentine?"

The tall woman handed over the shoe.

"I'll not give up the turpentine," she declared. "The fleas dread it some and it makes them skip though I must hobble."

Juliette thought they were pitiful in their sun-struck calico dresses and rusty black bonnets. They probed through the mission stores with long fingers and long noses. Even their eyes strained about with an elongated look.

Noble women once and noble still, in Christian conscience they tried to overcome the spirit of rivalry which years of privation finally had waked in them. Juliette sensed that they had a kind of inborn gumption that would not square with the communal rule under which they labored.

She reminded herself that she and Amos were pledged to a lifetime of obedience to this very system which held all joiners equally in thrall.

She looked to the wiry little man who had made her his bride and helpmate. Amos did not heed. His restless glance darted among the rows of boxes and barrels. He perceived a shortage here, an overstock there, and mentally he was dividing the lot.

Juliette thought he would like the business of counting and measuring and listing goods to be dispersed throughout the establishment. Already Amos had shown a certain aptitude for trade, though he had spent most of his youth laboring on a farm in Connecticut. For a time, he had studied for the ministry.

What tasks the brethren would require of such a disparate couple as the Cookes proved to be was still undecided. But in one visit to the Chamberlain house Juliette had witnessed enough to know that whoever dealt in this common stock system must wrestle with an unsolvable human dilemma.

To balance the scales justly, while competing families watched from all sides, would require the wisdom of Solomon. She thought Amos might better be employed at some duty which more urgently required his determination to "take hold, hang on and never let go." His exactitude hardly would pacify these sisters who had lived too long under penurious restraint.

She did not want to watch them any longer herself. Taking up Mr. Chamberlain's spyglass and training it from the second-story hatchway, Juliette scanned the shoreline from Waikiki to

Moanalua. Her curiosity was piqued by an incredible stir of human activity along that wide arc. She supposed it had to do with the much-talked-of decision of the chiefs to replace the grass church at Kawaiahao with a new one built of stone.

She saw thousands of native men wielding metal bars and axes on the fringing reefs. Their dark skin glistened through showers of ocean spray that leapt and fell with the breaking waves. Juliette studied the panorama and concluded that most of the able-bodied men on the island must be engaged in prying up the coral beds that lined the leeward shore.

She lowered the glass and focused on a little knot of workers some distance inland. A tall man in a sailor's blouse appeared to be fitting wheels on a wagon bed. Was that not Hiram Bingham? Recalling a discussion she had heard in General Meeting, Juliette was sure it must be the mission leader who toiled yonder.

Bingham had opposed the chiefs when he discovered they intended to order the natives to drag fourteen thousand reef rocks to Kawaiahao.

"We will furnish carts and teams to move the stone," he told them.

Next day he had set about constructing wheeled planks on which the slabs of coral could be drawn by horses. He had also devised a system of cranes and pulleys by which the stone blocks could be hauled up and set in place to form the walls of the church.

"Thus the people will benefit by first acquaintance with the mechanical powers—the lever, the wheel and the axle," he had told the chiefs.

Juliette tilted the glass and sighted a commotion far to leeward. Hundreds of native women streaked across the plain toward a sandy field at the center of which was a man astride a bucking horse.

That, thought Juliette, would be Dr. Judd who raised the dust. She had heard him say he would break wild horses to the harness and they would be ready to haul Bingham's carts and pulley ropes by the time the reef rocks were cut. Moreover, he vowed he would make the rawhide lines and drive the beasts himself.

Audacious band of preachers and teachers!

Though she marveled at all things proposed and all things accomplished, Juliette still could not reconcile the magnitude of their ventures with the grievances which were leading some of them to the verge of dissent.

That afternoon she and Amos attended another session at the meetinghouse. Again, they heard the note of antagonism when the brethren began a debate on ways and means to provide for their children.

Did those fathers who spoke out regard themselves as disillusioned men? They did not say so. They only reported that of the number of children who had been sent home to be educated in America, not all had fared well. Some of the sons and daughters of Sandwich Islands missionaries had become indigent orphans in their parents' homeland.

"Even now, one and another are handed about from farmhouse to farmhouse up and down the Atlantic coast!" cried a voice edged with bitterness. "Stories come back to us that for their keep some of our children must toil in the fields of taskmasters all unknown to us."

O God, how long?

The brethren proposed a school on mission ground for mission children. Again there rose the questions: Who would be their teachers? With what would they be paid?

The confoundment had not altered, except to worsen, since a decade earlier when the overburdened parents had exclaimed:

"If it should be said we ought to teach them ourselves, we would enquire what parents in America are the teachers of their own children, and is it to be supposed that the missionary is of all men the most free from care and labor?"

The fathers wrote a joint letter to the Board.

"Thirteen have been added to the number, since our last General Meeting," they reported. "Perhaps this fact may not be so welcome, if they are eventually to be sent to the land of their fathers for education.

"The churches may feel by and by that the children of missionaries are a great burden; and perhaps they begin to feel it already. We suppose however it will be granted, that the children, even of missionaries, have, as citizens of the world, a right to a support from some source...."

In seventeen years of pioneering, the brethren in the islands had written enough of ambition, innovation, requirement and requisition to paper the walls of the Mission Rooms in Boston, and ample to spare. Now the Reverend William Richards of Lahaina had the audacity to stand before the governing secretaries in their New England office.

On the one hand he brought visible reminders of a crucial provocation amongst the island families. He had landed on his native sod with six more children to be reared and educated in America. In his other hand he carried the Sandwich Islands Mission "Memorial."

In the eyes of his astonished sponsors, Mr. Richards plainly had overstepped bounds of propriety. As to the authors of the "Memorial," they had so far exceeded their warrant that it was thought the whole community of Sandwich Island missionaries ought to be reminded of where authority lay. Clearly, it was the secretaries' duty to dispatch a corrective admonition to the brethren in the field.

The island company was instructed:

"...No mission, or member of a mission, may print any letter, tract, or appeal at these establishments, at the expense of the Board, with a view to its being sent to individuals or communities in the United States."

The Board further decreed:

"It shall not be deemed proper for any missionary, or assistant missionary, to visit the United States, except by invitation or permission first received from the Prudential Committee."

The final blow could not have been avoided, for America in 1837 was reeling in the throes of financial panic. The missionaries were informed that whereas, in the previous year, seventy thousand dollars had been expended to sustain their families and their works throughout the Hawaiian archipelago, no more than thirty thousand dollars could be allotted for the whole in 1838.

"The whole" meant the building and support of churches, common schools and boarding schools for natives; the printing and binding of books; it also encompassed the costs of food, clothing, shelter, medicines, tools, lumber, glass, paint, nails and transportation between the islands for the brethren and their families.

Now, for Sandwich Island missionaries to speak of serving the native population in civic matters was utterly vain.

As to the plight of those missionaries' children, if the parents would train a spyglass on the rigging of almost any American vessel calling at island ports, they might see there the sons of once-prosperous Yankee merchants and farmers. Many a young gentleman lately had been reduced to the rank of a common seaman because his bankrupt father no longer could sustain him at home.

The mission families were given to understand that the time had come when they could ask for nothing more.

❀ ❀ ❀

At the islands, Hiram Bingham spoke of imperative duty to a threatened race and prayed God to hold back the gathering clouds.

Kinau sat in her office and listened with mounting resentment to the demands and arguments of hawk-nosed military men. White-gloved and gleamingly accoutered with pistols and swords and epaulets, they claimed to uphold the laws of civilized countries. They demanded that the Hawaiian government do likewise.

The proud-hearted chiefess turned contemptuous, then stubborn, then imperious. At every interview the seeds of conflict multiplied.

From Lahaina came a first clear sound of warning. David Malo, one of the Hawaiian scholars educated at Lahainaluna Seminary, sent a message to Kinau:

"... You must not think that this is anything like olden times, that you are the only chiefs and can have things as they are.... If a big wave comes in, large fishes will come from the dark Ocean... and when they see the small fishes they will eat them up.... The ships of the white man have come, and smart people have arrived from the great countries....

Therefore get your servant ready who will help you when you need him."

Time was running out.

From Tahiti came news that the French warship *Venus* lay anchored at Papeete and threatened bombardment. Within the year another French vessel *L'Artemise* dropped anchor opposite the mission houses at Honolulu. Its commander boasted:

"I have prepared forces sufficiently strong, that in giving a dreadful blow, the French shall be the masters and the protectors of the town at the same time."

He let it be known that his gracious mercy might be granted, but only if the king agreed to certain conditions.

Kamehameha III must assure him that henceforth no Frenchman accused of crime in the islands would be tried except by a jury of foreigners selected by the French consul. Land must be made available for the Catholic church, and French wines and brandies must be admitted at island ports.

As guaranty for future good conduct of the native government toward the sons of France, an indemnity of twenty thousand dollars was demanded and delivered aboard *L'Artemise*.

"France has done what she would not have done to Great Britain or to any other power that was able to defend itself," exclaimed Juliette Cooke.

British Consul Charlton viewed the matter in a different light. Kamehameha III stood more vulnerable now than ever before. Not again would he be able to raise a great coffer of silver money on demand. Late or soon, he would have to capitulate.

The long arm of power groped about through the Pacific. In time, it would reach out again for the Hawaiian Islands. The men of the mission, who could offer neither weapons nor dollars, advanced an extraordinary plan. It was based on their contention that if the kingdom of the Kamehamehas were recognized as a civilized nation, its independence must be acknowledged by the Christian powers on both sides of the Atlantic Ocean.

From the text of their defunct "Memorial," they now revived a single clause:

"They [the rulers] need competent instruction immediately in the science of government...."
On this the brethren resolved to act.

William Richards, returned from his galling errand in Boston, tendered his resignation as a missionary and entered the service of the king.

Kauikeaouli had all but abandoned Honolulu in favor of his royal bowers at Lahaina—and the lesser likelihood of confrontation with warlike foreigners. In that temporary retreat, Richards initiated daily classes for the king and chiefs in political economy, government and law.

"...Services highly important," Dr. Judd agreed. "But this did not silence my constant complaint that he should leave so important a port as Honolulu exposed to the liability of making the greatest mistakes, endangering, if not actually causing the loss of the king's sovereignty, unless I, who was still supported by the American Board, were constantly turned aside from my appropriate duties to attend to his."

How many more fixed intentions must be turned aside because of the baffling eddies that ran counter to the tide of destiny!

The leaders of the mission—headstrong visionaries attempting to bring forward an isolated race upon the stage of the civilized world—turned next to the juvenile heirs of the king and chiefs. They too must come under immediate instruction or all would be futile experiment and lost labor.

King, chiefs and missionaries, counseling together, fixed on Brother and Sister Cooke as a suitable couple to conduct a royal boarding school for the future rulers of the land.

Nonplussed, Juliette took up her quill and observed:

"Forty independent, enlightened men cannot get together even here at the Sandwich Islands and hold their tongues entirely still.... This meeting is likely to affect our situation materially."

"After the close of the afternoon meeting, Bro. Judd came to see if we would become teachers of the young chiefs," Amos confided in his journal. "...I lay awake almost all night laying plans, etc.

provided we should be chosen for that employment."

Three weeks later he recorded the decision:

"In the afternoon, the subject of our taking the Chiefs' children was decided. We were set apart to that work. The Lord God of Israel aid us."

Chapter 17

A mos drew a plan for the Chiefs' Children's School and helped lay up its adobe walls. Under the torrid sun he lifted and heaved and sweated until his tough little body withered to its frame and the lines of his face deepened in dry creases.

Mauka of the mission establishment the dun-colored boarding school began to take form. It was a quadrangle built around a central courtyard where the wind blew in circles and dust demons filled the laborers' mouths with grit.

Amos ground his teeth on it and toiled like a man beset. He was goaded by a sense of the enormity of the work laid out for him and Juliette. They were charged with training up a set of headstrong native children to the pitch of competent kings and queens and ministers. Moreover, Bingham and Judd had admonished them to do their work quickly.

If they should fail, as Amos thought they might, the consequence to the nation could be extinction. Nor did the expectations of his fellow missionaries rest lightly on his conscience. Twenty years' labor by scores of sisters and brethren, even children, seemed destined to culminate in this final exertion.

"God give me wisdom that my concerns may be managed with discretion," Amos prayed.

Juliette stood aghast at the very thought of managing such concerns. She who seldom minced words was tempted to broadcast her misgivings, but that would be unseemly in a mission sister.

Very well, then. She would have her say in private. She took to airing her views in letters that went the rounds of the Cookes and Montagues back in New England.

While native workers thatched and tied down a roof over the school, Juliette wrote to her sister Fanny:

"Providence permitting, we shall be in our house in three or four weeks. I dread the undertaking beyond all expression. Nothing but the conviction of duty could induce me to undertake it."

Duty prevailed. The Cookes set up housekeeping in April, and on the fourth of May, 1840, seven haughty scions of Hawaiian *alii* entered their home and custody, to remain there until they should be reared and educated.

Before the week was out Juliette flew to her writing box again and scrawled:

"Oh, my dear Mother, it is more than I feel as if my weak nerves could undertake to bring up in a proper manner these headstrong princes! I have been thinking it over tonight till it seems as if my heart would burst."

Another week passed and the heir to the Hawaiian throne, a child of six, arrived at school. It was the boy Alexander who one day would rule as Kamehameha IV. He was followed by a train of thirty *kahus* (attendants).

Pomp and royalty notwithstanding, Mrs. Cooke viewed the princeling with a sober eye.

"Alexander...and two other little boys have come to take up their residence with us," she announced to kith and kin in Massachusetts. Juliette-fashion, she added, "All the gold of the Indies would not compensate for the loss of the quiet hours in one's life."

The folks at home knew something of Alexander from earlier letters. On making first acquaintance with him Mrs. Cooke had written:

"Alexander appears to be a pretty boy now, but we fear for him some, the influence surrounding him being very bad. His father lives on Maui most of the time. He has houses and grounds of his own where he lives as he pleases with twenty or twenty-five servants whom he orders according to his fancy.... He generally has eight or ten natives to carry his things...one carries his books, another an umbrella, another a fly brush, and so on."

She mentioned a younger pupil, David Kalakaua, who was destined to become Hawaii's Merry Monarch. He was four years old when he came to live with the Cookes and Juliette noticed only that "little David was so shy he hid behind the door."

More scholars arrived. Alexander's future queen, Emma Rooke, who "has not yet learned to obey"; William Lunalilo who "cries considerable," and Bernice Pauahi, a gentle child of eight. The baby of the school was Liliuokalani who would reign as the last island queen. The eldest were Moses—irresponsible, outrageously spoiled and verging on a troublesome adolescence—and his brother Lot who, upon Alexander's death, would come to the throne as Kamehameha V.

They wore no crowns yet and Juliette remained skeptical. Writing to sister Fanny she confided:

> I have many fears about it, having seen the children when they seemed quite unmanageable. But Dr. Judd is to stand by us and says that if there is any difficulty we must send for him. He has great influence with the chiefs and is very anxious to have the school succeed.

Later, she exclaimed:

"It is teaching, endeavoring to correct, to fix principles of right and wrong, etc., from dawn until evening. People who say, do you have *only* so many, I would beg to undertake the task *one day*. Six of our family are under 6 years of age and I wish they *all* were. I think we should have more rational hope of success."

In some measure her doubts were justified. Of the sixteen highborn children entrusted to Juliette and Amos, some would have to be counted failures at the last. The race would be short and swift, the stakes enormous, and hurdles had to be set at the highest notch.

The marvel was that the Cookes did not lose every royal pupil as soon as he entered the school.

From the beginning, there was a plan afoot to lure the children from their teachers by means of a weird maneuver. It was the more insidious because it proceeded with primitive stealth.

Amos and Juliette discovered their antagonists among the horde of *kahus,* bereft not only of their charges but also of the gain and favor due them as guardians of royal children. Stripped of their sinecure, they commenced a slow bedevilment and waited for the *haole* teachers to yield.

The *kahus* would not quit the premises. Day and night dozens of them lurked outside the school wall. They preyed on the restless dormitory, never permitting the Cookes to settle their menage for more than a few hours at a time. By turns, as the homesick children left off weeping within doors, the *kahus* renewed their dismal wailing at the wall:

"*Auwe-e-e-e... Auwe-e-e-e... Auwe-e-e-e*"

The ghostly keening, punctuated by sudden outcries, raddled the nerves of teachers and children. Moses and Lot caught a sly message; they slipped over the wall and fled with their *kahus*. The little ones, frightened the more, cried the harder. Amid such turbulence there could be no school.

Still the chiefs said they wanted their children to be educated. They sent after the truants and led them back to the Cookes. For a little while the *kahus* subsided, but they would not go away. Forbidden to call or beckon to the children, they squatted in the mud with their backs against the outer wall. Juliette thought they looked like a flock of sullen, oftimes drenched ravens—watching and waiting.

Sitting at her work table, long past the bedtime hour, she kept her own vigil and pondered on the contenders at the gate. The air had turned chilly and a wet wind swept down from Punchbowl. Doors slammed and window sashes rattled. Juliette tried to sew, then to write, but the flame of her lamp rose and fell with the squalls.

"A night perfectly suited to the *kahus*," she began, but she made poor work with her pen. The lamp might be blamed some but, more than that, her nervous hand was at fault.

She tried to think of what else she might do to make the hours pass, yet still hold herself alert.

It occurred to her to repeat the psalms and proverbs. She could do that well enough, and with some comfort to herself, while she listened for the cry of a child. Much depended on her running quickly to her brood if one of them waked.

Like a sailor at the helm, thought Juliette, she must stand her watch. But she railed at the mischief which had brought matters to such a pass. She felt sorry for the little princes and princesses who had gone to bed terrified, and so needlessly.

It was the *kahus* again. Without entering the house, they had struck their most damaging blow and spread panic among the children. Young Moses, returning from his brief escape, had carried back the inflammatory tale by which the *kahus* meant to undo the school.

Akuas (ghosts) were coming to haunt the house of the Cookes, he said. The *kahus* had told him so.

"*Mea hoopunipuni*! A deceitful thing!" Amos had retorted. But the damage was done.

Juliette began a new letter, then gave it up abruptly:

"We have met with many things during the day to try our patience and grieve us, but I am too tired to tell mother about them tonight."

She may have seen that Amos already had set down the whole of the story in his journal. His closely written pages lay on the work table beside a heap of unfinished sewing, caps and collars, patterns and bombazine bonnets which Juliette was fashioning for the little girls.

The schoolmaster had recorded:

Moses & Lot were out at nine o'clock, & I extinguished their light. They soon returned & Moses went to bed with his pantaloons on. Took the back side of the bed & left Wm. on the edge.

Fearing he might fall out, I put two chairs to the bed, and about three o'clock he rolled out and was very much scared, as the children had been talking during the day about a god haunting the house.

I got up and after quieting him a little I returned to bed, and in about half an hour he got up again & cried "*He akua! He akua!*" (a ghost, a ghost!).

Moses & Lot then got up and I let them both sleep with William, & let the *Kahu* also sleep there. They probably slept little or none, and in the morning they were up before me & scared Wm. again very much.

I took each of them to a room and made them remain until prayer time, & tabued any more being said about it. I was afraid it would break up the school....

At noon I mistrusted Moses & Lot had gone into the rooms of the girls & went there and sure enough—they were there, and had gone to bed. They were much ashamed.

J. took the girls & talked with them & I the boys. This afternoon I tabued their going into each others' rooms—girls with the boys, boys with the girls.

Wm. is so afraid this evening that he stays in the bedroom with Mrs. C.

Amos and Juliette had no opportunity to dwell on the trials which began that night because scarcely a day went by without some new predicament. While they strove to instill virtue in the older scholars, and banish fear from the hearts of the tots, Crown Prince Alexander suddenly took it in his head to run off to the fort.

"Last evening we had some trouble with Alexander," Amos reported in his journal. "Indeed, during the day he made three attempts to escape and go to the Fort. When it was time to go to bed, he made some trouble and bit John's wrist. I went with my rule, and he got into bed and was soon asleep . . . ."

Poor Amos. His rule stick and his tabus were no match for volatile, self-willed proteges who never before had been governed.

"Our souls have been much tried this evening by the going out of some of our number. . . ." he wrote again. "I put Moses in the carpenter's room, Jane in the carpenter's shop, Abigail in her room, Polly in the bathing house & Emma in the grass house & punished her for several disobediences this day."

He grieved and worried and bridled. But since he could hope for no change of occupation, there was nothing to do but persevere. School must keep, somehow.

But how?

The shadowy ways of the *kahus* were beyond a New England schoolmaster's comprehension; nor could Amos outmaneuver his extraordinary foster children. So he banished every idle hour in which mischief was sure to hatch.

With his house still in a pother, Amos raised his voice above the tumult and forged ahead. He commenced teaching numbers and letters, spelling and defining and the proper use of tenses. Hour after hour he drilled the children, then he set them to doing penmanship exercises in their copybooks.

As soon as they dropped their quills and rushed for the door, they were told to alter their step and walk quietly to the family table. There they learned to say grace and, gracefully, to make proper use of spoons and forks and cups and tumblers.

On hot summer afternoons, all except the Sabbath, villagers stared as Amos Cooke shepherded his charges about on horseback expeditions or sailed with them off Waikiki. He walked them over hill and dale in troops. One day he led the lot of them into Honolulu village and weighed them on an old sandalwood scale. He recorded the statistics:

"Moses, 152 pounds; Lot, 96; Alexander, 82 ...." At the last, Amos put down his own weight: 107 pounds.

Evenings, when supper was over, the weary schoolmaster took his seat in the parlor. He crossed his narrow shanks and presided at a reading hour. It was planned so that the children might become acquainted with history and literature, and also that Amos might know where they all were.

If exhaustion overcame him, Juliette governed the school for a day. Otherwise she went about the tending of little children and food and fires. Betwixt times, she tailored new frocks and pantaloons to replace the masquerade of lace petticoats, velvet weskits and satin robes which daily passed before her.

With caterwauling and loud disputes erupting all around, she set down some practical admonishments:

Have a place for everything and everything in its place.
Never do what you know to be wrong, and if you do, go immediately and confess and resolve to do so no more.
Speak not too loud nor too low.
Answer not one that speaks to you till he has done.
Speak not without Sir or some title of respect which is due to him to whom you speak.

Go not singing, whistling or hollaring along the street or Road.
Quarrel not with one you meet.

Amos thought his more venturesome pupils might do well to copy and memorize Mrs. Cooke's every dictum. He set them to that task between the hour of evening prayer and the moment when they gladly escaped in sleep.

So long as Juliette kept adding to her list, not an idle hand could be found to engage in the Devil's work at the Chiefs' Children's School.

Under its thatched roof, chaos began to give way to order. Juliette reviewed their situation and wrote to the homefolks in New England:

"We find to our joy and satisfaction that the restraints which we are throwing around the children do not operate unfavorably by making them wish to forsake us.... They are very affectionate to us and think it the greatest privilege in the world to be allowed to come into our private sitting room....

"Frequently they knock at the door and say, 'I thank you walk in,' by which they intend politely to solicit the privilege of walking in and sitting awhile with us."

The cry of the *kahus* no longer shattered the bashful rapport springing up between the children and their teachers. For that blessing Amos and Juliette had to thank their arch prankster and trouble maker, Moses.

It chanced that when Moses read *Hamlet* his adolescent fancy stuck on two aspects of the story: the appearance of a ghost and the scene in which Hamlet pretends madness. In the boy's imagination, the roles merged and he visualized himself playing his own concoction of the drama. He could not have asked for a more responsive audience than that which awaited him just outside the school wall.

From his box of finery, he drew out a bolt of golden crepe and a scarlet Spanish shawl edged with heavy fringe. He wound the crepe round and round to make a turban. It grew to the size of a bushel basket.

When he set it on his dark brow it slid down over his ears. No matter. With a cavalier gesture he flung the shawl over his shoulders, muffled his nose and mouth in its forward folds and strode off to the outer gate.

Rounding the corner of the wall, he all but floated before the *kahus*. His bare feet and gliding tiptoe gait were hidden beneath the shawl. The turban rested on his shoulder blades and swallowed up his head. Through the furrows of his silken coif, lo, there came the hoarse cry of the ghost of Elsinore.

"*Akua! Akua!*" bawled the *kahus* and they fled the apparition. Their prophecy that the house of the Cookes would be haunted had taken a strange turn. It had fetched up the ghost of William Shakespeare.

When night fell the dolorous cry of the *kahus* was heard no more.

"Peace, how sweet it is," thought Juliette. But for her and Amos, how imperfect a thing was peace.

At two and three-year intervals Juliette brought forth five babies of their own. She lived in that "whirlpool of conflicting cares" which had engulfed Sybil Bingham and every other mission mother in the field.

"Now, could I feel that I have done all things well, I should go to bed happy and contented," she wrote at the close of a harrowing day. "Oh, could I know just what duty is, just how far the Lord would have me expose my own dear children for the good of these young Princes."

Amos plunged ahead in a race against the clock and the calendar, and Juliette observed:

"It has been rather heavy on Mr. Cooke having to teach subjects with which he is imperfectly acquainted, trigonometry, surveying, natural philosophy etc. He has been obliged to study nights in order to keep ahead of his class."

It was not a circumstance to keeping ahead of the Devil.

"Our scholars are getting older," reported the anxious foster mother, "and feeling their independence somewhat, they have made us more trouble of late than formerly. I speak of the three oldest boys. They have purchased wine secretly several times and twice have gone off in the night to drink it!!

"You must not be surprised to hear at some future time that they have fallen into the nets that are spread for their feet...foreigners have had a hand in what has been of late so saddening to our hearts...."

When Moses and Lot and Alexander were little boys, it had been Amos' custom to make his rounds after the children were in bed; he would bind up their cuts and sores and say a short prayer with them before he lowered the lamps.

One night, in the time of their youthful rebellion, the schoolmaster went his old route around the quadrangle. He paused at Alexander's door and knocked one sharp rap.

"Enter, sir!" the crown prince called out. He stood to receive his guardian.

Amos pushed the door open and walked in, a spindly little figure in faded black clothes that no longer fit but merely hung over his shoulders and hips.

He looked up at the boy he had reared. Alexander stood before him in the statuesque mold of the Kamehamehas. He faced his teacher with a lofty stance and his eyes gleamed defiance.

If Amos could have peered into the future he would have seen that no more than six years remained before this errant schoolboy would assume the crown and title of Kamehameha IV, monarch of Hawaii.

That night it was as well that he did not know it. He knew only that Alexander and his brothers were sheering off course so rapidly that he no longer could hope to govern them.

Since he had failed to regulate their conduct, he believed that all hopes concerning them also must fail. All at once the accumulation of trials and aggrevations seemed to have trammeled his spirit. He could not think what to do.

The prince stood stiff-necked and arrogant. He waited for Mr. Cooke to impose the old penalties for misbehavior. Instead, the unhappy man appeared to be looking for a place to sit down.

Alexander pulled his chair around, but Amos sat on the edge of the bed. He motioned to Alexander to take the chair.

A quarter of an hour passed. From every darkened room around the quadrangle the children watched Alexander's door. When it opened they saw the thin shadow of Mr. Cooke move along the courtyard wall until it reached his room. They

AMOS COOKE
with daughter Mary Annis
Hawaiian Mission Children's Society

heard the bolt of his door fall with a click. Very soon, all were lost in sleep except the schoolmaster and the heir to the throne.

Alexander lay in his cot and gazed at the moon as it rose over his window. He felt none of the resentment that put him in temper after he had been punished. This night he had received no punishment. Mr. Cooke had only talked in a low voice, saying some things that made the boy feel badly.

Alexander repeated to himself everything Amos had told him. It kept him restless till nearly dawn. He had got hold of an idea which in the years ahead, as man and king, he would call by the name of *moral responsibility.*

At the other end of the house Amos sat with sorrow in his heart and the conviction that he had fallen short in his duty. Tracking back through the years to see what he had done and failed to do, remembrance humiliated him all the more when he thought of the letter he had sent home when his school had just begun.

"My heart's desire and prayer to God has been and continues to be that I might be instrumental in setting a train of causes in motion that should be felt for good long after I may be laid aside...." were the words he had written.

"All, *all* must rest with the Lord!" Amos rebuked himself.

He tried to forget the vain pretension that once had allowed him to think that he would "set a train of causes in motion."

At last he ceased self reproach and sought comfort in prayer. Then he turned over the pages of his journal and took up his pen to record the events of the day:

Before retiring, I had an opportunity to testify to Alexander our great anxiety about him and Lot ...that I did not believe there would be a native King after the present one unless he or Lot were prepared for it; that their temptations were much greater than any one's & they could not stand against flattery and vices without Almighty aid; that a ship all sail & no ballast would soon be on her beam's end....

I also said that few princes would have submitted to teachers as they had, and stated that if my discipline had seemed too severe, I was sorry. I said that he and Lot ought to keep a journal & finally besought them to attend to religion *now.*

Amos had taught them better than he knew. Even in the time of their apparent failure Juliette caught an intimation of things to come and she ventured to speculate:

"Who can tell but what God has mercy yet in store for these people and that it may be communicated through these children."

Their mission, in a land that had never known other than despotic rulers, was to prepare the ground for benevolent government of a free people. Within the Christian home that was their school Amos and Juliette laid down the Golden Rule and they repeated to the children, times without number, the story of the Good Samaritan.

In the context of their teaching they sowed the seeds of liberal ideas: care for the poor and oppressed, comfort for the sick, education for the ignorant, humanitarian concern for the welfare and protection of all. They produced the first Hawaiian philanthropists to grace the island throne.

Five of their royal wards brought forth the fruit of their teaching when Alexander and Emma, reigning together, founded the Queen's Hospital;

JULIETTE COOKE
with son Clarence
Hawaiian Mission Children's Society

Bernice Pauahi made her gift of the Kamehameha Schools; William Lunalilo, the king who had been frightened by the *akuas*, provided a home for aged Hawaiians; and Queen Liliuokalani set aside royal treasure for the care of orphaned children.

Conceived in the hearts of the young *alii* who grew up in the Chiefs' Children's School, those humanitarian pillars of an isolated Pacific community gave evidence to the world of a civilized race of people who would in future command the respect of ministers and navies of nations around the globe.

Chapter 18

Lessons at the Chiefs' Children's School were well begun one morning when Kamehameha III arrived unexpectedly from Lahaina. He said he wished to inspect the school to see what advancement had been made by the princes and princesses.

Kauikeaouli presented a splendid figure in his white suit, but the brim of his Panama hat cast its shade aslant a dark and troubled face. The mouth, enhanced by beard and moustache, curved upward with a hint of scorn. The eyes were those of an offended man.

His majesty walked with Amos from room to room through the school. He stopped to hear the children sing and recite, and a little brightness seemed to relieve his sad spirit. When he examined their books and papers, perplexity clouded his eyes. Withdrawn and silent, he only nodded assent to Amos' invitation to share the scholars' noonday meal.

Juliette could not remember a more melancholy repast. When it was over and the king had

KAMEHAMEHA III
Drawing by Madge Tennent
Tennent Art Foundation Gallery

seen all concerning the school, and still he offered no word of sanction or reproof, her puzzlement came near to leading her out of bounds. She dared not attempt to alter the mood of a monarch, but she did contemplate some little query about his silence. In a moment Kauikeaouli took his leave and she was spared the shame of treading on tender ground.

Engrossed as she was with the care of royal progeny, Juliette had paid little attention to the sovereign who seemed to her little more than a myth. She could not reconcile her idea of kingly conduct with Kauikeaouli's habit of absenting himself almost wholly at Lahaina.

In the years ahead she would learn compassion for this fated man, and a first glimmer of understanding entered her heart when she heard him bid farewell to the princes at the Chiefs' Children's School.

The king stood at the gate with Alexander and his brothers. When he raised his hand to put on his hat he turned and looked back at the school.

"I wish my lot had been like yours," he told his heirs. "I deeply regret the foolish manner in which I spent the years of my youth."

Within an hour Kauikeaouli boarded his schooner. Like a dishonored man, he went back to self-imposed exile at Lahaina.

He had confirmed the truth of stories which had come to him there. He was told that sea captains and traffickers, looking in at the Chiefs' Children's School, opened their mouths in wonderment to see native children so quickly acquiring the stamp of civilized ladies and gentlemen. Foreigners who would threaten an older chief curried favor with the oncoming rulers. The royal scholars were as familiar with the protocol of nations as the adventurers themselves.

For Kauikeaouli, most of the transient *haoles* had only contempt. They castigated him for imposing primitive tabus on the land and labor of his people. Adroit foreigners, of course, were at liberty to coerce and plunder according to their own lights. When their greed provoked the king's wrath, they grunted "Heathen!" to absolve their transgressions.

They claimed that their property was subject to confiscation at the whim of a native, and they proposed to settle accounts by force. Other men called it intimidation with intent to exploit.

William Richards found a parable here.

Endeavoring to demonstrate principles of justice to his class of native chiefs at Lahaina, he asked:

"Do not these men from foreign countries abuse your king in much the same way that you oppress your own people?"

The corpulent old nobles sat cross-legged before him on the floor of the council house. They did not trouble themselves to answer, nor did Kauikeaouli who occupied a wooden bench in front of Mr. Richards. Instead of a textbook, the king held a handwritten translation of the American Declaration of Independence.

From the rear of the thatched pavilion two young natives looked over the backs of the silent assemblage. Their eyes had a lively look and there was some eagerness in their bearing, but they too remained mute. They sat with the ruling conclave only by virtue of being educated men, first graduates of Lahainaluna Seminary. It was not for them to speak except to answer the questions of the king.

"Every man derives his right to life and liberty from God," Mr. Richards continued.

"In enlightened nations the common people may engage in trade to their own benefit. But in countries where the right of property is withheld from the people in order to secure their obedience, the rulers are called unjust."

A doughty old chief cleared his throat. His voice rumbled up like thunder from the cavern of his chest.

"If we can not take away their lands, what will they care for us?" he growled. "They will be as rich as we!"

"The power of the law must be alike over rich and poor," Mr. Richards insisted. "In order to govern peacefully, the law must have power over all alike."

Richards rose from the mat and bade his pupils aloha. He stepped from the shade of the pavilion into the blazing sunlight and hurried off toward his house which stood just *mauka* of the council house.

His custom was to take his leave without ado, in the hope that Kauikeaouli and the chiefs would continue to discuss the things they had learned. Often they did, but on this day the king rose abruptly and beckoned to the educated natives. Boaz Mahune and David Malo came forward.

Kauikeaouli pointed to the place where Mr. Richards had sat. The young men dropped to the mat and crossed their legs in the posture of the chiefs. The king sat on the bench and said he wished to hear again the story of how the men of America had cast off the tabus of *Beretania* and made new laws for their people.

Mahune and Malo obeyed in the manner of ancient bards. Alternately they assumed the role of narrator and each vied for the honor of performing the most skillful rendition. Together, they conjured up an image of General George Washington and his Yankee soldiers as vivid, if not as authentic, as if the Hawaiian scholars had fought beside the rebels.

Mahune finished the story:

"The men of America were few, and they were poor in all things to make war against the men of *Beretania*. But God protected them because they obeyed His laws. And He made them a peaceful nation, where the chiefs cannot take from any man that which is his.

"No man may do violence to another without punishment, be he high or low, rich or poor. The laws must be kept by all men in America, and by all foreigners who come to live in their land."

Kauikeaouli stood again and faced the chiefs.

"I have sought for the *pono,* the right way," he said. "Yet men of many nations say we rule according to the laws of dark-hearted people, and they will not obey us.

"But if the law in my land were the same for every man, then I think that every man must obey."

Turning back to Malo and Mahune, the king held out the sheets on which William Richards had written the Declaration of Independence in Hawaiian.

"From this paper, and out of the book of God, take those laws that will end the quarreling and evil things amongst us. Set them down that I may see what they are."

He dropped the papers on the mat and walked away from the council house.

After several months, the scholarly young men announced that a code of laws had been prepared for the king. It was the work of Malo and Mahune, John Ii, Timothy Haalilio and other native men who had studied the history and government of nations. The writing of it fell to Boaz Mahune.

His first sentence professed the brotherhood of the Hawaiian race with all races of the world, after which he made a declaration of the rights of all people from every country:

> God hath made of one blood all nations of men, to dwell on the face of the earth in unity and blessedness. God has also bestowed certain rights alike on all men, and all chiefs, and all people of all lands.
> These are some of the rights which he has given alike to every man and every chief, life, limb, liberty, the labor of his hands, and production of his mind.

The document curtailed the power of king and chiefs in matters of life, property, taxation and punishment of the people. It provided for courts and judges and a legislative assembly to which the common people should send representatives.

Kauikeaouli called his chiefs together to judge whether it should become the law of the land.

The old men glared at the paper and looked from one to another. In a guttural harangue, one of the *alii* cried shame on young men who dared to tamper with the power of a king.

"My father ruled absolute. Tabu," Kauikeaouli replied. "After him, the *mana* is no more. What I desire is that all men live in peace."

Through the summer of 1840 Kauikeaouli and governing *alii* from all the islands pondered and argued and tried to find the *pono,* the right way to govern. Finally, the chiefs consented to the new constitution and Kauikeaouli proclaimed it to be the law of the land.

"Where," asked the justly-proud Hiram Bingham, "has the world ever seen a monarch so freely limiting his own power, inviting the common people to send representatives to aid him and his high-born counsellors in making laws...?

"In this particular, the king and chiefs of the Sandwich Islands stand unrivalled."

※ ※ ※

The first Hawaiian legislature convened at Lahaina on April 1, 1841. Fourteen chiefs and three representatives of the common people sat with Kauikeaouli to conduct the business of their troubled island nation.

The transition from feudal law to constitutional government had been achieved.... "Not by the noisy and turbulent demand of the people," Bingham noted, "...without a disastrous revolution, and without prostrating the feelings of loyalty, or evincing the slightest tendency to anarchy."

For the mission brethren and their wives who, step by step, had brought the nation forward in Christian conscience, the weary race seemed almost over.

Twenty-two years had passed since Kaahumanu had struck down the pagan idols of her people, twenty years since their first lesson pages were put into the hands of the natives. In two decades Hawaiian converts, with their teachers, had built eighteen Christian churches.

The Bible had been translated and twenty thousand copies were printed and bound.

Since 1820, when Sybil Bingham gathered together a band of orphans to make the first Hawaiian school, the mission had established the Chiefs' Children's School, Lahainaluna Seminary, four vocational boarding schools, twelve station schools and three hundred and fifty-seven common schools in which eighteen thousand children and adults were enrolled.

For their use, the brethren had written or translated—and printed in multiple copies—almost fifty text books and tracts. They included maps and illustrations which were engraved by Lorrin Andrews and his scholars at Lahainaluna. The mission press also had produced three newspapers and an almanac written in the native language.

One of the first acts of the constitutional government was to relieve the mission of the support and administration of elementary schools, island-wide. David Malo was appointed superintendent of schools and John Ii became administrator of Oahu schools.

Once again, the mission fathers met to consider the establishment of a school for their own children. It now seemed possible that one or two missionary couples might be diverted from other duties and set to educating the progeny of the lot.

A site was selected at the foot of Manoa valley. Kaahumanu had wished to give the land to Hiram

Bingham, but individual missionaries were not permitted to own land. Therefore the tract at Punahou had been given to the mission for some communal use.

The brethren envisioned a farm school to which mission families might send their children from all the islands. In some measure the scholars would earn their own keep; the boys would raise fruit and vegetables for their table and tend a small dairy herd. The girls would share domestic duties with the mothers.

"...Indeed we hope that light begins to dawn," Dr. Judd wrote to a secretary of the Board in Boston. "...There is a goodly number of the mission who are willing to keep their children here as long as possible, in the expectation that the time is at hand when God designs to open before them a field of usefulness in this their native country.

"Could their children be educated, and could they find employment here, there are many of us who would rejoice in such a prospect."

Chapter **19**

Many did rejoice in such a prospect, but for Sybil Bingham it had come too late.

She likened herself to a watch that was running down.

"Ere-long the mainspring must fail," she confessed. "If I should write just as I feel, I should write as I have not been accustomed to these twenty years.... My soul longs to lean on Jesus, that when his summons comes, I may calmly go and be at rest...."

Pain and weakness bore her down at last. Her lungs began to hemorrhage.

Dr. Judd told Hiram that a voyage to her native land might prolong Sybil's life. He appealed to the brethren concerning a leave of absence for the Binghams, "only for a season."

Permission was granted. The Reverend Richard Armstrong was summoned from his station on Maui to serve as pastor at Kawaiahao during Bingham's absence. Dr. Judd wrote to the gentlemen at the Mission Rooms in Boston:

"Little need be said on the occasion of the return of Rev. H. Bingham and family, as their features bear marks of having borne the burthen and heat of the day.... Our prayers and cordial sympathies attend them."

Supporting his invalid wife and followed by their three youngest children, Bingham, the prime mover of the Sandwich Islands mission, left his post. Among their fellow workers and throngs of natives who crowded round them at the harbor there were those who dared hope for Hiram's return. Most of them knew that Sybil was embarking on her last voyage.

The mission women bade her farewell and prayed she might live to see her firstborn Sophia and second daughter Lucy who, like her sister, had been sent to America when she was little more than a tot.

More than a year later the island families learned that parents and children were reunited at last. The Binghams had arrived in Connecticut where they found Sophia grown to womanhood, married and the mother of a baby daughter. Lucy was a sober New England school miss of fourteen years.

Sybil Bingham lingered for almost a decade, but with every passing year the hope that she and Hiram might return to the islands diminished. At last Bingham had to face the fact that time had passed him by.

He did not deny his bitter disappointment. Reviewing the turn of events which had ended his career in the foreign mission field, he wrote:

"Though as much had...been gained as the pioneers expected in their lifetime...yet, in some sense, the work of the mission was but begun. To lose health at such a time, or to be called to leave such a field in such a state, was a trial greater than that of leaving one's home and country to convey the Gospel to the heathen."

Nevertheless, he did not relinquish the cause. Still a handsome and commanding figure in his fifty-second year, Hiram Bingham traveled down to Washington to be received by President John Tyler and Secretary of State Daniel Webster. He visited Congress and presented the American statesmen with a copy of the Hawaiian Bible. He described to them the monumental advancement which had been made by the Sandwich Islanders between 1819 and 1841.

"Shall a nation be born in a day?" asked Bingham.

"However that question may be solved, the Hawaiian nation, after twenty-one years of acquaintance with Christianity, is but a youth...washed and trimmed, supplied with clothes and books, and endowed with a healthy and manly constitution, but...now needs the impress which the correct example and counsels of the older and more mature nations of the earth ought...to give it...."

Bingham's call for a "correct example of older and more mature nations" was timely. Several months before he presented his views in Washinton, the strife which erupted between a clique of Honolulu's foreign residents and the administrators of the native government made a mockery of his ambition.

The provocation was trivial. Kamehameha III had ordered two roads to be built: one leading up Nuuanu valley, the other from Honolulu toward Ewa. Governor Kekuanaoa had decreed that native men who were not otherwise taxed should work twelve days each month at road building.

Among those summoned were the household servants of certain British residents who protested to their consul Richard Charlton. He in turn upbraided Governor Kekuanaoa for daring to inconvenience Englishmen by such a levy.

"I tell you plainly that this work is for the Government...," the Hawaiian governor retorted. "I have not taken improperly, neither have I opposed, but you think to take away my works; and your communication is like opposing the command of my King to make the road...."

J. J. Jarves, a recently arrived Bostonian and editor of a newspaper in Honolulu, agreed with Governor Kekuanaoa that both sides of the controversy should be published. When it was done Charlton charged off to the house of the journalist and set upon him with a horsewhip.

Juliette Cooke described Charlton's assault on Editor Jarves and the fight that ensued:

"On arriving...he [Charlton] found Mr. Jarves, his wife and Mr. Marshall [a young American storekeeper]. They proceeded to business, but the Consul was laid sprawling by Mr. Marshall and received a pretty thorough drubbing, the young American not being careful of the hide of Her Majesty's Consul. He carries the marks of the conflict."

The British consul jotted down this latest episode in his book of grievances against the Hawaiian government.

No incident was too trifling, no trumped-up charge was too absurd to be recorded in it. He collected them all and enlarged on them. As a mason lays up brick upon brick, he set about building a dossier by which he meant to prove the unfitness of the native rulers to govern and, in particular, their unfitness to govern Englishmen.

Hawaiians and foreigners alike knew that Charlton's bullying was calculated—merely a prelude to the calling up of a British warship to deal with the natives. Repeatedly they had been threatened—by Englishmen, Frenchmen and Americans—and by 1842 William Richards reckoned that Kauikeaouli had been forced to pay nearly $30,000 in "reprisals." The Hawaiian government was almost impoverished.

The time had come to plead its cause, not with foreign functionaries in the Pacific, but with the heads of government in their respective countries.

William Richards prepared to embark on a diplomatic mission to Washington, Paris and London to ask for official recognition of Hawaiian independence.

Yet he must not leave the king without an advocate.

Kamehameha III sent word to Honolulu that he needed Dr. Judd. Gerrit answered the summons and when he arrived at Lahaina the king petitioned him to enter his service at once.

"Of one thing you may be certain," the doctor wrote, "I shall not consent to any arrangement which does not promise a greater sphere of usefulness."

Without much delay (and without waiting for the approval of his Board) Gerrit Judd agreed to quit the mission and devote himself to the cause of the Hawaiian nation.

At the same time he promised his offended brethren that he would not leave them comfortless. He would tend their families in illness and

TIMOTHY HAALILIO
Paris, 1843
Bernice P. Bishop Museum

WILLIAM RICHARDS
Paris, 1843
Bernice P. Bishop Museum

he would continue to dispense the mission medical supplies as long as his services were needed.

In May, 1842, the king appointed Dr. Judd to the first Hawaiian Treasury Board and commissioned him as the Government Recorder and Interpreter.

"His business shall be to superintend the arrangement of Government documents, and act as interpreter at all trials of foreigners before the Supreme Judges," Kamehameha III announced.

"He shall also give information as to the manner of conducting business in foreign countries. He shall also be present as interpreter whenever His Majesty transacts any Government business with any foreigner, and it shall be his duty to give information on the subject of that particular business as done in other countries. . . .

"It will therefore be particularly proper for foreigners who wish to speak to His Majesty on any business which requires official action, to first call on the legally appointed interpreter."

Dr. Judd planted himself directly in the path of all comers and William Richards took to the high seas with the exhortation "*E na hoahanau e pule oukou no makou.*" (Brethren, pray for us.)

Traveling with Richards as fellow emissary went Timothy Haalilio, Kauikeaouli's childhood companion. Like Obookiah, Haalilio was to capture the imagination and affectionate regard of his North Atlantic hosts. In their courts and assemblies he would win champions for his emerging race. Like Obookiah, he would not live to see his island homeland again.

Chapter **20**

By 1842 Honolulu was a frontier town filled with bickering exotics: Britons, Yankees, Spaniards, French and Chinese who mingled and married with Hawaiians, but who lived as Anglo-Saxons, Europeans and Orientals.

The outlanders did not call themselves colonists, yet neither were they vagabonds. Some had come to the islands with ambition and money; others brought only a skill and a strong back.

But those who stayed became investors in the ramshackle little market place of the Pacific. Amongst them were homesick men who went away for a season and returned with wives from their native lands. Their commitment in Honolulu was as permanent as that of the missionaries.

More than two dozen foreign merchants owned stores or warehouses and competed for the harbor trade. Scores of rugged workmen earned their keep as ship calkers, carpenters, sail makers, coopers, cabinet makers and cobblers. Or they set themselves up as saddle and harness makers, butchers, bakers, engravers and printers. Keepers of grog shops, boarding houses and bowling allies were as numerous as merchants.

The days of the sandalwood trade were gone, but the American whaling fleet had found a bonanza in the Pacific. In multiplying hundreds, whaling ships plied the seas off Japan and the Aleutian Islands in summer and hunted southern Pacific waters in winter. Twice a year, between hauls, the masters rendezvoused at the Sandwich Islands to buy provisions and refit their vessels.

At the ready was this community of tradesmen, prepared to meet the captains' demands and to supply the ribald pleasures for which many a sailor gave his last coin, or paid with his hat and his jacket.

The merchants and chandlers lived in shabby structures built along paths that lay shank-deep in mud or dust, depending on the rainfall. The best of their lodgings were two-story clapboard buildings with peaked roofs, or coral-stone cabins covered with thatching. The worst were rickety sheds around which were strewn dross and cinders, rags, bones and swill—offscourings of the day's toil in this jerry-built commercial outpost.

When the whaling fleet was out trade fell off. Boredom set in and, except for a few charitable fellows, the foreign colony livened up the winter and summer doldrums by baiting old Governor Kekuanaoa and castigating the missionaries. These diversions were eclipsed by an occasional stabbing or fist fight.

Except for MacAfee there was scarcely a white man on the island who could call to mind a time when Honolulu had no governor and no missionaries to belabor. MacAfee could, and often he thought of the days when he was rescued and nursed back to life by half-naked pagans on this very ground. If he counted aright he was sixty years old; it was more than half a lifetime ago that he had made his pact with "auld Tammie."

MacAfee's loyalty to the Kamehamehas remained unchanged. As to the missionaries, he owed them no allegiance nor would he care to be one. Nevertheless he held them in esteem. If Mr. Richards took it into his head to scud off to foreign courts and confront sovereigns and ministers on behalf of Kauikeaouli, MacAfee could not but admire him and wish him Godspeed. But the canny old Scot scented trouble.

A band of Honolulu merchants and functionaries was fanning up the old row again. They conceded that a civilized Hawaiian nation had been brought into being, but only by an insignificant parcel of Yankee psalm singers.

What of that? Other men from other countries served the Lord. They read their Bibles and often they prayed. But waking, sleeping or praying, more than one harbor entrepreneur nursed the obsession that hard work and enterprise (their own, not the missionaries') had made of these islands a commercial plum ready for the plucking.

With tactless gusto they harped on the seizure of other Pacific islands by foreign naval officers and they noted that in every case the thing had been done quietly, benevolently—almost unnoticed.

But what had they here? A zealous Yankee in almost every pulpit in the land. More of them hovering over the native schools. The heirs to the throne reared and indoctrinated by New England missionaries, and the ubiquitous Dr. Judd in constant attendance on the king and every phase of government. Now William Richards had turned his back on accredited consuls and sped off to claim sovereign independence for this recently barbarous race of people!

Damn the missionaries!

On a hot afternoon in August when Richards and Haalilio had been gone almost two months, MacAfee dragged his old chair out of the store and set it in the shade of his *hau* trees. He had planted a row of them in hopes that one day their tangling branches would form an arbor over the dooryard.

Sunlight flickered through the leaves and dappled the pages of a Hawaiian newspaper which he spread out on the butt end of a barrel. That his reading stand reeked of whale oil (betraying an earlier usefulness in the fishery) did not offend the old man. But he was vexed, and the source of his indignation was the newspaper.

He folded it in half and jabbed at the ill-fitting spectacles which slid down over the bridge of his nose. His eyes glowered as he reflected that in two decades he had listened to more than he cared to hear about the meddling of the missionaries in native affairs.

"'Tis a ver-r-ry great pity that no mon would come to the aid o' the poor heathen at the Marquesas Islands!" he snorted. "Nay but the French admiral would call it meddlin'!"

He re-read the brief report of the arrival of a French sloop of war at Honolulu harbor. The writer noted that the firing of an off-port salute had been omitted and that, on stepping ashore, the French commander had the honor to announce that his flag now waved over the Marquesas Islands.

MacAfee studied the final sentence:

"The French officers took possession of that land called Nukuhiwa and they placed there 500 soldiers and some sailors, and Captain Mallet is saying the French fleet will be coming to Hawaii . . . ."

A shadow fell over his paper. The Scot cocked one eyebrow before he looked up. Beside him stood James Marshall, the young American storekeeper who had earned MacAfee's good opinion the day he trounced Consul Charlton.

"Jamie lad!" MacAfee exclaimed. "Glad I am that ye walked this way!"

The young man stated his business.

"You may know, sir, that I've had no cargo these six months. Until we get another ship I am without tea, either to drink or to sell. Thinking you might relish a bottle of sherry wine, I've brought it along . . ."

"Tea he says!" hooted MacAfee. "Strong drink be more fittin' the lad that knocks m'lord Charlton sprawlin' in the dust! But aye, Jamie, ye'll have the tea an' I'll have the wine. Now lad, just open yer bottle an' we'll share a drap together."

The old fellow stumped off to fetch tumblers and a tea canister from his stores. Jamie took his seat on the barrel, though he had not been brought up to sit on barrels.

The son of a prosperous banker in Massachusetts, young Marshall had quit his studies at Harvard in favor of an ocean voyage. About a year since, he had chosen to try his luck as a Sandwich Islands merchant.

MacAfee credited the lad with a measure of sense and sobriety uncommon in most hazarding youths of his acquaintance. But he reckoned Jamie would need all his wits, and a stout heart too, to keep from foundering in this mud hole of contention. However that might be, as long as young Marshall cared to bide at Honolulu Mac-Afee was glad of his presence.

"Lad, lad!" the old fellow cried when Jamie rose and placed his wine bottle and three small coins on the barrel head.

"Ye've not pulled the cork! An' what be this money?"

"For the tea," Marshall answered, "though it's not full payment."

"Nay, Jamie. We did barter the wine for the tea, the tea for the wine, an' no more. Now then, just draw the cork an' tilt the bottle. Fix it in mind, lad, ye'll soon be a poorer mon than ye now are should ye persist in givin' out good coin for the likes o' yon tea canister."

"A man who cannot pay a debt ought not to multiply it," said Marshall.

"Tush! Belay that," MacAfee chided, "'tis a din to the ears. Sit a while now an' tell me what keeps ye in any kind o' funds."

Marshall poured the wine and handed a tumbler to his host.

"Why sir," he answered, "while the trade is poor I've found some employment with Dr. Judd at the government office. Copying documents for the king is the work he gives me . . ."

"So! Here's a shopkeeper hankerin' for adventure," cried MacAfee. "Now Jamie, cling on to the doctor's coat tails an' I warrant ye'll see a

242

bit o' hurly-burly."

"Trouble with the French?"

"Nay. 'Tis trouble he'll get wi' Charlton."

"With Charlton? But sir, the French threaten most. By spring you'll see their ships up from the Marquesas..."

"Exactly so, Jamie, exactly so! An' do ye not glimpse m'lord Charlton stalkin' the harbor like a shabby lion, growlin' an' snarlin' an' switchin' his tail?"

"I do."

"An' have ye not heard that a land called New Zealand far south o' here is lately possessed by the British? Think ye then that John Bull will suffer the Frenchmen to take *these* islands? He dinna forget how it were his own Captain Cook that found 'em first."

"Captain Cook is a long time dead," said Marshall, "and Charlton is a pretty long way from home."

"Ye may say so, right an' proper," MacAfee conceded. "But lad, 'twill ne'er do to misjudge the plaguesome mon. For nigh on twenty years his blood be all afroth an' aboil to make these isles the Great Britain o' the Pacific!"

"I would say then that he had overdrawn his bow," Jamie observed.

That the Hawaiian kingdom had no defense against foreign aggression, from whatever quarter, young Marshall understood as well as any man. But he had no conception of the virulence that sometimes may possess a man who has nursed ambition overlong and sees his time running out.

Before another month passed, Charlton was gone. He had been seen climbing up the ladder of a ship that lay off port. When the vessel sailed the pilot boat returned to harbor, but the British consul was not on it.

Rumor flew from tongue to tongue: Charlton had sailed for Valparaiso to rendezvous with the British Pacific fleet. Charlton had been recalled to London. Charlton had disappeared! How? Why?

James Marshall was one of the first to learn the truth. Dr. Judd called him to the government office to make copies of Charlton's last official letter to the king. Gerrit laid the document before him and Jamie stared at it, incredulous. The letter began:

Sir,
From the insults received from the local authorities of your Majesty's Government, and from the insult offered to my Sovereign, Her most Gracious Majesty, Victoria ... by Matthew Kekuanaoa, Governor of this island; and for other weighty causes affecting the interests of Her Majesty's subjects in these islands, I consider it my bounden duty to repair immediately to Great Britain, to lay statements before Her Majesty's Government, and have therefore appointed—as I am fully authorized to do—Alexander Simpson, Esquire, to act as Consul until Her Majesty's pleasure be known.
Your Majesty's Government has more than once insulted the British flag; but you must not suppose that it will be passed over in silence. Justice, though tardy, will reach you; and it is you, not your advisers, that will be punished. ...

The threat contained in Charlton's letter was compounded by his act of deputizing Alexander

Simpson, an Englishman whose conduct toward the native government was, if possible, more menacing than his own.

Kamehameha III decided to be rid of both of them. He declared that since Charlton had left his post, and since Alexander Simpson was a *Pelekane ho'opilikia*, the Hawaiian kingdom would do without a British consul. He refused to acknowledge the appointment.

Crusty old Governor Kekuanaoa sent off a note addressed to A. Simpson, Esq.:

> This is my fixed thought, which I now make known to you:
> It is not proper for you to perform the duties of Consul between this kingdom and the subjects of Great Britain, because you despise the authorities of the kingdom, and you say you are going to make a disturbance in the kingdom.
> If you think proper to go to Valparaiso to complain, then go; and, if proper to go quite to Great Britain, then go. Therefore I do not consent for you to work with me. No indeed.
> I am with respect,
>
> KEKUANAOA

Dr. Judd wrote to Richards and Haalilio, urging them to cut short their negotiations in Washington and to press on with all possible haste for London. He reckoned that a letter might reach them either at Washington or Boston, and to both cities he dispatched copies of his message:

> Mr. Charlton left the Islands for Mazatlan the last of Sept. bound to England for the purpose of pressing complaints against the government and to oppose the objects of your Embassy. You will therefore, in case this letter finds you in the U.S., hasten to England as fast as possible, and I shall accordingly send no more letters to you in

the United States at present. . . .

You cannot imagine how much anxiety I feel in the success of this mission and how anxious I am you should get to England. The efforts made here to thwart you will do mischief if they have the first hearing. . . .

Richard Charlton, bounding over the Pacific toward the coast of Mexico, felt a similar compulsion to be swift in his travels. However, since his ship touched at Mazatlan where he encountered several high-ranking officers of the British Pacific squadron, he tarried there long enough to pour out his grievances against the Hawaiian government.

He had just set forth again for London when Rear Admiral Richard Thomas, commander of Her Majesty's fleet in the Pacific, received an urgent complaint written by Alexander Simpson, the *persona non grata* British representative in Honolulu.

Outraged by the snub he had received from the Hawaiian king and chiefs, Mr. Simpson called for a British man-of-war to be dispatched to the port of Honolulu.

The admiral complied. On January 17, 1843, he ordered the frigate *Carysfort*, commanded by Lord George Paulet, to sail for the Sandwich and Society Islands. With respect to his mission at Honolulu, the admiral informed Paulet:

You are hereby directed to put to sea in Her Majesty's ship "Carysfort" under your command, and proceed without delay in the first instance to Woahoo, Sandwich Islands, where you will put yourself in communication with Her Majesty's Consul, for the purpose of affording him support in case he should require the same, for the more effectual performance of his duties. . . .

Chapter 21

H er Britannic Majesty's Ship *Carysfort* sailed into Honolulu harbor February 11, 1843. The Hawaiians said it was a "sick wind" that brought her and Levi Chamberlain noted in his journal:

"...ship of war entered the harbor this morning. The wind having changed to the southward, she came in under full sail."

Rain squalls obscured the masts and hull of the black frigate as she approached the island. At the mouth of the harbor the *Carysfort* emerged in sunlight and, turning broadside, showed the white wale of a British man-of-war. Along that horizontal stripe her gun ports gaped like teeth bared in a malicious grin.

For six days the errand of the Captain Lord George Paulet remained a mystery. He received no government agents aboard ship. When he was informed that King Kamehameha III was on Maui the British commander decreed that either his majesty must be sent for at once or the *Carysfort* would sail for the royal residence. Governor Kekuanaoa replied that the king would come to

247

the captain.

While all Honolulu waited, the American sloop of war *Boston* put in from China, Australia and Tahiti. Her officers carried the news that England's flag waved over Hong Kong and they confirmed another report: the tricolor of France had been raised at Tahiti.

Brooding over the plight of the dispossessed, and anxious for the security of Hawaii's king, Laura Judd exclaimed: *"Why can they not be let alone for a little while?"*

Kamehameha III no longer expected to be let alone. He also knew the hazard of being left alone with the captain of a war vessel. Therefore, when the king arrived from Maui and Lord George Paulet demanded that he name the hour for a private interview, Kauikeaouli refused. He informed the British commander that he would receive written communication from the *Carysfort* or he would send Dr. Judd to confer with his lordship.

A rude retort came back at midnight. Paulet wrote to advise the king that if the Hawaiian government did not comply with his demands by four o'clock next day the *Carysfort* would commence hostilities.

He stipulated the immediate acknowledgment of Alexander Simpson as acting consul for Great Britain, to be followed by a twenty-one-gun salute. Further, he demanded that the king satisfy the claims of Richard Charlton, Alexander Simpson, and all other aggrieved Englishmen, resident or transient, in the Sandwich Islands.

While he was about his official correspondence Lord George also penned a note to Captain J. C. Long, commander of the U.S.S. *Boston*:

"Sir: I have the honor to notify you that Her Britannic Majesty's Ship *Carysfort*, under my command, will be prepared to make an attack upon this town at 4 p.m. tomorrow (Saturday) in the event of the demand now forwarded by me to the King of these islands not being complied with by that time.

> I have the honor to be, Sir,
> Your most ob't Humble Servant,
> GEO. PAULET, Captain."

Next morning at dawn the English brig *Julia* was towed out of the harbor. Wives and children

HMS CARYSFORT

Hawaii State Archives

of British residents were hurried down to the wharf, put into boats and rowed off to take refuge aboard her.

Paulet gave the command to clear the decks of the *Carysfort* for action. He brought his ship into fighting position and ordered her guns run out. Opposite the native fort she lay in the water like a black monster bristling for the attack.

At ten o'clock Captain Long of the *Boston* was heard from. In a public notice which he caused to be posted in the town, he offered asylum to as many American families as he could accommodate aboard his ship. Simultaneously he addressed the commanders of all American vessels in the port of Honolulu:

"Gentlemen: I have to request that you will cause all the boats belonging to your respective ships to be manned...to render any assistance which may be required by citizens of the United States...pending the difficulties between this Gov't and that of Great Britain...."

From mid-morning until early afternoon Kauikeaouli sat in his straw palace at Halekauwila and watched while the harbor town emptied. Dust billows flew over the dirty little lanes along which white men pushed carts filled with money boxes and ledgers and clothing. Their women ran alongside, each clutching a child or an armload of pots and kettles, pillows and quilts to be carried aboard the refuge ships.

The natives, who were offered no sanctuary, abandoned their grass huts. Some of them scrambled to high ground above the valleys. Others flocked to Waikiki to play in the surf while the foreign *pilikia* was at Honolulu.

The mission fathers gathered their families together for prayer at Kawaiahao. They suspected Paulet of making an empty threat in order to bring Kauikeaouli to his knees without the necessity of firing a single cannon. They would not oblige his lordship by clambering up the ladders of neutral ships.

Lord George waited on his quarter-deck. He took no notice of the absence of missionaries among the throngs hastening toward the wharf; he was satisfied that the extraordinary spectacle already under way would be adequate to his purpose.

Shortly before two o'clock he was handed a message from Kauikeaouli:

"We have received your letter and the demands which accompanied it. ... We shall comply with your demands ... but we must do so under protest, and shall embrace the earliest opportunity of representing our case more fully to Her Britannic Majesty's government through our minister...."

Paulet turned livid. He heartily misliked the warp of this native king who had been forced to submit, but who still had the impudence to refute the fact. He would teach the ignorant creature how to defer to a servant of the British Crown.

Notwithstanding Kauikeaouli's note of compliance, it pleased Lord George to hold the *Carysfort* in fighting trim and keep the muzzles of her guns yawning over the port of Honolulu. When he renewed his demand for an interview with the king of the Sandwich Islands, Kauikeaouli had no choice but to yield.

Paulet and his lieutenants stood at attention to receive the native king aboard the *Carysfort*. In his military uniform, accoutered with gold lace, epaulets and sword, his Hawaiian majesty ascended the accommodation ladder to the deck of the war vessel.

Close behind him—uninvited, unexpected and unwanted by Lord George—climbed the stocky figure of Dr. G. P. Judd buttoned up in a shabby gray cloth coat. The doctor stepped aboard to the ruffle of drums and the piping of silver whistles, a glaring breach of protocol which even his lordship was at a loss to correct.

Paulet shot a contemptuous glance at the interloper before he turned on his heel and led the way to the great cabin. He stepped in ahead of his guests and showed Kauikeaouli to a sofa covered with pale golden India cloth. He seated himself before his chart table and ignored Dr. Judd. Unabashed, Gerrit strode across the cabin behind his unwilling host and squatted on the lid of a mahogany chest.

The captain's steward carried in a decanter and three silver goblets on a tray. Stiff as a pike, he waited while his lordship poured wine for the king. When it was passed to him, Kauikeaouli grunted *"Aole"* and waved the servant off.

"We will have no wine," Dr. Judd announced.

Lord George chose to disregard the voice from the rear. He filled his cup and raised it to the king. He paused and eyed him with a cold stare. Kauikeaouli, unmindful of his host, was leaning over, then under the table, the better to view a great terrestrial globe which stood beside the captain's chair.

When the king stood up to examine a barometer, then a marine compass that was mounted overhead, Paulet waived the amenities and drank alone.

DR. GERRIT P. JUDD
Daguerreotype, 1849
Hawaiian Mission Children's Society

He spoke at last and his utterance was like the clap of a pistol.

"I am told your majesty enjoys a fair comprehension of the English language! I am further informed that your majesty is quite able to speak it!"

Kauikeaouli merely prolonged his observation of Lord George, the cabin and all it contained.

Again came the voice of Dr. Judd behind Paulet's ear:

"His majesty is pleased to speak only in the native tongue. I am here to convey to you the sense of his remarks—and to acquaint him with the object of your visit."

Lord George swung around to rid himself of the intruder. He might as well have thought to remove an oaken beam from his ship. Dr. Judd, having lodged his broad seat on the lid of the chest, appeared to be as permanently situated as the coffer itself. He regarded his lordship with such a froward eye that Paulet abandoned his first impulse which was to order him off the vessel at once.

While the captain sought to quell the Yankee doctor with a glare, Gerrit took the measure of his adversary.

Rather undersized he was, and underseasoned too, thought Judd. He took note of the bold blue eyes, the fresh complexion and a tumble of chestnut curls which revealed the youth of this tormentor. There was a petulance about him which caused Dr. Judd greater anxiety than he customarily felt in the presence of foreigners who considered it their duty to chastise the natives.

His misgivings proved valid. A more preposterous confrontation than that which now took place aboard the *Carysfort* he could not have imagined.

He saw at once that Paulet would reap the fruit of Charlton's determination to bring the Hawaiian Islands under British rule. His lordship had only to "make assurance double sure"—to the everlasting glory of himself, his queen and country.

Paulet was armed with a list of Charlton's old grievances, of which he had neither personal knowledge nor proof of their validity. He commenced by demanding that Kauikeaouli ratify a 299-year lease (made out in favor of the British consul) to a tract of Honolulu beach land which Kaahumanu had left to her heirs.

The king replied that no chief could have leased the land to Richard Charlton without the consent of the old regent, and he did not believe she had granted it. Nevertheless he instructed Dr. Judd to say to Paulet, "There is the land, go and take it."

Lord George pressed on. The king must make amends to another class of Britons—merchants and captains—who claimed to have suffered loss because of Hawaiian court decisions, or the lack of them.

"How do you say the king has done wrong?" Dr. Judd demanded. "A sovereign is neither judge nor constable. He cannot be acquainted with the merit or the want of merit in every foreign contention."

"We deem it a strange neglect," Paulet remarked coolly. "It appears to us an acknowledgment of his incapacity to rule."

Gerrit clenched his fingers over the ends of the chest and strove to put a hobble on his temper.

He replied, "Sir, I know that you think you act on good testimony. But the opinion which has been presented to you is altogether erroneous.

"Therefore I propose that you, together with Captain Long of the United States Ship *Boston*, make fair examination of the evidence. We could hope that after the facts have been weighed..."

Paulet brought the flat of his hand down on the table and made the wine cups dance.

"I will brook no interference, Dr. Judd! No interference!

"Now, sir, you will inform your king that I demand an immediate reversal of the absurd and unjust decisions which have given my countrymen cause for grievance.

"Further, I direct that his majesty must pay damages. Mr. Simpson informs me that the very least of the bill of accounts will be four hundred dollars owing for a ship's chronometer. Beyond that he totals some eighty thousand dollars for loss of revenue and inconvenience to Englishmen doing business at these islands."

Dr. Judd sprang to his feet. He crossed the cabin and planted his bulk before the chart table. He looked at Paulet with such fierce contempt that for a moment the young nobleman felt on the brink of some discomfiture.

Outwardly, he remained impervious. While he waited for the king, or the king's man, to speak, Lord George savored another cup of wine.

He would not look at Dr. Judd but, glancing across the table at Kauikeaouli, his lordship saw that a most extraordinary change had occurred in the fellow's physiognomy. In place of the open, almost childlike curiosity which had marked his features a moment before, Kamehameha III now wore the mask of a barbarian.

The heavy eyelids were lowered, the mouth was hostile and the flesh of his brow and cheeks appeared bloodless, almost stonelike. Paulet saw imprinted on that dark countenance the bitterness of a wronged and helpless man. It was a sight which he found repellent. He chose to ignore it.

In his humiliation, Kauikeaouli reverted to a primitive means of communication among Polynesians—a curious telepathy in which the rhetoric of the eye serves in place of speech. Mute as a post, he conveyed to Dr. Judd his readiness to capitulate.

Lord George noticed but did not comprehend the subtle communion. He destroyed it with a single thrust.

"Now, sir!" he barked, "I cannot doubt that the king has heard and understood my demands. You will inform him that I am waiting for his answer."

"It will be my duty to do so," said Dr. Judd, "after the king has had time to reflect. His reply will be set down in writing and delivered to you aboard ship. But sir, I pray you will first consider the consequences to this struggling nation if the claims of Mr. Simpson are allowed.

"You have commanded his majesty to overturn the decisions of our court—a thing both illegal and oppressive. If you force him to such an act of injustice, his government and treasury must be exposed to attack from all sides. I leave you to judge with what alacrity French and American residents would press new claims.

"Were theirs added to yours, sir, the forced indebtedness of this government would soar to more than one hundred thousand dollars."

Paulet touched the terrestrial globe and set it in motion.

"Your king ought not to have allowed British interests to suffer," he replied.

Kauikeaouli watched the globe spin around. Dazed and distracted, in memory he saw himself a child again and he recalled the voice of Mrs. Bingham saying to him, "Kauikeaouli, here is a map of the world. You must repeat after me the names of the countries as I point to them."

For a moment he was struck by the sense of wonder he had felt when he first saw the whole world spread out before him. He remembered his pride when Mrs. Bingham said he might keep the map, and his little prayer that in the time of his manhood he would acquit himself as handsomely as the kings and chiefs of those great lands which lay at the other side of the world.

Paulet spun the wooden sphere again. It no longer waked in Kauikeaouli any sense of wonder or delight—or pride. He knew now that he could only watch while a white hand, reaching out from a gold-banded sleeve, manipulated the globe. His own hands, plump, brown and impotent, lay helpless on the stranger's table.

Dr. Judd and Kauikeaouli were rowed ashore in the captain's gig. No sooner had they returned to the straw palace than they were confronted with the work of other pale hands. Yankees and Frenchmen, having got wind of the new impasse, and fearful lest the guns of the *Carysfort* blast their homes and shops to rubble, had united in the hour of crisis.

"Let the king cede the islands to the United States and France!" they had cried. "Let him seek a joint protectorate!"

To hurry him toward that compromise, they had drawn up a deed of cession. It was delivered to the palace and its authors withdrew to await the king's decision.

Kauikeaouli held the document in one hand and with the other he divested himself of sword, braid and epaulets and unhooked his collar. He made slow work of reading while he tried to unfasten a row of gold buttons at the front of his coat. Vexed with his multiple chores, he thrust the paper into Dr. Judd's hand and asked for his *manao*.

Gerrit scowled at the thing, tossed it aside and seated himself on the mat beside a pile of the king's trappings. Kauikeaouli stripped to the waist and lay face downward before the *mauka* doorway. Trade winds, soothing as a tepid bath, caressed his bare flesh; for a moment he might have slept if the doctor had not spoken:

"To solicit the custody of other nations is to step on dangerous ground. Would the United States be party to a joint protectorate? Forlorn hope! Would France, once invested with the power to protect, ever relinquish her hold on these islands?"

The question hung in the air.

"Yet to provoke the British is to invite a bloody collision. Some well-aimed broadsides, a landing party to take possession . . . the reign of the Kamehamehas would cease forever. There would be no redress."

Kauikeaouli made no sign or sound and almost half an hour passed in silence. At last the king heaved a dreadful sigh and his whole body shuddered.

"I will not die piecemeal," he muttered. "Let the men of *Beretania* take all."

When he had said it he pressed his face into the mat and breathed the musky scent of *hala,* sweeter and more pungent in the small depression where the plaiting was damp with his tears.

Could Gerrit Judd or any of the mission brethren deny the mischief which would strip this tormented king of land and money, perhaps his crown? Could they dispute the necessity which forced Kauikeaouli to bow to his oppressor? They could not.

They could raise up a proud race of men, turn them from heathen ways and build them a nation that was grounded in law and letters, schools and churches. Like their fathers before them, God had made them draftsmen and craftsmen of Christian dominions where none had been before.

But when their work was almost done, did the Lord intend that they should stand mute before the usurper and "let the men of *Beretania* take all"?

Mistrusting with every fiber of his being that Lord George Paulet had been sent to do the will of God, Dr. Judd began to entertain similar doubts concerning the will of Paulet's fleet admiral.

Certain aspects of his lordship's conduct seemed not altogether in keeping with the limited resources at his command. A single frigate (Gerrit judged the *Carysfort* to be a war vessel of no more than the sixth class) was ordered to the Sandwich Islands—but for what purpose?

Considering that the French had employed a fleet of seven men-of-war to subdue Pacific island kingdoms more remote and less protected than that of Kamehameha III, Dr. Judd suspected that Lord George might not have been vested with unlimited authority when he sailed for Honolulu. He guessed correctly that Paulet carried no orders to take possession of the islands.

However that might be, his British lordship now stood on the brink of conquest. Ambition drove him and discretion was not in him. Let the Hawaiian monarch or Dr. Judd make a single misstep and he would seize the kingdom entire. They did not need to be reminded of the fate of Tahiti and the Marquesas Islands.

Gerrit knew that the English nobleman could overreach himself with impunity, but only if Kauikeaouli gave him cause to act. If Paulet took the islands without provocation, even his own government must charge him with an act of flagrant injustice.

Judd leaned forward and touched Kauikeaouli's back.

"We'll bait the hook with a fish too big to swallow," he said. "Paulet will not refuse if we offer to cede the islands to Great Britain. But mind, a cession made under threat of hostilities. We will debate the issue then, not with this hothead, but with Her Majesty's government in London."

Kauikeaouli raised his face. Gerrit saw only sorrow on the heavy features. The king could not fully share the expectation that Queen Victoria would restore his sovereignty because he had been dealt with unjustly. Or because the queen's ministers might consider it inexpedient to tilt the balance between three maritime nations. Or because the United States would certainly object, might even interfere, if the whole story were told in America.

"To delay is to lose all," Gerrit warned. "The thing must be challenged at once, on both sides of the Atlantic. A protest to Her Majesty's government in London. Full accounts of the cession to be carried posthaste to Washington and Paris. We will set up such a hue and cry as will yet mend the wrong done here today."

Gerrit Judd believed that whatever he could conceive he could accomplish. From a distance of more than twenty thousand miles he proposed to beard the British lion in his den, cry shame before the world and thereby see an end to the coercion of this struggling race of islanders. It was a plan to tempt Providence, but clearly it was England that flew in the face of Providence, not Dr. Judd!

"Richards and Haalilio, if they live, will have reached London by now," he told the king. "Already they may have achieved some recognition. If so, they will have only this transgression of Paulet to dispose of. If not..."

Kauikeaouli lifted his hand in a gesture of resignation. He was exhausted by the week's grinding debate and he could endure no more.

"Let it go," he repeated. "If I get help, I get it; if not, let it go. I can do no more."

Dr. Judd, having decided on the remedy, set about effecting a cure at once. He stepped to a long table at the center of the palace and reached for pen and paper. Dating the top sheet February 25, 1843, he began to draft the official document of cession:

"In consequence of the difficulties in which we

find ourselves involved...we do hereby cede the group of islands known as the Hawaiian (or Sandwich) Islands, unto the Right Honorable Lord George Paulet, Capt. of Her Britannic Majesty's ship of war *Carysfort,* representing Her Majesty Victoria Queen of Great Britain and Ireland from this date and for the time being...."

Kauikeaouli listened to the relentless scratching of the pen. Grief stifles the heart and numbs the tongue; still the king wished to speak to his people before they heard the deed of cession read and saw the Hawaiian flag hauled down from its mast at the fort.

He raised himself from the mat and approached the table. He would put down his thoughts in Hawaiian; what he had to say need not concern the Englishmen. To those men who understood his language and grieved for the *pilikia* that had come among them, Kauikeaouli wrote:

Where are you, chiefs, people, and commons from my ancestor, and people from foreign lands? Hear ye, I make known to you that I am in perplexity by reason of difficulties into which I have been brought without cause; therefore I have given away the life of our land, hear ye!

It now devolved on Dr. Judd to find the means to justify not only the conduct of the king, but his own as well.

Chapter 22

Victory for Paulet was not sweet. It was "conditional" and it hung like a millstone round his neck.

He had raised the British flag over Honolulu—and ordered every Hawaiian flag destroyed—and Yankee merchants still prattled about "when the truth is told...an appeal to the honor of the English queen...peaceful intervention by the United States or France."

Rushing to defend both *coup d'etat* and career, Lord George began to weave a tangled web.

He was obliged to dispatch an account of his proceedings to the admiral of the British squadron in the Pacific. Paulet deemed it more politic to report direct to England.

His story of the possession of the Kamehameha kingdom in the name of Queen Victoria must be hand-carried to Her Majesty's foreign minister in London—and by no less a contender for British rule in the islands than Alexander Simpson.

Three Hawaiian schooners lay in the harbor. Commandeering the lot and renaming them the

Albert, the *Victoria* and the *Adelaide*, Paulet ordered the *Albert* made ready to sail. He assigned junior officers from the *Carysfort* to command the native crew. Their orders were to transport Mr. Simpson to a Mexican port, first leg of his journey to England.

Now let Dr. Judd hold his tongue and his pen! He'd get no document of protest dispatched aboard the *Albert*, and the remaining ships would be impounded. Lord George resolved to cut off every channel of communication by which the native king (or his meddling missionary henchmen) might present his case abroad.

The Hawaiian chiefs withdrew. Kauikeaouli returned to Lahaina. Dr. Judd stalked the harbor like a sentry. Still the *Albert* did not sail.

The first British midshipman to step aboard her was met by a company of American merchants who challenged his right of access. They claimed custody of the vessel until she made a run to the Gulf of California and returned with a shipment of gold coin.

To support their contention they showed a sailing charter granted by Kamehameha III prior to the date of cession. They sent the British seaman off with a warning to Paulet; it referred to the folly of attempting to seize American property, even that of temporary status.

Lord George was quick to alter course. He conceded the right of the Yankees to control the vessel, but he offered to strike a bargain with them. If they would relinquish their charter he would order the *Albert* to whatever port they designated. He would permit them to send one passenger, an agent approved by his lordship, who would conduct their business on the coast. He added that since the ship would sail under British colors, the American traders would be spared the expense of sending her out and back again.

His offer was accepted and officers and crew went aboard the *Albert*.

From chandlery to warehouse the story was told: Paulet had been challenged and the Yankees had got the best of the bargain. A loud hurrah went up along the waterfront where knots of grim-faced men stood in front of their stores and jeered at the *Carysfort* marines on patrol. Native boys, scampering through the harbor lanes with handfuls of mud and stones, played a nimble game with the "lobster backs" and the Americans roared at the skirmish.

Jamie Marshall pushed his way through the guffawing crowd and made for the wharf. Probably he would not have been noticed if he had not carried a small cowhide trunk on one shoulder.

"So it's you, James Marshall!" shouted a hairy giant of a blacksmith. "So it's Mr. Marshall goin' to sea under the British flag!"

"An' what be *ye* doin' under the same banner?" retorted old MacAfee. He pointed a crooked finger at the Union Jack that jerked and flapped over the fort.

From across the path the eye of Dr. Judd fastened on MacAfee and flashed a warning. Marshall slackened his pace, then moved on without glancing at the old man. MacAfee watched him and guessed that Jamie had been chosen to slip through the British embargo. He framed the silent message "Fare ye well Jamie lad, an' God speed ye home agin."

A red-coated marine stood on the wall of the fort and blew a bugle call that signaled the end of day. Marching two abreast, fresh troops of *Carysfort* marines swung out of the main gate and tramped off to patrol the harbor. The night watch was doubled. Paulet's orders were to seize any person found loitering near the water's edge.

A crew of kanakas, conscripted to load stone ballast aboard the *Albert*, was watched by a lynx-eyed old man-of-war's-man who counted the natives every time they boarded or left ship. James Marshall was ordered off by a midshipman. The American agent, though his passage had been approved by Paulet, was not permitted to put his trunk aboard until the next day.

The *Carysfort* swung gently at anchor and her lamps cast trails of light on the darkening water. In the great cabin Lord George sat at dinner with Alexander Simpson. Paulet's report to the British Foreign Office lay on the chart table and the Englishmen drank to the success of their maneuver. Within twenty-four hours, Simpson would be on his way to London.

That night nothing disturbed the peace of the quiet village. When James Marshall left the wharf he went to his lodging and ate a solitary meal of beef and taro. Afterwards he extinguished his lamp and walked up the road from the harbor toward the new stone church at Kawaiahao.

Just short of the church he turned *mauka* and made for a low coral blockhouse—the resting place of Hawaii's departed rulers. At the door of the mausoleum Jamie found Governor Kekuanaoa waiting for him.

Kekuanaoa thrust a long iron key into the lock. The bolt tumbled and the door swung open on creaking hinges. In a yellow light that glowed at the center of the chamber Dr. Judd stood before a coffin.

Kekuanaoa nudged Marshall's elbow and the young man stepped forward. The door was pulled to and locked behind him.

Jamie stood still in his tracks. Dr. Judd acknowledged his presence with a glance and bent over the coffin again. Its crimson velvet lid was strewn with boxes and pens, crumpled paper and sheets of foolscap. The doctor jabbed his pen at a brass inkstand and resumed writing.

His whale oil lamp shed a dim glow on the other furnishings of the sepulcher. Jamie observed three long boxes draped with purple satin which he presumed to be the cribs of Liholiho and his queens Kamamalu and Kinau. Judging by its size, Marshall was sure the central coffin contained no less a friend to her physician than the regent Kaahumanu. It occurred to him that in this hour of crisis Dr. Judd could not have found safer refuge or a quieter office than this crypt of the departed *alii*.

"You were not seen walking this way?" Gerrit asked.

"I think not, sir," replied Jamie.

"You have thought the matter over?"

"I have."

"You are prepared to make your way to London and lay these documents before the proper ministers?"

"I have not the means to go to London, sir. But if they are provided I am ready."

"Paulet has not the means of dispatching Alexander Simpson without also sending you," Gerrit retorted. "Your transit to the Gulf of California is assured."

Jamie nodded.

"I understand that, sir. But you have not told me how I should buy passage for England. I am mindful that the treasury is all but drained..."

"Firewood, young man," Judd interrupted. "Firewood will take you to England. These islands abound in trees, do they not? Captain Brewer will take the wood. He'll get a profit fueling whale vessels. In return I have from him the price of your passage to London and back."

He leaned over the coffin and peered at Jamie.

"Step forward, Marshall!" he commanded. "How will you know what you're about if you hang back there in the dark?"

Jamie moved toward Kaahumanu's coffin and the doctor reached for a tin box that was half hidden among the paraphernalia on his makeshift desk.

"There is your money box," said Gerrit. He lifted the lid and ran a finger over the gold coins that were stacked in rows. A packet of bank notes was stuffed in one end of the rectangular case.

"Here, your credentials."

Judd stepped aside and motioned Jamie to read the document which he had addressed from Kamehameha III, Native King of the Sandwich Islands, to Her Most Gracious Majesty Victoria the First, Queen of the United Kingdom of Great Britain and Ireland:

Great and good Friend,

We have made choice of   as our Envoy Extraordinary and Minister Plenipotentiary to Your Majesty.

He is especially charged in relation to recent occurrences which have transpired with us, and is expected to act in unison with the Rev. William

Richards, whom we have previously appointed our Envoy to Your Majesty....

We therefore request Your Most Gracious Majesty to receive him favourably, and to give full credence to what he shall say on the part of our government....

Marshall stopped reading and eyed Dr. Judd.

"The government must depend wholly on the justice of its cause, not the experience of its ambassador," he protested. "You know, sir, that I am no wise versed in diplomacy..."

"If an experienced ambassador could be found we would send him," Gerrit answered. "Do what you know is right, Jamie, and trust to God, not your worldly wisdom. Now attend to what I say. Much needs to be done before sunrise."

Jamie waited. Dr. Judd was preoccupied with sorting his papers. He separated draft copies from pages that were unmarred by corrections and arranged the lot in orderly piles.

"Here," he began, "a first draft of your credentials. Here, my draft of a letter of protest to Queen Victoria. Another to President Tyler. One to King Louis Philippe.

"I have to leave you for a while, Marshall. Employ yourself at copying. When you have written three perfect manuscripts of each document, destroy my drafts. But mind this, Jamie. Lest these papers fall into the hands of the British tonight I have not put your name to the credentials. Do not write it yourself until after you have got to sea."

At the center of the coffin lid there remained one immaculate copy of each document written in Judd's hand. The doctor folded these separately and stuffed them in the breast pocket of his coat.

Scanning the jumble of objects which lay before him on the red velvet cover, he selected two pens, a vial of ink and a handful of lucifer matches and packed them in a wooden box.

"If you finish writing before I return, snuff out the lamp," he said. "It consumes the air and inflames the eyes."

He thrust the box under his arm, made for the door and drummed on it with his fingers. The key rattled in the lock and the door opened. Dr. Judd stepped out.

The lock fell again and Marshall, left alone in the sanctum of the dead, bent to his task of reproducing appeals for justice for a native king whose existence the world had hardly heard of.

❋ ❋ ❋

Dr. Judd walked past the mission houses. He had a rendezvous at Waikiki where, despite a bright moon, British sentries would not distinguish a king's canoe from those of native fishermen.

A crew of paddlers, which he had dispatched before dawn, had left Oahu by starlight and steered for a bank of hanging clouds to the southeast. By noon they should have beached at Lahaina. Now he reckoned that the great koa canoe, with Kauikeaouli as passenger, would be gliding toward Diamond Hill.

At Waikiki Gerrit hid himself in the coconut grove and gazed seaward through its leaning pillars. He watched the lines of silver breakers advancing over the bay. Almost an hour passed before he spied the glint of a paddle and the hull of the canoe as it rose on a swell, then dropped out of sight. For a time he saw nothing more.

The king's paddlers, waiting for a long comber that would carry them in, held their craft as quiescent as a seabird resting in a trough of the ocean. The canoe rose again and angled on a wave. White water curled beneath the prow. The wave broke and it bore the Kamehameha canoe shoreward on a line of alabaster foam.

Gerrit kicked the litter underfoot and found a dry coconut frond. He bound the leaves native-fashion and, striking a handful of matches across the sole of his boot, he fired the brand and held it aloft.

Six figures jumped from the canoe. They ran across the beach and made their way through the grove toward the flare.

The king arrived like a fugitive, barefoot and clad in the dark wool blouse and trousers of a common sailor. His paddlers were naked except for *malos* that were soaked with sea water. In the torchlight their bodies gleamed like sculptured bronze.

One of them took the flare from Gerrit's hand, and in this strange place and circumstance, with a thousand dark plumes swaying overhead, Kauikeaouli and Dr. Judd sat down to conduct the affairs of state.

Gerrit planted his wooden box on the ground between them. He noticed the king's hands were wet and offered him a handkerchief to dry them before presenting letters addressed to the heads of nations.

Kauikeaouli took the pages and read them. He nodded and repeated, *"Maikai, maikai... ae."*

Judd studied his features to see if anything in the documents perplexed the king.

"*Papa hana maikai,*" Kauikeaouli answered the unspoken query.

"Then they need only the signature and seal," said the doctor.

He took from his box a pen and the vial of ink. Replacing the lid, he offered it to Kauikeaouli for a writing board. Gerrit laid the sheets before him and dipped the pen. The king wrote at the end of each document:

Judd glanced at the kanaka who held the torch. He made a downward gesture with his arm. The other natives seized dry palm fronds and dug a furrow in the sandy soil. The torch was thrust into it and covered with sand.

As silently as they had come into the grove, Kauikeaouli and his men moved out to the beach. Gerrit waited until he saw the canoe drive through the silver breakers and the paddlers, steering by a star, set a course for Lahaina.

❋ ❋ ❋

Several hours after midnight young Marshall heard the door of the tomb swing open again and the voice of Dr. Judd ordered him to light the lamp. In its dingy yellow glow the haggard men bade each other a hasty farewell and Jamie stepped out alone. In his blouse he carried the documents which bore Kauikeaouli's signature.

He made his way back to his lodging and waited there for daylight. When it came, he fell into a doze from which he woke with a start. His room was flooded with sunlight.

Jamie sprang from his cot and dressed in a black suit. Beneath the ruffled bosom of his shirt he stowed the king's messages and, without waiting to eat a breakfast, he shouldered his trunk, walked to the wharf and boarded the *Albert*. The schooner sailed at midnight.

❋ ❋ ❋

The pages which Jamie had copied remained in a stack on Kaahumanu's coffin. One night, when Marshall had got well on his way to England, Dr. Judd went to the native administration office and dismantled it. He carted all Hawaiian government records off to the mausoleum.

As the state papers disappeared overnight, so did the remainder of the king's treasury. Old Governor Kekuanaoa escorted the doctor on his pre-dawn foray and the two men lugged a strongbox full of specie into the tomb. They set it plumb with Kaahumanu's bier. There it would remain as long as the British held the islands.

Gerrit looked at the money chest and reckoned it might serve as a place to sit while he did the work of king's deputy. To try its height, he straddled the lid and hooked his heels over the iron hasps. It would do, just as the regent's coffin would do for a desk. He adjusted his lamp and set to work.

"Kauka okole kala" (doctor who sits on the money) grunted Kekuanaoa and he unlocked the door and let himself out of the musty cell.

As the months dragged on and Britain's flag still flew over the islands, Dr. Judd went about his business in daylight hours. At night he sat firmly astride the money chest and managed Hawaiian government affairs incognito. He labored over the velvet-covered coffin until his whale oil lamp did "consume the air and inflame the eyes," and the ghastly expedient began to take its toll.

Chapter 23

Five days after the *Albert* sailed Dr. Judd delivered his wife of their eighth child. In the months that followed, Laura was left much alone except for the brood which swarmed round her for every necessity. But she took up her recording pen and wrote an account of the predicament "in which husband placed himself for the sake of the nation."

For five long months we ground in the prison-house, like poor blind Samson. After the cession my husband came home and threw himself down, utterly exhausted in body and mind....I sat by him two hours, ransacking heart and brain for arguments of consolation.

There was no stain on his character; he had committed no crime. No blood had been shed. He had done his best, and what more could be required? I advised him to lie down in the arms of a kind Heavenly Father, and in good time he would come forth with new strength for the conflict; and it was so....

We had just risen from family devotions one morning...when we were startled by the native

LAURA JUDD
Daguerreotype, 1849

Hawaiian Mission Children's Society

cry of "sail ho!" An immense man-of-war hove in sight, floating the flag of an English rear-admiral of the white....

The errand of Rear Admiral Richard Thomas, commander-in-chief of Her Britannic Majesty's naval vessels in the Pacific, was to remedy the "unlooked-for" blunder of Lord George Paulet before news of it should rouse all Christendom.

In London, James Marshall, William Richards and Timothy Haalilio were challenging the right of Paulet to take possession of the Sandwich Islands. In Washington, Richards and Haalilio had pleaded the cause of the Hawaiian people with the heads of American government. President Tyler told Congress:

> It cannot but be in conformity with the interest and the wishes of the government and the people of the United States that this community, thus existing in the midst of a vast expanse of ocean, should be respected, and all its rights strictly and conscientiously regarded...while its nearer approach to this continent...could not but create dissatisfaction on the part of the United States at any attempt, by another Power...to take possession of the islands, colonize them and subvert the native Government.

Reports of rising antagonism in America moved the Earl of Aberdeen, Queen Victoria's minister of foreign affairs, to pen a note to the Honorable Mr. H. S. Fox, British ambassador in Washington:

> Her Majesty's Government have received, via Mexico, information...that Lord George Paulet, of Her Majesty's ship "Carysfort," took possession of the Sandwich Islands, in the name and on

the behalf of Her Majesty the Queen, on the 25th of February last.

I have to desire that you will lose no time in officially assuring the Government of the United States, that this Act was entirely unauthorized by Her Majesty's Government, and that they purpose, with the least practicable delay, to call on Lord George Paulet to render an account of his conduct.

Admiral Thomas had arrived in Honolulu to do precisely that. Obedient to British Foreign Office policy, he informed King Kamehameha III and the principal chiefs of the Sandwich Islands:

...The Commander-in-chief of Her Britannic Majesty's ships and vessels in the Pacific...as the highest local representative of Her Majesty Queen Victoria, Queen of the United Kingdom of Great Britain and Ireland, hereby declares and makes manifest that he does not accept of the provisional cession of the Hawaiian Islands, made on the 25th day of February, 1843, but that he considers His Majesty Kamehameha III, the legitimate King of those islands....

The disclaimer was sent to Dr. Judd with instructions that its contents be made known to the Hawaiian people in their own language.

Admiral Thomas then ordered his lieutenants to see to the manufacture of a new Hawaiian flag. Paulet had left not one intact.

Aboard the admiral's ship *Dublin* British sail makers fashioned the banner from strips of bunting. On the morning of July 31, 1843, it was taken ashore in the admiral's gig and carried to an open field beyond Kawaiahao.

"...Marines from the *Dublin, Carysfort,* and

other English ships, under their respective officers, were ordered to be on the parade ground on the plain, in full uniform, at eight o'clock A. M., under Lieutenant Frere," Laura Judd wrote.

Out of the valleys, up from the bays and beaches, throngs of natives and foreigners hurried to the arena. Laura, joining her husband and the sisters and brethren of the mission, walked to the place where all Honolulu awaited the restoration of the Kamehamehas.

"Admiral Thomas preceded the king in the carriage of the latter." Mrs. Judd continued. "When the king, on horseback, arrived upon the ground, the admiral gave him a salute of twenty-one guns from the field artillery of the squadron. Lord George was not present.

"At a signal given, the English flag-officer advanced toward the king, surrounded by his guards, bowed his colors most gracefully, while the splendid Hawaiian standard was unfurled, and, as the breeze caught its ample folds, displaying the dove and olive branch in the center, the guns from the *Carysfort* fired first, then the *Dublin,* and the other English ships, followed by two American ships-of-war. Each poured forth a salute of twenty-one guns, which was responded to by the fort and battery of old Punch Bowl."

MacAfee, who lay on a pile of mats in his trading shack, heard the uproar and cursed his feebleness. The old Scot was ailing. Sweat streamed from his body; his head seemed to be turning in a whirl and he could not get his bearings. When the dizziness passed he struggled up and made his way to the dooryard.

A pall of smoke hung over Honolulu. Under the eerie canopy MacAfee spied more than a hundred

British marines moving in retreat from Punch-bowl toward the harbor. They tramped past his dooryard, every man resplendent in white trousers and scarlet jacket crossed with white braces. Burnished caps and firearms glistened beneath the banners that rippled over the marching corps.

Looking after them as they neared the wharf, the old man saw that the yardarms of all the ships in port were manned by blue-jacketed sailors ordered aloft to salute the king of the Sandwich Islands. MacAfee thought himself the only man in Honolulu who did no honor to Kauikeaouli that day.

He turned and hobbled back into his store. From beneath the trading counter he pulled out a white bowl and a bottle of brandy.

Not since he had gone to bid Hiram Bingham farewell had MacAfee walked out to Kawaiahao, nor had he ever visited the stone church, but the people were called there now to give thanks and he felt a hankering to be there too.

He swallowed some brandy and felt his heart-beat quicken. When he had taken half the bowlful some little strength seemed to flow into his arms and legs. He poured another tot and carried it to the back room.

Fumbling through a pile of trade goods, he found a coarse linen blouse and a pair of trousers that was clean and whole. Slowly he discarded his ragged togs and clad himself anew. The exertion made cold sweat start from every pore.

He plunged a hand into the brandy bowl, scooped up some liquor, swabbed his face and neck with it and drank the remainder. Thus cleansed and fortified, MacAfee emerged from his shack and started for the church.

When he got there the service had commenced. MacAfee climbed the steps of the church and stood outside the vestibule door. He felt ready to faint. He shaded his head from the sun with one bony hand and steadied himself against a pillar with the other. When he peered in at the congregation he could scarcely credit his eyes.

In his weakness and confusion he was like some old Rip Van Winkle of the south seas whom time had passed by but who, when he woke, found astonishing changes all around him. Within the wide sanctuary foreign merchants dressed in suits of fawn-colored broadcloth sat beside pale ladies who wore lace collars and plumed bonnets. Ships' officers, stiffly arrayed in dress uniforms, mustered together in cliques of two and three.

A thousand natives—every man breeched and jacketed, every woman gowned in silk or calico—sat in orderly rows. Along the side walls, crowded against the window casements, portly troops of the king's regiment stood at attention.

The central aisle presented a spectacle such as MacAfee had never laid eyes on before. A wooden arch spanned the passageway and over the heads of the people there floated the flags of many nations. The Hawaiian standard was flanked by the Stars and Stripes of the United States, the Union Jack of Great Britain, the colors of France and Belgium and more which the old fellow could not distinguish.

Beneath the flags Kamehameha III sat with a concourse of native chiefs: the governors of the four principal islands and the *alii* and commoners of the first Hawaiian legislature.

MacAfee could hear the voice of Dr. Judd. Gerrit stood facing the king's party; he was reading his translation of Admiral Thomas' declaration, a public acknowledgment that the people of Hawaii had learned to read and to write, to govern equitably and treat with foreign nations.

"...To the illustrious circumnavigator Captain Cook, as the first discoverer, the inhabitants of the Sandwich Islands owe their admission into the great family of civilized man," ran the admiral's summation, "...and by the well-directed energies, the ceaseless perseverance of the American missionaries to the establishment of a religion...accompanied by the advantages of instruction and civilization...."

"Oh, aye," thought MacAfee, "An' 'tis Dr. Judd been the stumblin' block o' the likes o' Lord George Paulet!"

The king rose and stepped forward under the galaxy of flags. As his majesty advanced so did MacAfee, for the old sailor was all but bewitched by so grand a sight. He edged his way to the entrance of the center aisle and stared down the passage at the stately figure of the king.

Kamehameha III wore the uniform of a European monarch. His coat of scarlet twill was buckled with gold. The breast and collar gleamed with thread-of-gold embroidery. From waist to knee he was clad in white breeches and his legs were encased in high black boots that shone like mirrors. The hilt of his sword and his epaulets glittered with gold filigree. In the crook of one arm he carried a tall black cap embellished with white cock feathers.

Kauikeaouli glanced at the apparition standing at the other end of the aisle; he recognized the *haole* whom his father had befriended. MacAfee, gazing back at the splendid king, forgot himself and mused aloud: "Auld Tammie would ne'er ken the lad!"

"Auld Tammie" had been dead not yet a quarter of a century when Kauikeaouli, the child of his last years, stepped upon the stage of modern history.

The king spoke with the mellifluence—and the charity—of Polynesians. He uttered no vindictive word to shame those foreigners who, from his childhood, had made him an uncertain wanderer in his own land. When he had finished, he pronounced a benediction:

"*Ua mau ke ea o ka aina i ka pono.*" (The life of the land is established in righteousness.)

"So it be, lad. So it be," whispered MacAfee and he bowed his head in prayer.

He did not care to invoke the Lord overlong. When it appeared that one and another would take a turn in the pulpit to recount the blessings of the day, MacAfee faced about and made his way down the long steps of the church. He moved slowly, for the mid-day sun beating on his head made him dizzy again.

He reached the ground and bore off to the *mauka* side of the church where he stood in a sliver of shade cast by the wall of the great temple. He decided to rest there, out of the way of the crowd, until he could make his way home alone. He had no wish to mingle with a celebrating multitude.

The populace began to emerge from church. They overran the steps and churned up the white coral gravel in the dooryard. MacAfee turned to make a further retreat and it vexed him to discover that he was being followed. The persistent footfalls advanced. When he had walked the length of the church wall the old fellow stepped aside to let the trekkers pass.

A group of men and women walked by, looking neither to right nor left. They were a dour lot, buttoned up in rusty black gowns and coats and trousers made of threadbare woolen stuff. Their thin bodies and angular faces looked as haggard as their garments.

MacAfee had no doubt they were missionaries. But so many of that ilk had come and gone, and the years had so altered their appearance that he no longer recognized them. Likely he had known these weary souls once. He tried to recall something of the look of their faces before they were aged by toil and illness.

He watched them until they passed beyond the adobe walls of the mission compound and went their ways among the dwelling houses. Some of the men stopped at the mission print shop. Others climbed the awkward stairs of the book bindery. There were two who entered a strange slope-roofed edifice which MacAfee knew to be the depository of their goods in common stock.

The old man wondered how many more of their band still labored on the islands to north and southward. He did not know. He could not remember. Nor did he want to think of it now. He wished only that the crowd would disperse so he could go home.

Taking refuge behind the church, MacAfee discovered that he was standing near the place where, some twenty years before, his friend Bingham had opened the ground to bury two infant sons. He searched about and found the barrows.

"Poor, wee sickly babes," he said as he stepped around the depressions in the ground. "Did the Lord allow, ye'd be braw young men ere now."

Yet all around him lay the graves of other mission lads—and more of the lasses.

"So little time..." he thought and he called to mind the day when he had walked out to make acquaintance with Bingham and the brethren. Just here, he remembered, stood the grass huts where they lived and taught a school and where the young brides were put to bed to bring forth the first white infants in the land.

MacAfee had thought their footing in this raw, alien land was so precarious that it was only kindness to warn them off.

"'Tis no the natives will hate yer teachin'," he had said to Bingham. "'Tis the men o' yer own race. They do not love the gospel here."

But Bingham had already entered into his labor. Against those who detested his presence he had no power except his will. They could not bend his will.

"I say to you that the word of God must command the respect of all men," he had told the Scot.

At dusk that evening MacAfee fell asleep sitting in his old round-backed chair. Before morning he died.

His body was found by a sailor off a whaling vessel. The lad had received liberty to go ashore and he ran up to MacAfee's to barter a piece of scrimshaw, in return for which he had been promised a stick of tobacco and a new cap.

The bargain had been made a fortnight earlier when the youth wandered up to the trading shack and said to MacAfee that his ship would sail soon and he was in need of a woolen cap to cover his ears when he would have to run aloft in freezing winds off Cape Horn. He held out his palm and showed MacAfee a few coins.

"Will it be enough, sir?" he asked.

The old fellow cocked a bristly white eyebrow and peered first at the small sum, then at the boy who proffered it. A wight of no more than fifteen years, his face was framed by a cluster of yellow curls. His eyes, dark and forlorn, implored the old man.

MacAfee lowered his gaze and stared at a trinket which hung from a cord around the lad's neck. It was a piece of ivory on which was etched the form of a spouting whale.

The boy moved his fingers and the coins clinked.

"'Twill no be sufficient!" said MacAfee. "But should ye care to part wi' that bit o' scrimshaw, I might give ye the cap an' a stick o' tobacco."

The sailor's hand darted up and covered the ornament.

"I'll not trade this one, sir. But there's another aboard ship. 'Tis a piece of whale tooth, fine and white and most as long as your foot. On its side is drawn the likeness of a vessel, full-rigged."

"A vessel full-rigged!" exclaimed MacAfee. "Now there's a pretty sight! Bring it, lad. Bring it. I've just a hankerin' for such."

When he brought it he found the old man slumped back in his chair. MacAfee's limbs were stiff and his eyes gazed up in a wild stare. The fingers of one hand were drawn up like a bird's claws and in them was clutched a small paper book. It was his Hawaiian hymnal.

The boy laid his scrimshaw in a pile of flannel

on the trading counter. Squatting on his haunches, he studied the corpse. When he was sure it would not move or speak, he faced around and began to search through the goods under the counter.

He pulled out a black worsted cap, shook the dust from it and drew it over his curls. Without rising, he shifted his supple little body along the length of the counter and his hands made quick thrusts among MacAfee's stores of tea and sugar and knives and brandy. At last he discovered a box filled with tobacco. As he pulled it forth his elbow touched the hand of the dead man.

He heard a faint thump and whirled around. The hymnal had dropped out of MacAfee's hand. The sailor glanced at it. He would have been glad to have a book, but he could not read the Hawaiian words on the pages that lay open before him.

A scrap of loose paper peeped from the edge of the little volume. He pulled it out and read the lines that were scrawled across it:

If I should die in this land Whatever I possess in Trade Goods and Eatables shall go to Hiram Bingham to share with the mission families. For they do Labor hard without a farthing to call their own.

Ian MacAfee, Sandwich Islands trader
January 1, 1830

The boy slipped the paper back between the pages of the hymnal and set it on the mat where it had fallen. Quick as a monkey, he grabbed half a dozen sticks of tobacco, stuffed them under his cap and jumped to his feet. As he ran for the open doorway he caught up the scrimshaw from its bed of flannel and hid it in his blouse.

He stopped at the threshold and, seeing he was

not observed, sauntered forth under the bright morning sun. Stepping along toward the harbor, he whistled a merry tune. He had made a three-years' voyage in a Pacific whaler and his ship was homeward bound.

EPILOGUE

Seventy-one men and seventy-four women served in the American Mission to Hawaii from 1820 to 1848.

They established twenty-two mission settlements on five islands, built forty dwelling houses and filled the land with churches and schools for native children and adults.

The men of the mission operated two printing offices and four presses on which they produced in the Hawaiian language twenty thousand Bibles, thirty thousand New Testaments, three newspapers and more than seventy texts on history, science, government, geography, mathematics, medicine, surveying, navigation, grammar, religion and morals.

In 1841 they built Punahou School, a thatch-roofed boarding school for their children.

By some mission parents the undertaking was termed an "experiment"; by all it was hailed as a blessing. It ended the sad necessity of parting with their sons and daughters of tender years in order to give them uninterrupted schooling in America.

Early the next year the Prudential Committee of the American Board of Commissioners for Foreign Missions voted to abolish the "common stock" method of supporting missionaries in the Sandwich Islands.

Henceforth, married males received $450 per year and those stationed at Honolulu were allowed an additional $50 annually. The work of unmarried males was valued at $275 per year; unmarried females received $175 per year. Allowances for the support of mission children were set at $30 per year for a child under ten years old and $75 per year for children over ten and under eighteen years of age.

By 1848 the ABCFM was ready to release its laborers in the Hawaiian field. The islands were recognized as a literate nation of free Christian people.

Members of the mission who had survived their errand in the Sandwich Islands (only six years of which had brought them any financial remuneration) faced a critical decision. They could return to America, but the Hawaiian government and the Board in Boston encouraged them to remain in the islands.

To stay would be to risk the future of their children in a land where industry scarcely existed and where the opportunity to earn a living still had to be created. Most of the retiring missionaries were past middle age and their health was impaired.

They were offered the houses which they had built and the use of a few horses, carts and cattle which were owned by the mission. As laymen they would be free to engage in trade, a privilege which had been denied them as long as they labored under the rule of the ABCFM.

Fifty missionaries chose to remain in the islands. To support themselves they farmed, sold beef and butter, preached, taught school, surveyed, dug ditches and took in boarders. A few entered government service.

There were four who bought and sold merchandise. Others who were adept at printing, engraving or book binding employed those skills which they had learned during their mission service.

The years of the fathers were numbered and they died poor. In the land where they had raised up the pillars of religion, education and democratic principles of government, some of their sons—no more than a dozen—joined the ranks of the pioneer builders of Hawaii's economy.

They began as wage earners and manual laborers in the second half of the nineteenth century; their contribution to the development and civic improvement of each of the major islands can scarcely be estimated.

Among them were men who engineered irrigation systems which turned masses of worthless land into productive sugar fields. Others improved harbors, increased trade and shipping, built a railway and initiated the first labor-management profit sharing system in Hawaii.

By dint of hard labor and ingenuity, some of them made money. Those who did, remembering the cause to which their parents' lives had been dedicated, multiplied their works throughout the islands.

Prosperous sons and daughters of missionaries continued to build new schools and churches, medical and cultural facilities, welfare centers and homes for the indigent.

When they died most of them left trust funds which, having increased in value over the years, provide several millions of dollars annually for the support of religious, educational, humanitarian and cultural institutions throughout the modern state of Hawaii.

Island business enterprises which missionaries or their children pioneered in the years of their poverty include Alexander & Baldwin, Inc., Castle & Cooke, Inc., Kohala Sugar Co., Grove Farm

Plantation and *The Honolulu Advertiser.*

Schools and other institutions which they established, and which still serve the people of Hawaii, include Punahou, Mid-Pacific Institute, Mauna Olu College, Lahainaluna School, the Hawaiian Evangelical Association (Hawaii Conference of the United Church of Christ), *The Friend*, the Kindergarten and Children's Aid Association, Kauikeolani Children's Hospital, the Honolulu Academy of Arts, the Hawaiian Mission Children's Society, Daughters of Hawaii, Moanalua Gardens, the Aquarium at Waikiki, Lyman House Memorial in Hilo, Lihue Parish House on Kauai and the Waioli Tea Room, founded for the benefit of the Salvation Army in Honolulu.

Countless other agencies which missionaries or their children initiated have merged with, or been taken over by newer organizations.

... they may rest from their labors, and their works do follow them.

BIBLIOGRAPHY

Unpublished Material

American Board of Commissioners for Foreign Missions annual reports and letters to Sandwich Islands missionaries

Early Hawaiian government documents

Journals and diaries of Sandwich Islands missionaries

Letters and journals of traders and foreign residents of the Sandwich Islands, other than missionaries

Levi Chamberlain's account book

Memoirs of children of Sandwich Islands missionaries

Personal letters of Sandwich Islands missionaries

Records of general meetings of the Sandwich Islands Mission

Reminiscences of Honolulu 35 Years Ago by Henry Sheldon (typescript)

Reports and letters from Sandwich Islands missionaries to the American Board of Commissioners for Foreign Missions

Unpublished Minutes of the Prudential Meetings of the Mission

Published Material

Alexander, Mary Charlotte, and Dodge, Charlotte Peabody, *Punahou—1841-1941* Berkeley, 1941

Ancient Hawaiian Civilization Honolulu, 1933

Anderson, Rufus, *History of the Sandwich Islands Mission* Boston, 1870

Ballou, Howard M., and Carter, George R., *The History of the Hawaiian Mission Press, With a Bibliography of the Earlier Publications* Honolulu, 1908

Bingham, Hiram, *A Residence of Twenty-One Years in the Sandwich Islands* Hartford and New York, 1847

Bishop, Sereno E., *Reminiscences of Old Hawaii* Honolulu, 1916

Bradley, Harold W., *The American Frontier in Hawaii* Stanford, 1942

Brookes, Jean I., *International Rivalry in the Pacific Islands 1800-1875* Berkeley and Los Angeles, 1941

Byron, Rt. Hon. Lord George, *Voyage of H.M.S. Blonde to the Sandwich Islands in the years 1824-1825* London, 1826

Campbell, Archibald, *A Voyage Round the World, From 1806 to 1812* Honolulu, 1967

Castle, William Richards Jr., *Life of Samuel Northrup Castle* Honolulu, 1960

Castle, William Richards *Reminiscences of William Richards Castle* Honolulu, 1960

Coan, Mrs. Titus, *A Brief Sketch of the Missionary Life of Mrs. Sybil Moseley Bingham* Honolulu, 1895

Correspondence Relative to the Sandwich Islands 1824-1843 [London, 1843]

Damon, Ethel, *Koamalu* Honolulu, 1931

Damon, Ethel, *The Stone Church at Kawaiahao* Honolulu, 1945

Diary of Andrew Bloxam Honolulu, 1925

Dictionary of American Biography New York, 1957

Dibble, Sheldon, *A History of the Sandwich Islands* Honolulu, 1909

Dibble, Sheldon, *History and General Views of the Sandwich Islands Mission* New York, 1839

Dodge, Ernest Stanley, *New England and the South Seas* Cambridge, 1965

Fragments II Honolulu, 1911

Fragments IV Honolulu, 1928

Frear, Walter F., *Anti-Missionary Criticism with Reference to Hawaii* Honolulu, 1935

Halford, Francis John, *9 Doctors and God* Honolulu, 1954

Hawaiian Club Papers Boston, 1868

Haynes, Merritt Way, *The Student's History of Printing* New York, 1930

Hobbs, Jean, *Hawaii: A Pageant of the Soil* Stanford, 1935

Ii, John Papa, *Fragments of Hawaiian History* Honolulu, 1959

Instructions of the Prudential Committee of the American Board of Commissioners for Foreign Missions to the Sandwich Islands Mission Lahainaluna, 1838

Judd, Gerrit P. IV, *Dr. Judd, Hawaii's Friend* Honolulu, 1960

Judd, Laura Fish, *Honolulu* Honolulu, 1928

Kamakau, Samuel M., *Ruling Chiefs of Hawaii* Honolulu, 1961

Kuykendall, Ralph S., *The Hawaiian Kingdom, 1778-1854* Honolulu, 1957

Loomis, Albertine, *Grapes of Canaan* Honolulu, 1966

Lyman, Henry M., *Hawaiian Yesterdays* Chicago, 1906

Macrae, James, *With Lord Byron at the Sandwich Islands in 1825* Honolulu, 1922

Maurer, Oscar E., *Three Early Christian Leaders of Hawaii* Honolulu, 1945

Melville, Herman, *Typee* New York, 1962

Memoirs of Henry Obookiah Elizabethtown, N.J., 1819

Missionary Album Honolulu, 1937

A Narrative of Five Youths From the Sandwich Islands New York, 1816

Pacific Islands Year Book and Who's Who, 9th edition Sydney, 1963

Paulding, Hiram, *Journal of a Cruise of the United States Schooner Dolphin* New York, 1831

Pukui, Mary Kawena, and Elbert, Samuel H., *Hawaiian-English Dictionary* University of Hawaii Press, 1957

Polk, Ralph W., *The Practice of Printing* Illinois, c1952

Report of the Proceedings and Evidence in the Arbitration Between the King and Government of the Hawaiian Islands and Messrs. Ladd & Co. Honolulu, 1846

Reynolds, John N., *Voyage of the United States Frigate Potomac* New York, 1835

Richards, Mary Atherton, *Amos Starr Cooke and Juliette Montague Cooke* Honolulu, 1941

Richards, Mary Atherton, *The Chiefs' Children's School* Honolulu, 1937

Simpson, Alexander, Esq., *The Sandwich Islands* London, 1843

Smith, Bradford, *Yankees in Paradise* Philadelphia, 1956

Smith, Lucius E., *Heroes and Martyrs of the Modern Missionary Enterprise* Hartford, 1854

Stewart, C.S., *A Residence in the Sandwich Islands* Boston, 1839

Stewart, C.S., *A Visit to the South Seas in the U.S. Ship Vincennes During the Years 1829 and 1830* New York, 1831

Sullivan, Josephine, *A History of C. Brewer & Co., Ltd.* Boston, 1926

Taylor, Albert Pierce, *The Rulers of Hawaii* Honolulu, 1927

Thurston, Mrs. Lucy G., *Life and Times of Mrs. Lucy G. Thurston* Honolulu, 1934

Van Loon, Hendrik Willem, *Ships and How They Sailed the Seven Seas* New York, 1935

Wight, Elizabeth Leslie, *The Memoirs of Elizabeth Kinau Wilder* Honolulu, 1909

Wilkes, Charles, *Narrative of the United States Exploring Expedition, 1838-1842* Philadelphia, 1845

Williston, Samuel, *William Richards* Cambridge, 1938

Periodicals and Reports

Annual Reports of the Hawaiian Historical Society

Annual Reports, Minutes and other publications of the Hawaiian Mission Children's Society

The Friend

Hawaiian Historical Society papers

Hawaiian Spectator

Hawaiiana

Journal of the Polynesian Society

Ka Nonanona (Hawaiian newspaper)

The Maile Wreath

Mid-Pacific Magazine

Missionary Herald

Pacific Commercial Advertiser

The Polynesian

Proceedings of the Massachusetts Historical
   Society

Thrum's Hawaiian Annual

GLOSSARY

In Hawaiian the vowels are pronounced:

    a as in "far" or "ah"

    e like "ay" in "day"

    i like "ee" in "bee"

    o as in "low"

    u like "oo" in "moon"

Consonants are pronounced as in English, except "w" which may be pronounced as "v."

The accented syllables are underlined.

The glottal stop indicates a break, as in "oh-oh."

ae (eye): yes

akamai (ah-ka-mī): smart

akuas (a-ku-as): ghosts, also gods

alii (a-li-'i): royalty; chief

aloha (a-lo-ha): love; farewell; greetings

Beretania: Hawaiian pronunciation of "Britain"

Binamu: Hawaiian form of "Bingham"

Boki (Boh-key): a high chief of Oahu

ewa (e-va): west in relation to Honolulu, toward the region known as Ewa

Haalilio (Hah-'a-li-li-o) Timothy: companion of Kamehameha III and envoy to foreign nations

hala (hah-la): pandanus

Halekauwila (Hah-le-kau-wi-la): name of a street in Honolulu where the thatched palace of Kamehameha III stood

haole (how-le): foreigner; now applied to Caucasians only

hau (how): plant belonging to the hibiscus family

Hawaii (Ha-wī-'i or Ha-vī-'i): largest island in the Hawaiian group

heiau (hay-ow): Hawaiian temple

hele mai (he-le my): come

Hilo (Hee-lo): a district on the island of Hawaii

himeni (hi-may-ni): hymn

hoike (hoh-'i-ke): exhibition

holoholo (ho-lo-ho-lo): to go out for pleasure

honihoni (ho-ni-ho-ni): to kiss a number of times

Honolii (Ho-no-li-'i) John: member of the first company of missionaries to Hawaii

Honolulu (Ho-no-lu-lu): capital of the Hawaiian Islands

Honoruru: early spelling of "Honolulu"

Hopu (Ho-pu) Thomas: member of first company of missionaries to Hawaii

hula (hoo-la): dance

Ii ('Ee-'ee) John: Hawaiian leader during late mission period period

imu (ee-mu): underground oven

io (ee-o): true

Iolani ('I-o-lah-ni): a second name of Liholiho (Kamehameha II)

Kaahumanu (Ka-'ah-hu-mah-nu): favorite wife of Kamehameha I and first regent of the Hawaiian kingdom

kahu (kah-hu): honored attendant; a royal person's attendant

kahunas (ka-hoo-nas): priests

Kailua (Kī-loo-a): village on the island of Hawaii

Kalakaua (Ka-la-kah-u-ah) David: scholar at Chiefs' Children's School; later king of Hawaii

Kamamalu (Ka-ma-mah-lu): favorite wife of Liholiho (Kamehameha II)

Kamehameha (Ka-may-ha-may-ha): dynasty of five rulers beginning with Kamehameha The Great

kanaka (ka-nah-ka): man, native

kanalua (kah-na-loo-a): doubtful

Kanui (Ka-noo-i) William: member of first company of missionaries to Hawaii

kapu (kah-pu): forbidden

Kauai (Kau-ah-'i or cow-eye): fourth largest island in the Hawaiian group

Kauikeaouli (Kau-i-ke-a-ou-li): Kamehameha III

Kawaiahao (Ka-wī-a-hah-'o or Ka-vī-a-hah-'o): name of the church and location of mission headquarters on the island of Oahu

Kealakekua (Ke-ah-la-ke-koo-a): a bay on the island of Hawaii

Kekuanaoa (Ke-koo-ah-na-o-'a) Matthew: governor of the island of Oahu

kihei (kee-hay): cape; shawl; blanket

Kinau (Kee-now): second regent of the Hawaiian kingdom

Koolau (Ko-'o-lau): mountain range on Oahu

kua leho (koo-a lay-ho): callous back

kuleana (koo-le-ah-na): title; piece of property

Lahaina (La-hī-na): port on the island of Maui; early capital of Hawaiian kingdom

Lahainaluna (La-hī-na-loo-na): upper Lahaina

lalo (lah-lo): lower; down

lana (lah-na): buoyant

lauhala (lau-hah-la): pandanus leaf

lei (lay): garland, flowers strung together

Liholiho (Lee-ho-lee-ho): Kamehameha II

Liliuokalani (Li-li-'u-o-ka-lah-ni): scholar at Chiefs' Children's School; later queen of Hawaii

Lumiki: Hawaiian form of "Loomis"

luna (loo-na): a head man who gives orders; upper

Lunalilo (Loo-na-lee-lo) William: scholar at Chiefs' Children's School; later king of Hawaii

Maka-lolo (Mah-ka-lō-lo): paralyzed eye

Mahune (Ma-hoo-ne) Boaz: one of the early scholars at Lahainaluna Seminary

maikai (mī-kah-'i): good; nice

maile (mī-le): twining shrub with fragrant shiny leaves

makai (ma-kī): toward the sea

malo (mah-lo): loin cloth

Malo, David: one of the early scholars at Lahainaluna Seminary

mana (mah-na): power

mana kia'i (mah-na ki-ah-'i): guardian power

manao (ma-nah-'o): thought; idea

Manoa (Mah-no-a): valley on the island of Oahu

Maui (Mau-i): second largest island in the Hawaiian group

mauka (mau-ka): toward the mountain

mea nui (may-a noo-i): great thing

Moanalua (Mo-ah-na-loo-a): a district on the island of Oahu

Namahana (Nah-ma-hah-na): sister of Kaahumanu

Niihau (Ni-'i-hau): island to the west of Kauai

Nukuhiwa (Noo-ku-hee-va): place in the Marquesas Islands

Nuuanu (Noo-'u-ah-nu): valley on the island of Oahu

Oahu (O-'ah-hu): third largest island in the Hawaiian group

Obookiah (Opukaha'ia - Oh-poo-kah-ha-'i-a): name of foremost Hawaiian student at the Foreign Mission School in Connecticut

oukou ('o-ko): you, plural form

Owhyhee: early spelling of "Hawaii"

pa'akiki (pah-'a-ki-key): hard and stubborn

palaoa (pa-<u>lau</u>-a): whale bone pendant

palapala (<u>pah</u>-la-<u>pah</u>-la): document of any kind; scriptures

pali (<u>pah</u>-li): cliff; precipice

papa hana (<u>pah</u>-pa <u>hah</u>-na): agenda; order of business

pa'u (pah-oo): woman's skirt, in olden times made of tapa

Pelekanes (<u>Pay</u>-le-<u>kah</u>-nes): Britons

Pelekane ho'opilikia (<u>Pay</u>-le-<u>kah</u>-ne <u>ho</u>-'o-<u>pee</u>-li-<u>kee</u>-a): trouble-causing Britons

pilikia (<u>pee</u>-li-<u>kee</u>-a): trouble

Poalima (Poh-'a-<u>lee</u>-ma): Friday

poi (poy): taro pounded into a gray paste (the Hawaiian staff of life)

pono (<u>po</u>-no): goodness; uprightness

Pualani (<u>Poo</u>-a-<u>lah</u>-ni): name of a mission scholar

Sandwich Islands: name given the Hawaiian Islands by Captain James Cook who discovered them in 1778

tabus (tah-booz): prohibitions (see "kapu")

tapa (<u>tah</u>-pa): (kapa) bark cloth used for clothes or bedding

taro: starchy edible root

ua loa'a iau (oo-a lō-ah'a ē-ow): I have got it

wahine (wa-<u>hee</u>-ne or va-<u>hee</u>-ne): woman, also Mrs.

Waialua (Wī-a-loo-a or Vī-a-loo-a): district on the island of Oahu

Waikiki (Wī-kee-kee or Vī-kee-kee): district on southeast shore of Oahu

Wailuku (Waī-<u>loo</u>-ku or Vī-<u>loo</u>-ku): district on the island of Maui

wela (<u>way</u>-la or <u>vay</u>-la): hot

Woahu: early spelling of "Oahu"